Insanity

Insanity

Susan Vaught

BLOOMSBURY

NEW YORK   LONDON   NEW DELHI   SYDNEY

First published in the United States of America in February 2014
by Bloomsbury Children's Books
www.bloomsbury.com

For information about permission to reproduce selections from this book, write to
Permissions, Bloomsbury Children's Books, 1385 Broadway, New York, New York 10018
Bloomsbury books may be purchased for business or promotional use. For information on bulk purchases
please contact Macmillan Corporate and Premium Sales Department at specialmarkets@macmillan.com

Library of Congress Cataloging-in-Publication Data
Vaught, Susan.
Insanity / by Susan Vaught.
pages   cm
Summary: The intertwining stories of three teenagers who find themselves haunted beyond
imagining in the depths of a Kentucky mental institution.
ISBN 978-1-59990-784-0 (hardcover) • ISBN 978-1-59990-839-7 (e-book)
[1. Psychiatric hospitals—Fiction.   2. Haunted places—Fiction.   3. Horror stories.]   I. Title.
PZ7.V4673In 2014   [Fic]—dc23   2013034321

Book design by Amanda Bartlett
Typeset by Westchester Book Composition
Printed and bound in the U.S.A. by Thomson-Shore Inc., Dexter, Michigan
2 4 6 8 10 9 7 5 3 1

All papers used by Bloomsbury Publishing, Inc., are natural, recyclable products
made from wood grown in well-managed forests. The manufacturing processes
conform to the environmental regulations of the country of origin.

For my sweet Frank, always and forever the best parrot ever.
I believe birds go to heaven, and you're flying with the angels.

What hills, what hills, my own true love,
What hills so dark and low?
That is the hills of hell, my love,
Where you and I must go!

—"The Daemon Lover," folk ballad, author unknown
Version recorded in Harlan County, Kentucky

Insanity

PROLOGUE

Levi

There was something wrong with the dog.

I saw it when I left the store, nothing but a little thing. I would have stopped to give it some love, but I had to get back before Imogene started to worry.

Don't go out tonight, boy. Death's walkin' on two legs.

But I had gone out, because I wanted some Slim Jims and peanuts and a Coke, and now I had a mutt following me home. It was a beagle with floppy ears and a tail that didn't wag. Its eyes were too black, or maybe its teeth were too white.

I kept hold of my bag and walked faster, cutting in front of Lincoln Psychiatric Hospital. My breath made a fog. It was November and already cold in Never, Kentucky. Above the trees on my left, the old asylum's bell tower hid the stars. It was dark, but the moon was bright, and I knew the way.

Behind me, that dog let out a growl.

Don't look back. Something might be gaining on you.

Somebody famous said that, not Imogene. Maybe it was a

baseball player, but I couldn't remember which one. Something flickered in the distance, winking between black pines and oaks.

Flashlight?

I glanced toward the psychiatric hospital. The back of my neck got the shivers, and that idiot dog growled again.

The bell tower. Had the light come from way up at the top? I slowed down, even though I knew I shouldn't, and got a new case of the shivers.

Nothing good ever came from the top of that bell tower, or from any of the thin spots in that hospital. Imogene looked after the place as best she could, but sometimes—

"That's about enough, Levi," I told myself, mocking my grandmother's voice. I shook my head to rattle out the stupid thoughts and headed for home again.

Something at the top of that tower turned with me. It was watching me. It was staring at my back, just like the dog was.

"Knock it off," I muttered, and the mutt growled, and I walked so fast I was almost running.

My steps echoed on the path across the hospital grounds. Everything got quiet except the dog. It panted way too loud.

Light flashed across my face and I stumbled, blinking until I could see again, and then I stopped. The dog had gotten itself in front of me, its eyes wide and its mouth open and its tongue lolling to the ground. In that weird yellow light, its shadow rose across the trees behind it.

The shadow was giant and black and wolf-sized.

The shadow had red eyes.

Don't go out tonight, boy. Death's walkin' on two legs.

"You got four legs," I told the creepy dog. I barely heard myself for the blood hammering in my ears.

Leaves crunched nearby.

I whipped around and fixed on the sound, expecting to see— what? A real wolf? Some crazy freak with a flashlight? Lincoln Psychiatric didn't have murderers and bad criminals now. At least, I didn't think they did.

Spots danced across my eyes as I squinted at the woods. Nothing. Just trees, and that old stone bell tower standing watch over Never. A single yellow light flickered way up at the top, like somebody was swinging an old-timey lantern.

I'm not crazy. I puffed out more fog. I'd told myself that same thing a lot of times.

A twig snapped on my right, and I jumped again.

"It's okay," I told myself, watching the mist rise in front of my nose. The night smelled like wet leaves and grave dirt. "It's just the dog."

The beagle stood in that strange lantern light from the bell tower. It was wagging its tail, but that didn't seem friendly. Its shadow still had red eyes, and the shadow wasn't wagging its tail.

I backed away from the dog.

It followed me, pace for pace, its lips pulled back to show fangs as big as my fingers. The wolf shadow rippled across the trees, huge and black and bristly, and the tower watched like a menace at the edge of my thoughts. My breath came shorter and my blood pumped faster.

The hound opened its mouth and let out a howl so loud it rattled my skull. My feet tangled, and I fell backward against something warm and solid.

A man?

"Easy there," said a voice deep enough to give me more shivers even as its owner kept me from spilling ass-over-teakettle and set me on my feet again.

"The dog—" I started to say but stopped, because I had Imogene's blood and she had raised me to use it since my parents died, and people didn't always see what I saw. If I asked him about his shadow, the man would think I was a runaway from the hospital. What was he doing here, anyway? Most people stayed off these paths.

"Sorry," I said. "Just trying to get home."

The man let me go, and then he laughed at me.

I didn't like the sound.

The guy, he was tall and mostly bald, but muscled like a runner. His dark skin didn't have any scars, and he was wearing suit pants and a nice shirt with a tie, but no jacket. Church clothes. He looked like a preacher.

"You're one of them," he said. "That's too bad. But better now, before you're old enough to make real trouble."

The beagle snarled, and the man's black eyes flicked to the dog. He muttered something I couldn't hear, but I felt the power in every word. The mutt's growl turned into a whine, and it shrank away and faded into the trees like a ghost.

Cold truth settled on my skin, and my teeth started to chatter.

That dog hadn't been growling at me. It had been growling at the preacher-man. Thunder rumbled from somewhere far away, and the light from the bell tower flashed before it went out.

Did the lunatics in Lincoln Psychiatric still run screaming through the halls when it stormed? I saw that on a news special one time. It used to be that way a hundred years ago. Imogene said so, and my grandmother always told the truth.

Run, her voice whispered in my brain, but it was too late.

The man moved when I did, grabbing me and yanking me backward. My bag went flying as I crashed to the hard-packed ground of the path, spilling peanuts and Slim Jims all over the ground. Agony tore up my right arm as my bone snapped at the elbow. It hurt so bad I went dizzy and dumb. My face bashed against pebbles, and one of my teeth broke.

My thoughts knotted up and I yelled, but I didn't hear anything because my throat didn't work. I used my good arm to push myself up, but the preacher-man threw smelly powder in my face.

I coughed.

It burned. I couldn't breathe.

Was the preacher-man saying a prayer? He rambled on about forgiveness and duties and saving souls. The guy was nuts.

It's okay. I'm still breathing. I'm still alive.

I blinked up at the man, who had daggers in his big hands.

I'm still alive, I told myself again.

And then, I wasn't.

Part I
Unforgiven

Forest

Her face reminded me of black marble, carved with wrinkles and frowns and sad eyes, always looking far away like she could see things I'd never understand.

Her hands—now those were cypress roots, dark and knobby, and rough when I had to touch them.

She never let go of the picture.

The photo was older than me, and she talked to it as though it were a person, down low where nobody could hear. It was laminated, and when I bathed her I'd wrap it in a plastic bag, because take that picture away from Miss Sally Greenway and she'd be throwing everything on the ward straight at your head. I never really looked at the photo, because I was too busy to pay it much mind.

How stupid was that? Stupid and wrong. That picture was the most important thing to the eighty-seven-year-old woman I dressed and fed almost every day. I should have looked at it.

When I finally did, I almost lost my mind.

CHAPTER ONE

$\mathbf{B}$e careful, Forest!" Leslie Hyatt slapped my hand so hard I almost dropped the comb I was trying to wedge into Miss Sally's stubborn white hair.

Leslie's dark eyes narrowed, doubling the wrinkles on her forehead. When she lifted her arm to point her finger at me, her oversized black scrubs fanned out until she looked like a giant bat. "What if she was your grandmama, girl? Would you want her hair pulled by some fool teenager can't make a braid without yanking the poor woman bald?"

She stepped toward Miss Sally, who sat in her wheelchair without moving or speaking, holding that black-and-white picture of a man she hadn't seen since she was young. "Give me that." Leslie took the comb away from me. "I done told you, it's like this."

She worked the teeth of the comb, gently teasing smaller and smaller sections of hair. For her, they stayed right where she put them.

I fiddled with the rowan-wood bracelet on my right wrist, running my fingers across its familiar carved surface and smooth iron beads. "Sorry." I managed a smile despite my stinging knuckles. I liked Leslie. She'd been helping me learn since I first came to work on second shift at Lincoln Psychiatric Hospital.

That was six months ago—two days after I turned eighteen, aged out of foster care, and had to take my GED and find a place to live. When I wasn't pulling hair, I was bottom-of-the-line staff at Lincoln, nothing but a bath-giver, a bed-pan scrubber, a bed-changer. I clipped fungusy nails, changed stinky clothes and disgusting diapers, made beds, fed patients, got spit on and bit and kicked and called names—whatever it took to keep nineteen elderly folks clean and comfortable in a forgotten basement ward in a double-forgotten state psychiatric hospital. If it paid me a salary and provided insurance and earned me overtime privileges so I could make more money, I'd do it, and I'd smile and mean it. Every dollar I got to put into savings instead of spending on rent and food was a dollar toward getting to college—and getting out of Never, Kentucky.

While Leslie worked on Miss Sally's hair, something rumbled outside the cedar-colored limestone walls. It came on slow and quiet, but it built and built and *built* until the barred windows rattled and the fluorescent lights flickered. All along the single hallway of Lincoln's geriatric ward, patients grumbled or whimpered or shifted in their wheelchairs. A few started rolling toward their rooms.

"It's all right," Leslie told them, easing up on her combing. "It's just Maintenance caving in those old tunnels under the

Administration Building." Her deep tone rippled across the stone floor like the kind of thunder that made people smile and sleep deeper at night. She was around sixty years old and had come to work at Lincoln when she was twenty-three. She had known some of these patients for most of her life—and theirs. They stopped rolling, or at least stopped fussing and looking worried.

The building rattled again, and this time the lights blinked off. The few seconds of darkness before the backup generator kicked on made me gasp. We had no real windows down here, just a few rows of glass panes so high they touched the ceiling— and it was October, so it got dark almost as soon as we finished serving dinner.

When Leslie grabbed my arm, I jumped.

"You got to stay calm," she told me in a gentle voice lined with steel. "They're helpless, and they don't know what's going on. All this jackhammering and blasting, it's likely to give some poor soul a heart failure." She handed the comb back to me. "As nervous as you get, you really planning to work your first double tonight, this close to Halloween?"

Why was my heart beating so hard? I tried to answer but worried I would squeak at the thought of spending the night in the hospital, so I nodded instead.

"Well, okay." Leslie shook her head. "You're cut out to work with my little peoples down here, but I don't know if you got what it takes for night shift. When the bells start ringing and you're runnin' the dark halls pissin' yourself before you can get to a bathroom, you remember I warned you."

"The bells don't ring." I went back to combing Miss Sally's

head, careful not to tangle my bracelet in her hair. "They told us so in orientation. Hasn't been a sound out of Tower Cottage for thirty years."

Miss Sally started talking to her picture, all little whispers and laughs. I caught "bells" a few times.

"Thirty years is what they *say*." Leslie winked at me and headed back to the patient whose hair she'd been combing out before she came to help me with Miss Sally.

"Bells," Miss Sally whispered again, staring down at her photo.

When Lincoln was built back in 1802, the superintendent's residence got a tower that had three big bells at the top. They rang for wake-up, meals, and bedtime, five times a day, regular as the clock on the face of that odd-colored limestone. If the bells rang any other time, people in Never were supposed to bolt their shutters, lock their doors, and come help look for whichever patient had escaped. Back then, four thousand patients lived at the hospital, some from the day they were born to the day they died. Today, we had maybe three hundred patients, mostly people too old or too sick to go to placements in Never or the surrounding towns in southern Kentucky. Tower Cottage was closed around 1980 because it cost too much to keep it in good repair. Lincoln used it to store files and records now.

"Don't walk at night," Miss Sally told her photo as I finally got a good start on a braid. "If the bells ring, *don't walk at night.*"

My fingers went still.

Did I hear that right?

wearing a hat and maybe overalls. His head was turned looking toward a shack next to a little cornfield.

I squinted. The picture seemed to get a little clearer. Definitely a hat. Overalls for sure. His hair was cropped close to his head, and he had big ears. Kinda cute. The overalls were dark blue and looked new, and his shirtsleeves were clean, as if he'd gotten all dressed up to come see Miss Sally. The shack was more like a small wooden house. The corn was healthy. I could smell it, sort of a dirty, earthy scent, and I could smell new jeans, too, the cotton fresh and still stiff and itchy.

Do you know who you are? The voice in my head didn't even scare me, because I knew he would talk like that, all deep and playful. *Do you know what you can do?*

And then the man in the picture turned to look at me.

The world shook.

Chairs rattled against the ward walls, and the lights went dark with a loud fizz and pop. I dropped the photo like it was made of blue fire, and Miss Sally let go of my bracelet and started wailing.

"Bells!" she shrieked. "Bells!"

The hospital bells were ringing.

My right mind told me it was just the bell clappers jittering like the chairs had done because of the explosions Maintenance was setting off down in the tunnels. My idiot mind told me a picture talked to me, then looked at me and made the bells start ringing.

"You have got to be kidding," Leslie muttered.

The sound of her sneakers squeaking as she ran to calm

scared patients was the only thing that kept me from breaking into shrieks louder than Miss Sally's. I felt around wildly in the dark, scooting my hands across the floor until I found her picture. I snatched it up and pushed it into her hands.

"Here it is. It's okay." God, I didn't sound calm at all. "It's okay, Miss Sally." She kept screaming. My heart thumped in my throat so hard it hurt. "Miss Sally." I held on to her fingers, closing them gently around the picture. "I hear the bells," I told her, "but they're just moving because of that explosion."

"Don't walk at night," she shouted.

The backup generator hummed to life, and the lights came back on. Miss Sally stared at me, but the white film of confusion was closing over her eyes again. She pulled her hands away from mine, glanced at her picture, then smiled and gazed off into the distance like she always did.

Before I could react to or even try to understand what had just happened, the nurse came flying out of the office at the far end of the hall. Arleen looked like a mean pumpkin in her orange scrubs, and I almost groaned at the sight of her fuzzy blond hair. She wasn't my favorite person. Always loud, never paying attention to the patients—

"Leslie," she yelled, obviously jacked up about something. "Leslie!"

I heard Leslie's irritated "What?" from inside a patient's room to my left.

Arleen bounced up and down on her toes like a little kid. "They found a body in the tunnels!"

I got up slowly, not believing that at all, but Arleen was

chattering about the Kentucky State Police coming as fast as they could get here and there being bones—a pile of bones.

Leslie stuck her head out of the patient's room. Her usually calm face was twisted in complete annoyance. "Say what, woman? We got a situation going on here—"

"A body." Arleen talked right over her, clapping her hands together once. "There's a body in the tunnels underneath Lincoln Psychiatric!"

CHAPTER TWO

It was one o'clock in the morning before I got my first break on my overtime shift. Leslie was long gone, and I was on my own as I walked the long corridor between the geriatric ward and the canteen. The hospital basement was quiet, with only a single strip of night lamps glowing along the baseboards.

Flashing blue police lights punched through the windows near the ceiling, keeping a clockwork rhythm on the walls. The Kentucky State Police had been on campus all night so far. Arleen, who was working a long shift, told me they had roped off Administration and the tunnel with the bones.

Bones.

I didn't want to go there. I had never been so aware that Lincoln Psychiatric Hospital was five miles from anything, smack in the middle of six hundred acres owned by the state, surrounded by a big stone fence. The patients sensed how nervous we were, and they knew the blue lights didn't mean anything good. We'd had to climb on chairs and hang sheets over the ward windows so they would stop crying and screaming and settle in for bed.

My footsteps banged too loud against the stone floor, and my breathing seemed to echo. The hallways weren't heated in non-patient areas, so every time I blew out air, fog trailed across my vision. When I rubbed my palms against my blue sleeves, the flashing police lights made me look dead and alive, dead and alive.

The picture. Miss Sally talking in sentences. The Tower Cottage bells ringing. The *picture*. What had I really seen? I rubbed my arms harder, trying to ignore the freaky blue lights. I wasn't—well, I didn't like to use the word "crazy," because it seemed disrespectful now that I worked at Lincoln. I didn't have a mental illness. At least, I didn't think I did. Okay, so I got a little jumpy sometimes, but I was trying to eat and pay rent and save for college. I had a right to be jumpy.

Forest.

The whisper came from behind me.

I stumbled, then stopped and turned quick to look.

The hallway behind me was totally empty. Nothing but closed office doors, blue lights strobing against the dark walls, and at the very, very far end of the hall, the clothing room where we kept donations for the patients. That door was shut, too, and locked, like it was every night from end of day shift to the start of the next.

As I stared at it, it seemed to move out, then in, like the room was breathing.

Pain stabbed into my chest, right where my heart throbbed. *This isn't happening.*

I sucked in a breath and let it out. Fog swirled around my face. The air smelled like . . . pine? Cleanser, maybe. But it seemed fresh and not as strong as the stuff Housekeeping used to scrub the bathrooms.

"Nothing," I said out loud, and almost screamed at the sound of my own voice.

The door at the end of the hallway stayed still, like doors are supposed to do.

I was creeping myself out. I spun back toward the canteen and started walking faster. I tried not to think about the door or imagine something in the hall behind me, walking quietly, ghosting my steps, moving forward, moving faster, faster—

I hit the canteen door with both palms and shoved it open as I ran inside. I didn't even give it time to swing shut, slamming it myself and holding on. I even thought about using my keys to turn the lock.

Nothing pushed against the door.

Of course it didn't.

I hadn't just heard a whisper in the hallway, and Miss Sally's picture did *not* look at me and talk to me.

So why was I shaking?

Because I was cold.

Time to jam my quarters into the vintage beverage dispenser, get my hot chocolate, and take my meal break. Except I couldn't make myself stop holding the canteen door shut.

Oh, jeez. What if there were people in here watching me act like an idiot?

I turned to my left and glanced down the long, semidark room. Tables lined the right-hand side, built into the walls with booth seats, all secured so they couldn't be knocked over or picked up and thrown. More vending machines were on the left. Nobody was watching, thank God.

Seconds passed. I made myself breathe, then finally took my hands off the canteen door. It was hard to walk away without first dragging something over to block the door, but it's not like I actually could—even the trash bins were bolted to the floor.

I walked slowly, quietly, listening for extra noise each time I took a step. I didn't hear anything, though my heartbeat was loud enough to drum for a metal band. The hot-beverage machine was at the end of the row, and as I passed the first soft-drink machine, lights flashed and gears whirred, and I almost died right there.

"Crap!" I banged my hand against the machine's plastic picture of a soft drink, and the motion woke up the dispenser next to it, and then the next one, on down the line. "Crap, crap!" I hit the machine again, even though I knew all these contraptions "slept" like computers with their lids closed until they sensed somebody walking by, and then popped to life with moving parts and glowing pictures of icy drinks or potato chips. Energy saving. Economically efficient. Whatever. It was a *stupid* thing to have in a psychiatric hospital.

It was all I could do to get my hot chocolate, sit at a table, and drink it. The hot liquid burned my mouth, and it felt good. I held the cup so tight I almost squashed it, letting the heat seep into my fingers. The iron beads on my rowan bracelet seemed to absorb the warmth, tingling against my wrist until I started to think straight again. Rowan was supposed to be enchanted wood, protecting against everything from getting lost to getting stolen by evil fairies. The trees grew mostly in Britain and Europe. One of my high school biology teachers figured out what my bracelet was made of and asked me where I got it. No idea. I just knew it was the only thing I had from my real family, whoever they were. It made me feel better.

In half an hour or so, I'd have to go back into that long, dark hallway where I did not, did not, did *not* hear something whisper my name or see a door breathing. I closed my eyes and rubbed the bridge of my nose.

Just my luck, to work my first night shift after Maintenance finds a pile of bones in a tunnel. In orientation, we learned that the tunnels were built during the Civil War so patients and staff could move around campus without getting shot by soldiers battling in nearby fields. Those bones could have been there a hundred and fifty years.

Or just a few months.

Was there a killer wandering through the tunnels under Lincoln Psychiatric?

The smell of fresh pine wafted through the canteen, and wild geese started honking in the distance.

My eyes popped open.

Geese?

But it was the middle of the night, and way past migration time.

Honk, honk, honk . . .

I stood up so fast I knocked over my cup, spraying leftover drops of hot chocolate across the table.

Dogs started howling, sudden and so loud they had to be right next to me. I backed against the table, looking everywhere but seeing nothing except drink machines still whirring and blinking.

The police brought dogs. Yeah. That was probably it. Right?

Blood blasted in my ears, but not loud enough to blot out the dogs and birds—and the bells. The bells were ringing.

Don't walk at night! my mind screamed in Miss Sally's voice.

"Decker!" a guy hollered from the hallway outside the canteen. I heard each syllable and letter in my brain, in my clenched teeth, in my toenails. I smelled them, too.

They smelled like pine.

Chills ripped across my skin, and all my hair stood up like I'd been hit by lightning.

Another guy yelled—only it was more like a scream.

Sweat broke across my forehead and neck.

Patient, my thoughts managed to sputter. *Patient in trouble.*

The dogs barked. The geese honked. The Tower Cottage bells rang and the lights blinked and went out and there were bones in a tunnel, and I ran through the pitch black for the canteen door like a nightmare dancer, staggering and jerking and not really sure what I was doing. I yanked the door open so hard I nearly fell when it swung, then lunged into the hall in time to see a silvery glow explode through the whole space, turning the limestone walls to polished stardust. Everything looked sparkly and new and unreal.

A guy ran past me. Jeans. Dark skin. Screaming. He wasn't anybody I knew from the wards.

Dogs charged after him, yelping like they were chasing a fox, and goose shadows slid along the ceiling where the lights should have been.

And behind the dogs—

Who was *that*?

My hands curled into fists as he came toward me. I opened my mouth to yell, but no sound came out.

He was six feet tall, maybe taller. Thin. Black jeans, black shirt, black coat dusting the floor. His hair was black, too, and longer than mine. Massive winglike shadows arced into the nothingness behind him.

He was glowing. He was both the light and the darkness, and he had teardrops etched under his right eye—so, so red and terrifying, and I knew in my guts they weren't made with ink. They were some kind of blood tattoos.

The hounds cornered the first guy at the clothing room door, and the dark-light guy passed me by as if I didn't exist.

"It's time to go, Decker," he said to the guy cowering from the hounds.

"No!" the man he called Decker yelled, and I figured he was a patient, even if I couldn't remember him. I was shaking so hard I couldn't think. I couldn't even walk.

The dark-light guy got to the dogs and waded through them.

He grabbed Decker with one hand, and with the other he ripped open the clothing room door.

"Leave me be!" Decker yelled. He beat against the dark-light guy, and I tried to clear my thoughts, because at Lincoln Psychiatric we didn't lay hands on patients except to provide care, and whoever this jerk with the coat and dogs might be, I couldn't let him hurt some helpless sick person.

"Stop!" I shouted, stumbling away from the canteen door. "You with the dogs. Knock it off!"

The dark-light guy was in the clothing room now, dragging Decker after him. The dogs streamed inside along with the goose shadows, and the bells kept ringing and ringing.

"Hey! Guy in the duster. I'm talking to you!" I picked up speed and reached the clothing room just as Decker's feet went sliding across the threshold.

I pitched myself forward and got a grip on his ankles. I expected to get pulled inside and eaten by a thousand dog teeth, but Decker stopped sliding like he'd hit a solid wall.

From inside the clothing room came the sound of a body hitting the floor and noises of surprise—dog and goose and human, too. I didn't stop to think about it. I kept my stranglehold on Decker's ankles, struggled to my knees, then leaned back and used my body weight to haul him out of the clothing room. He came without fighting, eyes wide, mouth hanging open in shock.

Dark-light guy came with him, still holding Decker's arms until he saw me and turned loose.

I'd had hours of training on separating patients who were fighting, so I risked letting go of Decker long enough to scramble past his legs and shoulders until I could force my body between the two people. As they stood I straightened up with them, straddling the entrance to the clothing room. My left hand rested on Decker's chest, and my right stretched toward dark-light guy.

Dizziness made me blink, and my head swam like I'd been punched—but at least the bells stopped ringing. Lights flickered back to life. The dogs and the goose shadows vanished, and the walls weren't made of stardust anymore. Dark-light guy looked like an escapee from a vampire-movie casting call, and he really was wearing black jeans and a black shirt with long sleeves, but he didn't have any wings.

Man, did he look pissed.

He stepped forward, his chest meeting my palm with force. Lightning shocks made my arm jerk as he bounced backward from the contact. Rainbows shot through my vision, and I winced at the sharp scent of mothballs and dusty old clothes. The room felt cold and weird and . . . wrong, and it didn't help when dark-light guy growled like one of his dogs. I widened my stance, ready for him to come at me again, but he reeled back like I'd hit him with a cattle prod.

"Don't let him out of that room," Decker whispered. "Please!"

My breath echoed in my ears, but this was getting easier. A pissed guy, a scared guy—but no dogs, no geese, no bells, no glowing crap. Things were making more sense, and I knew what to do. "Mr. Decker, which ward are you from?"

Decker gazed at me, slack-jawed. He had dark, curly hair trimmed close to his head, flawless skin, and an attractive face, but his eyes were wide and scared like a lot of the psychotic patients I'd worked with before. I figured he was about thirty, maybe older. His jeans and white T-shirt were filthy. Who let him out after hours—and who on earth hadn't given the man a shower and helped him put on clean clothes?

He didn't answer me about the ward. Maybe he didn't know.

As for the guy in the clothing room, I needed to figure out where he belonged, too. I glanced in his direction. "What's your name?"

He was younger than Decker, maybe not much older than me, and wickedly handsome. He didn't seem psychotic, but he had his hand pressed against the spot on his chest where he'd made contact with my palm, and he acted like he was in pain.

"Levi," he said, as though my question tore the word right out of him. Southern accent, but he so didn't look like a Never farm boy.

He blinked in surprise, as if he hadn't meant to answer me. Then his eyes narrowed, and he seemed to be cataloging everything about me, from my curly hair to my shaking hands to my rowan bracelet.

I knew enough to treat patients with respect, and I recognized fear when I saw it, even when it was painted over to look like anger. "I usually work on the geriatric ward, mostly second shift. That's why you don't know me. I promise I'll take good care of both of you."

"Sure you will," Levi murmured, fixated on my face with an intensity that made me nervous.

"I need to get you back to your wards," I told them both. "It's late, and there's a lot going on tonight. You need some rest, up where it's safe."

Neither guy said anything.

I let out a breath I hadn't known I was holding. "Come on," I said. "Let's go. Now."

When I risked lowering my hands, Levi turned, walked a few steps farther into the clothing room, and vanished.

Like, *poof.* Just—*poof*!

I stared at the place where he'd been, not believing what I had just seen.

Then Decker started to cry.

When I turned toward him, he dropped to his knees, like he was bowing before me.

"Hey, look. It's okay." I shoved away the image of Levi vanishing and got down next to Decker to put my hand on his shoulder. Too much weirdness. Too much not-realness.

I was at work. I had to keep working. I needed to take care of crying guy first, then . . . there was no way Levi had just disappeared. He had to be in that room somewhere.

"Mr. Decker, come with me to the switchboard, and we'll figure out where you belong."

He kept his head bowed like he was terrified to look at me.

"Mr. Decker—"

"Do you know what he was?" Decker looked up so suddenly I almost fell backward, but I held it together, at least until he asked, "Do you know what *you* are?"

That question struck me like a fist to the chin, and I sank back, staring at him, taking in his perfect skin and his powerful build, and his now-clean clothes. Not jeans anymore, but over-alls. Pressed, maybe even new. His shirt was clean.

He looked familiar. Was he—

No.

"Do you know what you can do?" he whispered, keeping his eyes fixed on mine—eyes I had seen earlier this evening, gazing up at me from a picture I held in the palm of my hand.

I was talking to the man in Miss Sally's photograph.

CHAPTER THREE

An hour." Arleen pretended to sound sad for me as she wrote me up for being late from my meal break. "A whole hour, Forest!"

Tears prickled in my eyes. I was still breathing hard from running from the clothing room all the way back to the geriatric ward. I didn't think I was late—I just wanted to get away from . . . whatever had happened. Get back to the real world.

But I hadn't found the real world at all. Just more craziness.

No way was I late coming back, not one minute, not five minutes. I should have been early, but Arleen and the clock said I was an hour past my report time. I'd been working since I was fifteen—odd jobs, then fast food, then stocking shelves at a grocery store, then here, and I'd never been written up. I couldn't comprehend why it was happening now.

Arleen had her back to me as she filled out the disciplinary action slip, but Decker Greenway was facing me in his clean shirt and overalls, smelling like new denim, grinning and being friendly.

Arleen couldn't see him.

"You're losing time because of the thin spot," he explained. "That's what they call them, Levi and his grandmother. Lincoln ain't nothing but a giant thin spot between our world and the other side, and places in this hospital get even thinner due to all the sadness it sees. Time can't help moving funny around thin spots."

Arleen was talking about "youth" and "irresponsibility" and "maturity." Decker Greenway was talking about madness.

All-over shaking made my teeth chatter until I set my jaw. I didn't want the tears to escape my eyes, but they did. I wiped them away quickly. "It was a mistake," I told Arleen and my hallucination. "I—I guess I fell asleep. I won't be careless again."

"If you were still on probation, you'd be fired for this." She turned and waved the yellow slip at me. "Even as a full-time employee, a second time AWOL from assigned duty and you'll be terminated." She smiled, all teeth and no heart.

I said nothing, because what could I say? I was due back at 2:00 a.m. It was now 3:15 a.m. How had an hour passed? It couldn't have been that long.

"It's because you got too close to a thin spot," Decker insisted. "You really don't know what you are, do you?"

I kept my eyes on Arleen. Maybe if I didn't look at him, didn't pay any attention to the weirdness, it would go away.

Arleen made a few shaming noises, and heat rose to my

cheeks as she deposited the yellow slip in the wall box, where the director of nursing would collect it tomorrow, dock my pay for the hour, and enter the disciplinary action on my record.

"You're distracted tonight," Arleen said. Then her tone swapped to sickly sweet. "Doubles are hard. I know. I've worked a million of them."

"May I go back to the hall now?" My voice shook like the rest of me, which made me that much madder. I wasn't one of those totally-scarred-from-foster-care people, but I didn't bother much with friends or attachments, and I had learned to keep my emotions to myself. When I couldn't, it scared me and made me want to be alone.

Arleen dismissed me with a wave of her orange Halloween nails, and I all but ran out of the station, leaving her and Decker behind. When I got to the table where night shift sat to monitor patient doorways, Decker was somehow already there, two doors away, gazing in at Miss Sally.

I sat at the table, grateful I was the only one assigned to the hall, and refused to look at him.

After a few seconds, he said, "You need to see Miss Imogene over in records. In the cottage with the bell tower. You know the place?"

My eyes darted up and down the hall to be sure nobody was around to hear before I shot him a look and whispered, "Whatever you are, go away."

Decker's eyebrows shot up. His eyes flashed—literally—and his friendly expression gave way to a darkness I associated with foster brothers who lit fires and stuck pins in kittens. The hairs on my arms stood up at the sudden energy in the hallway.

His voice took on an echo as he pointed toward Miss Sally's sleeping form and said, "I'm not leaving without her."

The sound made my ears ache, and all up and down the ward, patients whimpered in their sleep.

"Stop that!" I stood and faced him, suddenly more pissed than scared. "You're upsetting them."

Arleen stuck her head out of the station at the end of the ward hall. "Everything okay, Forest?"

"Fine," I told her, sounding harsh even to my own ears.

To Arleen, it would have looked like I was checking on Miss Sally. Perfectly normal. I hoped. She lingered for a moment, then withdrew, no doubt to keep updating her Facebook page.

"Sorry." Decker pulled back on whatever had made him go all exorcist-devil. "It's just—I thought I was done for. If you hadn't stopped that haint, I'd be on the other side right now." His head drooped. "Probably already forgetting about my Sally. I can't let that happen."

Haint. The other side. My pulse accelerated. I had caught Miss Sally's mental illness.

"I didn't send anybody anywhere," I told my hallucination, but he just laughed.

"You got guts, girl. Thank you for what you did. I just hope it don't bring you a world of hurt."

When I just stood there with no clue what to say or ask, Decker kept talking. "My Sally's hours are counting down. That's why I risked coming out of the tunnels to see her, but they found my bones today, so the haint knows I'm here. He'll come after me again."

It must have been clear that I still didn't get it, still couldn't pull myself together enough to grasp Decker's meaning or any of his reality, because he sighed. "If the haint sends me to the other side without her, I might start to forget, Forest. I can't forget my Sally. I been hiding all this time, 'cause we'll be going together or not at all."

From inside the dark room, Miss Sally started to sing—a real tune, with real words. "Swing low, sweet chariot . . ."

Her old voice pitched high and quavered, but she hit each note clear and right. "Coming for to carry me hoooooome . . ."

Her music made my bones tingle, and I swear it had a scent like lilac, or some flower I'd never smelled before—something purple and sparkling and bewitching to the eyes and nose and fingertips.

"Swing low, sweet chaaa-rioooot . . ."

The walls and floors around me turned liquid, and I could see things on the other side of the shadowy water. Big things. Dark things. And they were trying to come through.

"Jeez." I jumped away from the wall, then got up on my chair when something long and cold-looking slithered past my feet, barely contained under the translucent floor tiles.

"You stop that, now," Decker murmured, and Miss Sally giggled. She started spluttering on the words, and the walls and floors turned solid again. I couldn't see the monsters anymore, and the scent of lilac faded back into the more normal hallway smells of bleach, stone, and a hint of new denim.

"Madoc blood gave my Sally the power to make folks see things," Decker explained. "She could sing any reality she wanted, but the power turned on her and tore up her mind. I couldn't keep her off the streets, so the law took her from me and locked her up here."

Madoc? I stood on my chair, gazing first at Decker, then at Miss Sally, who turned over in her bed and snuggled deeper under her blankets.

What did that mean?

Madoc. I pushed it sideways in my head and fixed on the fact that Miss Sally hadn't been born with her illness. She got sick because she had some special ability, and she couldn't manage it?

I didn't believe in special abilities or magic. Or ghosts. Or that I could ever go crazy. But here I was, talking to . . . *something* . . . that wasn't real.

"I was coming to get her that night." Decker sounded sad now, and he wasn't looking at me anymore. "Halloween, nineteen and fifty-two. I couldn't stand being away from her anymore, so I was going to cross us over together on All Hallows'. The blood gave me the power to blend. I could make myself look like whatever was around, so people with no Madoc in them, they wouldn't see me at all."

"What does 'Madoc' mean?" I asked.

Decker didn't answer.

I shifted on the chair and thought about getting down, but what if Miss Sally started singing up floor monsters again? I was probably safer where I was.

Decker gazed through Miss Sally's door, then leaned against the frame. "Part of the main tunnel gave way and trapped me inside."

He glanced at his fingertips, which turned ragged and more bloody each second. I caught my breath because I could see it happening, him sneaking through Administration, being part of the wall, part of the floor, part of some bookcase until he got to the elevator and rode it down to the level below the basement. I could see him easing into the main tunnel, heading toward her ward, ready to slip up some shaft and snatch Miss Sally away to . . . to whatever the other side might be. Then a rumble and pop, some falling dirt, some crashing rocks.

He would have tried to dig himself out.

It would have been terrible.

My stomach heaved as I stared at his hands, at the grisly stumps his fingers had become. "I'm sorry," I whispered.

He shrugged. "She was worth it."

His fingers gradually re-formed, but he was frowning, and his eyes were doing that flashy-colory thing that meant he might scare the old folks—and me—again. "When I first died, there was no haint to hunt me. I don't know why Imogene lets him stay here, except he's related to her. She took him in when his folks got killed in a car wreck."

I thought about the bells, the flickering lights, and the Kentucky State Police. "Your bones were discovered tonight, after the explosion. The, um, haint—he knows you're here now because of that?"

Decker nodded. "He must have gone to the bones and sensed me."

Images of the guy in the black jeans flicked through my mind. His grim expression. Those creepy blood tears tattooed on his face. So dark. So unbelievably handsome—and callous and cold. Who was Levi, really? *What* was he?

Haint. Yeah, yeah. I'd heard that word before. It was some kind of ghost who was up to no good, but Levi hadn't felt like a ghost to me.

"Forest, who are you talking to?" Arleen asked. I registered her voice, that she had come out of the office again, but I ignored her. She didn't seem important anymore.

"He'll get me before Sally dies." Decker looked at me, his eyes nothing but wild darkness that made me imagine caves and holes in the ground. "He'll come for you, too—even here, out in the world. Haints can go anywhere. You ain't safe from a haint, no matter where you hide."

"Forest!" Arleen seemed louder and more insistent now, but even less important. My heart swapped between pounding and flooding. I felt so sorry for Decker and Miss Sally I didn't know what to do.

Decker hung his head. I watched the hope drain out of him, and with it went his color, his solidity, until he was nothing more than the blurred lines I had seen in Miss Sally's photograph.

"Wait!" I stood straighter in the chair. "I don't want to hide. I want to understand."

"You got to be careful," he murmured. "You're my only hope. You're *our* only hope."

And then he faded into nothing, leaving behind only a light scent of new denim.

Heavy fingers closed around my wrist, and I let out a yelp.

"What are you doing on that chair?" Arleen gave me a little shake, glaring at me. Her eyeliner was painted on thick.

"I—uh." Yeah. I shut my mouth and got down from the chair thought about it a second. "I think I saw a mouse, that's all."

Arleen frowned at me, then glanced at the clock.

Time had passed too fast again. My shift was almost over. I realized I hadn't turned any patients to prevent bedsores or checked diapers or swept or done anything I was supposed to do since I got to the hall.

My insides turned heavy.

"It's probably best you go home now," Arleen said, giving me that sharp-toothed grin as she reached into her pocket and withdrew another disciplinary action slip. "You better show up on time for your next shift. If you still work here."

CHAPTER FOUR

Madog ab Owain Gwynedd.

Otherwise known as Madoc.

"Found you," I whispered. I was staring at the screen of a computer in the Never Public Library, at a thumbnail of an oil painting of a Welsh prince stepping onto American shores. I tugged at the sleeves of my wrinkled blue blouse and tried not to notice that it smelled like the geriatric ward. My jeans were grimy from wearing them for twenty-four hours, and I knew I needed a bath, but I didn't have time.

Well, I had time. I just didn't know how long I'd get to keep it.

Wikipedia informed me that Madoc fled violence in Wales to come to America in AD 1170, a full three hundred years before Columbus floated by. Madoc's crest was a bloodred griffin on a field of gold. I stared at the lion face and huge crimson wings. My heavy lids tried to close, but I jerked myself awake. I had bought a cheap watch at the dollar store on my way here from

Lincoln and put it on my left wrist. I never usually bothered with watches, because they always stopped when I wore them. This one was no exception. The hands were frozen at around 8:00 a.m., but the library clock told me it was actually 10:30 a.m., Halloween day. Four hours until my next shift was supposed to start, assuming Arleen hadn't tried to get me fired. I hadn't stuck around to find out. The thought made me sick.

I kept glancing from the wall clock to the computer clock, terrified that time would slide past me again. I needed to finish my googling and get more coffee if I wanted to have a prayer of staying awake at Lincoln this afternoon. Clumsily, I clicked through a few more links. Some sites said Madoc's journey was a legend, with no proof behind it. Other sites carefully detailed the stories claiming that Madoc and his forces came to what would become the United States and settled near present-day Louisville, just over the border with Indiana, in an area called Devil's Backbone. There was a lot of talk about tribes of "blond Indians" speaking Welsh in that area, and they left behind forts that later explorers discovered.

Devil's Backbone. That was about an hour from here. I looked at the clock. Looked at the clock again to be sure time wasn't moving freaky-fast.

In 1799, six skeletons wearing brass armor emblazoned with a griffin were found near Devil's Backbone. A dig around Columbus, Indiana, turned up a nine-foot skeleton wearing Welsh jewelry. Then, in the late 1800s, a guy dug up a bronze helmet and shield in a vacant lot on the Kentucky side of the line. Another dig found piles of human bones near Clarksville, Indiana, like some massive battle took out an entire population. Huge floods from the Ohio River in the early 1900s washed away all that proof—but then in 1925 in Walkerton, Indiana, a group of archaeologists discovered another bunch of giant skeletons wearing heavy copper armor. Those skeletons and the armor vanished shortly after, but some researchers swore the breastplates were marked with Madoc's griffin.

Even though I might have imagined everything that happened at Lincoln, this Madoc thing seemed real enough. What it had to do with me, I had no clue. I was pretty sure one of my parents was Hispanic, since my real name was Forastera, which had gotten shortened and fixed up to Forest to make it easier for me in school. My first caseworker taught me that Forastera was a Spanish white grape that grew in the Canary Islands. One of my foster sisters used to tell me it meant that I'd grow up to be a giant yellow wino.

As for the race of my other parent, who knows. I was average height, average weight. Nothing blond or tall about me, with my dark, curly hair and dusky brown skin.

My nerves jumped, and I looked at the clock. It was a little after 10:45 a.m. I had to force myself to look away, because I was so worried time would move too fast if I stopped paying attention.

One part of this Madoc legend didn't make sense to me, though. Back in medieval times, nutrition sucked, so people didn't grow to be so tall. Folks in Europe were usually short and skinny unless they were rich, and then they were short and fat.

I yawned, then muttered, "So what's with the tall skeletons?"

"They were different," said a voice from right next to me at the computer table.

I jumped and looked to my left as the scent of fresh pine washed over me.

"They had power inside." Levi gazed back at me, his blood tattoos as vivid and shocking as the red griffin on Madoc's coat of arms. He pointed to the article about the tall skeletons. "Imogene says maybe they were magic people, running away from all the people settling in Europe."

My fingers curled into fists, and I sat very still, not even breathing. From somewhere far in the distance, I heard dogs howling. *Baying.* I'd heard that term before about dogs, the kind that hunted things.

Like . . . me?

You ain't safe from a haint, no matter where you hide.

Levi's black eyes blazed, and my whole body twitched like he had singed my skin. "You aren't dead, but you can see me even when I don't want you to," he said. "How?"

This guy—ghost—hallucination—whatever—was unhinged.

The dogs got louder. Closer. I imagined dozens of them charging toward the library, teeth gnashing, rabid for my blood.

"Maybe you're close to dying." Levi sounded so arrogant I wanted to punch him. "That's gotta be it."

How was I supposed to respond to that? Besides, there were people in the library. If I said anything at all, they wouldn't see the murderous prince of darkness sitting next to me, they'd see me talking to nothing.

Levi frowned. "You think you might have Madoc blood? Who are your parents? What's your name?"

My eyes darted around the library. None of the other patrons seemed to be hearing the dogs. My heart seized, and I looked at the clock. Still not 11:00 yet. Time was okay. I was okay— except some freak was threatening my life, my mouth was dry, and I felt dizzy enough to faint.

Levi's lips quirked into a feral smile. "You can stay quiet if you want, but when you die, I'll take you to the other side whether you want to go or not."

The baying of the hounds reached a crescendo. I ground my teeth, sure they'd come busting through the library walls any second. A flicker of shadow across the ceiling caught my attention, and the honks of wild geese added to the dogs, overwhelming everything else in the universe. All my instincts screamed at me to run, but I was in a library. What was he going to do, let his dogs eat me in front of everybody?

My heart beat so hard my chest hurt with each thump, but fear was just fear. I could think through it, and when I did, it usually pissed me off. Anger was a lot safer than being scared. I embraced it, let the heat fill me and chase away my shakes. After a quick glance around to be sure most normal people were far enough away from the tables not to hear a word, I told Levi in a low voice, "I haven't had a chance to search for 'other side' or 'haint' or 'monsters who run with hounds and geese,' but they're on my list."

His smile shifted and his lips parted, like he might be

surprised. The goose shadows moved crazily on the walls and ceiling. I tried not to look at them, but they weren't honking anymore. The hounds seemed to run right by the library, still baying but moving on, farther and farther away, until the noise eased and I could think more clearly.

Levi's eyes bored into mine, and his brows pulled together. "You really don't know anything, do you?"

I heard wonder in those words. I also heard danger. I had changed homes and schools often enough to know that ignorance about situations was a good way to get my ass kicked. I stood just as his long fingers snaked toward my broken watch. When he made contact with my wrist, an electric jolt slammed my teeth together. He grunted with pain and pulled his hand back fast, but not before I saw welts rising along the pads of his fingers.

"Don't touch me," I said, too loud for the library.

At the main desk a few rows away, the librarian raised his head and glared in my direction.

Levi glared, too, and the computer in front of me let out an electronic whine. The screen turned blue, some kind of error message appeared, and it shut down with a sickening shriek. This brought the librarian at a gallop, and the little guy pushed past me to punch the tower's on button two or three times before turning his attention to me. "What did you do? Miss—what did you say your name was?"

I had already grabbed my bag. Time to go.

"You signed a usage agreement," the librarian called after me as I hit the door. "I have your address, you know!"

I burst outside into the early afternoon sun, and the fall air immediately chilled me as I walked away from the library and Levi as fast as I could. They could look at the computer's activity log or its software, hardware, or whatever. I didn't hurt it. They'd figure that out. I couldn't handle any more problems right this second.

Lincoln was less than a mile from the library. I could make that in twenty minutes, easy. I glanced at my watch, which was still just as broken. A clock in the window of a convenience store said it was noon.

Crap!

I had lost an hour during all that goose-and-dog chaos in the library.

But I wasn't late to work. Not yet, anyway. I needed to get to the hospital and see this Imogene person my hallucinations kept talking to me about. Maybe she could help some of this make more sense.

I hadn't gone a block when the sharp tang of pine made my eyes water. Satan put in his appearance, popping out of swirling air near a holly bush and matching me step for step on the sidewalk as I made tracks toward Lincoln.

Without looking at Levi, I snarled, "Go away."

"I scared you." All the sarcasm and nastiness had left his voice. "I didn't mean to. No, wait. I did mean to, but I shouldn't have. I'm—sorry. Please, let me help you figure this out."

"Go. Away." I desperately searched for another clock face somewhere to make sure his appearance hadn't skewed time again and screwed me completely.

He stayed quiet for a few strides, then said, almost gently, "At least tell me your name."

Oooh. The devil wanted to know my name. In the movies, didn't that give him all kinds of power? But this wasn't a movie, and identities were easy to come by, especially since he could just wait a few hours and materialize on the ward when I was wearing my name badge.

"Forest," I told him. "Now will you go away?"

"You need to come with me and see—"

"Imogene, in Tower Cottage. Yeah. Already heard that. Headed there now."

Levi stopped talking, but he didn't go away. New energy seemed to radiate from his black-clad arms and shoulders, wrapping around me like a relaxing blanket. The sensation didn't give me the shivers. It warmed me and cooled me at the same time, helping me focus. It felt almost protective.

"Stop," I told him. "Whatever you're doing. I don't need your help. I don't even want you here, okay?"

He stayed quiet. The sensation didn't go away. He matched my pace all the way to Lincoln, straight up to the big wooden front door of Tower Cottage.

I stood outside the entrance, breathing hard and feeling way weird. I had lived around Never my whole life, as far as I could remember. I had grown up with the bell tower as part of my landscape, but I'd never actually come this close to it. The tower was part of a hospital where everything was confidential, so it wasn't like they offered tours. Even though I worked at Lincoln, I had never been inside Tower Cottage before. Direct-care staff had no reason to pull charts or look up old records. I had never seen the dark wooden front door face-on like this, and I had never seen the gleaming brass door knocker. It was formed in the shape of a griffin, with a flowing mane and large, feathered wings. I stepped in for a closer look, then got terrified it would turn to look at me like the man in Miss Sally's picture.

Before any weirdness could attack, I grabbed the big brass handle and pushed open the door, letting myself in to an impressive entry hall with a white marble floor that had the seal of the State of Kentucky tiled into the center. The walls were red limestone like those in the basement ward where I worked, but these walls were lined with portraits—probably previous facility directors, or "superintendents," as they used to be called. Four hallways led off the entryway, and I saw stairs in two of them. A clock over one hallway let me know it was 12:30. I had two hours until my shift—assuming nothing went loopy.

Levi must have slipped in behind me, because he got my attention by clearing his throat. He gestured upward and said, "Third floor."

I glanced where he was pointing and caught my breath.

The cottage didn't have a ceiling.

It opened straight up toward the tower roof, where a layer of wood painted like sky and clouds blocked my view of the bells. I felt like I was staring up a giant steeple. Balconies overlooked the entryway on all sides, and here and there people were walking. The perspective seemed off, as though the tower reached all the way to somewhere else. I felt like I could almost see it, like when you squint at shapes way off in the distance. I swayed, exhausted and impressed and dizzy all at the same time.

Levi lurched to catch me, but stopped before making contact. He looked pained at his inability to touch me, but I righted myself without any help from him. The pine scent that clung to him got stronger, and his eyes brightened with . . . concern?

I was tired. Probably imagining things.

"This is the oldest building at Lincoln," Levi said in that soft Southern accent of his. "And the grounds are way older. Old places can mess with your head."

"The tower's not normal," I muttered, glancing at the fake sky again but looking away quickly before I threw up. "It goes places it shouldn't."

Levi frowned at me. He stared at the painted clouds. "You can *see* that? Imogene can, but I never see the thin spots, just feel them when I'm close. You can see it? Really?"

Great. Now I was doing something the devil himself couldn't manage.

Not okay.

I walked away from him again and headed to one of the stairways, aiming for the third floor and hoping some magical barrier would stop the Prince of Darkness from following me.

Of course I couldn't be that lucky.

I checked the clocks on each landing, then checked again when I walked onto the third floor with Levi trailing after me like a Goth puppy.

Signs on the wall guided me to various parts of the hospital records department. By instinct, I picked the arrow reading MAIN and followed the circle around to the right until I got to the suite with the DIRECTOR OF MEDICAL RECORDS plaque on the outside.

The heavy wooden door pushed open easily, and I let it swing shut on Levi as I walked into a room full of bookshelves. Out of the corner of my eye, I saw him catch the door easily. It actually stopped when he touched it, which made me stop. My heart thumped once. Twice.

The door . . . stopped moving. When he touched it.

My head swam.

Heaviness claimed my legs, my arms, and gravity dragged hard on my shoulders and head. I bent forward, smelling pine and old books and musty air.

He's solid.

He's actually real.

Until that second, I thought Levi was like Decker Greenway—some kind of spirit or ghost or hallucination.

Haint.

My knees hit the wooden floor, and I started to fall forward onto my face, but strong hands caught my shoulders. I felt the jolt of contact with Levi, heard him suck in a breath as the pain hit him, and then smelled something burning. His skin?

Oh God.

He eased me to the floor, then pulled his hands off me. His fingers were smoking. His silvery, pale face seemed translucent, and his black eyes gleamed with agony. He grimaced but didn't make a sound.

"Idiot," I murmured, visions of large brown volumes filling dozens of shelves swimming through my awareness. My words came out thick because my tongue and lips didn't want to move. "Why did you touch me when you knew it would hurt you?"

"You were falling." His voice sounded deeper from the pain. "I didn't want you to hurt yourself."

"You chase people with dogs and ghost-geese and scare them to death. Why do you care if I bump my head?"

"My job isn't that simple, Forest."

"Chasing terrified men through the halls of an ancient mental hospital is a *job*?" I sounded sarcastic, but what I was really thinking was, *He said my name.* Even though I felt goofy from no sleep and so much shock and confusion, that gave me shivers—and not the bad kind.

"Everybody needs to work, right?" Levi said. "I owe my grandmother a debt I can't ever pay, so, yeah, it's what I do."

I sat up and found myself beside him, face-to-face, my hip almost touching the outside of his knee. He was so close I could feel heat radiating between us, and his dark eyes seemed impossibly large. His tattoos filled my awareness, so perfect and colorful I wondered how I could have ever thought they were creepy.

I was filthy compared to him. Dirty and unwashed and plain. Shame made my cheeks flush, and he lifted a hand, holding his fingertips a hair's breadth from my cheek.

"Forest," he whispered. "I like your name."

From somewhere behind us, a door opened. Moments later, a woman walked into the room, talking to two older men. The two guys shut up in a hurry and eyed me, obviously not seeing Levi.

"You okay?" one of them asked.

I did my best to force a smile. "Yeah, sorry. I just, um, tripped. Didn't want to get up too fast."

My attention shifted to the woman. She was pretty, but I couldn't tell how old she was, or what she actually looked like. One second she seemed to be tall and middle-aged, with blond hair and tanned skin, and the next, she was tiny and old and wrinkled, with the sharpest eyes I had ever seen. I blinked.

Tall and blond again. Wearing a navy pantsuit. She carried herself like somebody who knew a lot, somebody used to giving orders. I could tell the men respected her by the way they glanced at her to see what they should do about me.

"She seems fine," the lady drawled in a kind voice, but I heard the steel behind each word. "I'll see to her."

She barely gave me a glance as she led the men back to her office door, saw them out, and slid a bolt to lock them out—or to lock us in.

I got to my feet, feeling unsteady and off-balance all over again. Levi stood next to me, staying so close his black shirt brushed the sleeve of my blouse.

As the woman turned to face me, she started to glow and shrink. Her pantsuit turned into an old-fashioned dress with an apron, like the ones pioneer women wore. Her hair rippled, then seemed to braid itself into a thick, white rope. Her eyes—her eyes! So gray and bright and intense I could barely stand to look at her. Some kind of power shimmered and rose around her like a fog on a mountainside.

I felt it.

I felt *her*, somewhere way down in my bones.

She was trying to tear me apart!

My knees almost gave out as I mentally pushed back, and the bracelet on my wrist hummed and crackled. I tried to scream, but all I got out was a coughing squeak. I backed away, and Levi stepped around my outstretched arm, putting himself between me and—and whatever the old woman was.

It was like he broke a circuit, and the power invading me snapped away. Fog parted around him, rolling back toward the woman.

"Levi," she said in a voice that reminded me of deep caves and hollows. "You get away from her. *Now.*"

CHAPTER FIVE

N o," Levi told the woman in a tone that made my teeth hurt, and the scent of pine went to war with moss and rivers and really old wood. He had his arms out like he was shielding me, which I was grateful for and pissed about all at the same time.

"Her name's Forest, Imogene. Ease up on her. She doesn't mean any harm, and I think—I think she might be like you. This whole time I've been helping you, nobody but her has been able to see me, not when I've had my glamour on."

I wanted to ask Levi what *that* meant, but the old woman kept staring at me. She looked breakable and terrifying, and my insides were shaking even as her foggy power started to sink back into her skin. "Don't go meddlin' with what you can't control," she said to Levi. "This one's more than you can handle."

Levi didn't respond, except to let his arms fall to his sides.

My blood was pounding, and my eyes teared from the power still roiling around the old woman. My attention kept yanking to the clock over the office door, measuring each minute. I was terrified that all this weirdness would steal minutes and hours, and I'd be late and lose my job and my apartment and everything I was working for. College. My ticket out of Never. My future. What was I thinking, coming here, anyway? This wasn't any part of the real world. It wasn't any part of sanity.

"Is Forest your real name?" the woman asked.

I gaped at her.

Levi cleared his throat. "Better answer, Forest. My grandma doesn't wait well."

Rage bubbled through my veins and swept into my brain. "You try to kill a man in my hospital, then you threaten to kill me. I come here for answers, and *she* tries to kill me, too?" To him and the old woman both, I said, "Get out of my way. I'm done with this."

Levi just looked surprised.

I reached for him. He jumped out of my way, and I stalked forward, intending to see if I could burn Imogene with a touch, too.

She didn't budge from in front of the door as I approached, and she didn't look afraid—more amused. My mind calmly reminded me that she had some kind of freaky power that tried to tear people apart from the inside out. I slowed to a stop a pace or two in front of her. She was shorter than me, so I had to glare down at her. It made me feel like a bully.

She raised her hands above her head to the shelf next to the door, and came down with a huge brown volume identical to those on the other shelves lining the room. It was some kind of oversized ledger with the year I was born stenciled on the spine in black letters, and she opened to its center pages. She kept her gray gaze fixed on me. "Speak your name, child, so I can see where you came from."

I turned until I could see Levi, who had his arms folded. His expression was both intense and unreadable, and I could tell he was waiting for my answer.

My eyes darted to the clock.

Ten minutes until the start of my shift. Crap! How did that happen? How did time just *escape* like that?

"Forest Anderson," I told Imogene, so that maybe she'd get out of my way faster. "But don't expect the 'Anderson' to be much help. I got it from my first foster family. Whoever abandoned me just scrawled my given name in black marker across the front of my shirt. Happy now? Please move."

"Forest." Imogene held the big book in one hand and slipped the other into her pocket, producing a pen. She put it to the paper but didn't start writing, and she didn't move away from the door. "That don't ring true. Is it your second name—a nickname, maybe?"

"Actually, it's Forastera," I said, my anxiety ratcheting two levels with each tick of the clock above her head. "We Americanized it so I'd fit in better at school."

Imogene held her pen and stared at me. Her eyes widened, and her thin lips pulled apart into what might have been a smile. "Forastera. Well, I'll be."

I glanced at Levi. He looked even more surprised.

"You've got my name." I stepped to the side of Imogene. "So you can research me or look me up or whatever. Now I need to get to work."

"Forest," Levi said. "Please stay. We need to talk."

"No." My nerves twanged, and I hurried to check the clock. Eight minutes to get to the ward. "I don't have time for any of this." I lifted my hands again and wiggled my fingers. "Let me go, or we can do this with a lot of blistering."

Imogene's attention fixed on my bracelet. "That wood's from the other side. And the beads are pure iron. Did it grow up with you?"

That question startled me into stillness. I'd always thought it was a little weird that my bracelet never got too small, but I loved it. I didn't want anybody to think I was foolish—I just never mentioned it, really. My left hand wrapped around the smooth wood and iron beads, caressing them, which probably gave away how much it meant to me.

"It's all I have from my real parents," I muttered, saying way more than I meant to, and hearing heavy feelings lace through each word. I had a bracelet that wasn't normal. I had known that for a long time but hadn't admitted it to myself. I sure didn't want to admit it to this woman.

"You know what your name means?" Imogene asked, her drawl getting more relaxed.

I couldn't look at her. I could only stare at the clock. Seven minutes to get to the ward. "It's a type of white grape grown on the Canary Islands. Someday I'll be a giant yellow wino."

She didn't laugh. " 'Forastera' means 'foreigner.' " With her accent, it came out as "fur-ner." "Stranger. Whoever put you out didn't name you, child. They branded you."

"Branded me as what?"

Six minutes to get to the ward.

Imogene gave me a scary smile. "Snake-bit, like me." She cocked her head, and fog seemed to rise off her again. "I ain't seen another in over a hundred and fifty years."

A hundred years? Okay, yeah, sure. Snake-bit. That was old Southern for crazy as hell, cursed, full of bad luck—whatever. And this woman was nutty enough to act like she was hundreds of years old or something.

"I'm leaving now." My voice sounded low and shaky. "One way or the other."

"Maybe you ought to pull off that bracelet," Imogene said, "so I can get your measure."

"No," Levi said.

"Boy, don't you take that tone with me," Imogene snapped.

My pulse thundered in my ears, and I clenched my hand around my bracelet, ready to go to war.

"Don't touch her bracelet," Levi said. "And don't touch her."

Imogene stared at him, clearly stunned by his talking back to her. Levi seemed to be radiating a power of his own—only the fog clinging to him was darker than any night I had ever seen.

"What *are* you people?" I whispered, but neither one of them paid any attention to me at all.

For a few long seconds, they faced each other, and I saw how the lines of Imogene's face matched Levi's. Grandma, he'd called her. Only she seemed so much older now, like a great-grandmother, or even a great-great. Matching wills with Levi, it was sapping her somehow, and making her sad. Almost making her sick.

I had to fight a sudden urge to reach out and put my hands

on her, to ease the ache I sensed in her knotty joints. Her trembling frown reminded me too much of the patients I took care of, and even with the way she had treated me, I didn't want her to be in pain.

After what seemed like forever, she nodded once, and the battle between her and her grandson seemed to ebb.

"Imogene's a granny-woman," Levi said, shifting his eyes from his grandmother to me. "That means she can do some healing on the living, and spot folks with Madoc in them, and cross spirits to the other side when they have trouble going on their own. Since I got . . . well, something bad happened to me, and since then I've been helping her."

"Doing your job?" I asked, my voice sizzling with sarcasm. "Scaring poor spirits to death with dogs and birds so they freak out and run away from you?"

"I upset Forest," Levi said to his grandmother, almost like an apology. "She needs a little time to get used to how things are, that's all."

Imogene rubbed the sides of her face, like she was tired and getting a headache. "I guess that ain't unreasonable."

Levi let out a breath. "Okay, then. She needs to go to work."

Imogene moved aside without another word. She didn't so much as spare me a second glance.

I didn't stop to tell her off or thank Levi or punch him in the nose or anything.

I just ran.

CHAPTER SIX

She's been that way all day," Leslie told me as we stood in the doorway of Miss Sally's room. "Talking to herself and smiling and singing when she's awake like now—but her breathing's bad and her pressure's up and down."

Leslie had on black Halloween scrubs dotted with smiling white ghosts. Her sneakers were white, too, and she had fixed her hair in dozens of skinny braids, each tipped with a happy little ghost barrette. Just seeing her, standing next to her, I felt more normal.

She walked into the room and lifted the sheet so I could see Miss Sally's swollen feet. "All that puffiness, it's one of the signs. And touch her."

When I rested my fingers on Miss Sally's toes, they were cold.

"Decker," Miss Sally murmured as I took my hand away. She smiled, then squeezed her vacant eyes shut and seemed to fall straight asleep again, her breath whistling in and out like she was snoring, but the rattle sounded deeper.

It sounded bad.

I fidgeted with the sleeve of my dirty blue blouse, thinking how frail Miss Sally looked in the bed. Her skin had gone ashy, and her hands twitched like she was working hard in her dreams. Her picture slipped from between her fingers, but I caught it before it hit the floor and tucked it between her arm and the bed.

"Is she sick?" I asked Leslie as I walked into the hall.

Leslie snorted. "That's what that idiot in there's gonna call it." She gestured toward the nurse's station. Arleen was working again tonight, and the door was closed. She hadn't said a word to me, but I had found the two yellow write-up slips waiting in my box, with a warning that the next slip would be pink.

"Arleen won't want to do the extra care and paperwork," Leslie said. "She'll be trying to pack Miss Sally off to the medical hospital. Then they'll be sticking my poor baby with needles and poking tubes down her throat, trying to stop what can't be stopped. Seen it time and again at this place—it's a crime, if you ask me."

I glanced into Miss Sally's room again. "But what's wrong with her?"

"Honey, ain't nothing *wrong*." Leslie caught my right hand in hers and patted the back of it as though she could ease the sadness of what she was telling me. "She's passing. Nobody don't get in her way, she'll be gone by morning, and probably peaceful in her sleep, in this place that's been home to her for longer than she remembers." She let go of my fingers, then narrowed her warm eyes at me. "And you . . . you don't look much better. Get yourself to a bathroom and wash your face."

Before I could move, she reached up and ran her thumbs under my eyes, then gave me a frown so full of worry that it almost made me cry. "Them's some deep circles. You not sleeping?"

"I—" Oh, I wanted to cry *so* bad. I wanted to throw myself into Leslie's grandmotherly arms and let her hug me, and I wanted to tell her every crazy, impossible thing I had seen in the last day or so.

"I didn't sleep at all last night." I barely kept my chin from shaking as I spoke. "The double shift. And then—um, no. Didn't sleep this morning, either."

"Not sleeping, not changing your clothes, not taking care of yourself. That's how it starts, getting sick like these folks." She gave my cheek a loving pinch. "You watch that, you hear?"

I nodded.

And then I went to the bathroom and washed my face like she told me to do.

And then I went to work.

I changed sheets and bedpans. I made beds and gave baths and trimmed nails. I washed and combed and braided hair, and with every minute that passed the way it should, the world seemed calmer and more real. This was what I needed. This was what I had to have. I didn't even take a break, because if I didn't leave the ward, there was no chance I wouldn't get back on time.

Between each task, I checked on Miss Sally, and I whispered to her that Decker was close by and waiting for her, and that he loved her. This seemed to ease her mind a little bit when she woke and got worked up.

Getting on toward the last hour of my shift, the facility's

general practitioner came on the ward. She was older than Leslie, and looked enough like her to maybe be an aunt or a big sister. The two of them spoke in hushed tones, occasionally checking to be sure the nursing-station door was still closed. The doctor pulled an order sheet off her clipboard, scribbled a bunch of stuff on it, and then left as Leslie carried the orders to the station.

"This will help Miss Sally be comfortable," she told me as she passed Miss Sally's door, waving the orders. "Ought to piss Arleen right off, too, because Doc wouldn't sign off on the transfer to medical. Makes my night."

I realized Arleen would be bustling my way to do whatever Doc had ordered, so I slipped out of Miss Sally's room to check on the patient who slept in the room nearest the exit door. As I pulled up his sheet to cover his shoulders and keep him from getting chilled, I heard a muffled but unmistakable howling.

All the hairs on my arms and neck stood up at the same time, and my stomach flipped.

Levi.

Levi was in Lincoln's hallways again, and he was hunting.

But he wasn't hunting me.

I don't know how I knew that, but I had no question that the dogs weren't coming in my direction. But if Levi wasn't after me, then who—

My Sally's hours are counting down. Decker Greenway's words from the night before ran through my mind. *That's why I risked coming out of the tunnels to see her.*

"The haint knows I'm here," I muttered aloud in imitation of Decker's deep drawl, and slapped my hand against my forehead.

Miss Sally was dying. She was dying right now, and Decker intended to come here to meet her spirit.

Levi didn't understand that. He would do his "job," helping his grandmother or the granny-woman or whatever she was, and chase Decker to the other side, leaving Miss Sally all alone, with nobody to meet her.

"No, no, no!" I ran out of the patient's room and headed straight for the ward door.

"Forest?" Leslie's worried voice trailed after me, but I didn't stop—just yelled something about needing to get a soft drink and go to the bathroom.

This couldn't happen. It would be a tragedy. I wouldn't allow it—not without doing everything I could to make Levi see the higher right and wrong in Decker Greenway's situation.

I ran up the stairs to the main basement level and pounded down the long, long hall that led to the building with the canteen and clothing room. The tile seemed to stretch forever ahead of me. I doubled my speed, but I didn't seem to be going anywhere. The hallway just got longer, and the air got thick and heavy.

It smelled like pine.

Decker started screaming.

"Levi!" I yelled. "Stop it! You have to stop!"

I held out my right arm, leading with my bracelet as I ran, and the hallway around me shivered and shimmered. My muscles burned from pushing against the air, but I only shoved harder, hunting the hunter, tracking the dogs. My bracelet burned against my skin, each iron bead like a tiny poker, branding me with heat.

I kept pushing and running, running and pushing. It felt like the hospital itself was trying to keep me from getting to Levi—but I was moving. The hall shimmered again, and then the air barrier gave way with a soft pop. I slammed directly into the double doors separating me from the clothing room. Pain ricocheted up my arms and lodged in my elbows and shoulders, but I shoved it out of my mind.

As I finally burst into the hallway, stardust walls and floors and ceilings tied my senses in knots. Shadows of geese streamed around and around the silvery surfaces, screeching and honking and flapping blurry wings. Hounds crashed into my legs, snapping and snarling, but I kicked them away and staggered forward, yelling Levi's name until my side ached and I couldn't yell anymore. I saw him standing in front of the open clothing room door, radiating dark fog and holding Decker Greenway in a headlock and dragging him toward what looked like a black hole torn directly into the real world.

"Levi, wait!" I shrieked as the hounds swarmed me again, growling and biting and tearing at my ankles. They took me down like a graceless deer, and I hit the stardust floor so hard my head bounced with a crack. I saw flashing lights. Then all I could see was fur and teeth and blazing red eyes.

I beat at the crazed hounds, smashing my rowan bracelet into jowls and ears and clawing paws. Fur caught fire. Some of the dogs yelped. Blood streamed from my wrists, my arms, my cheeks, my legs, but I kept fighting. It felt like the hounds were three times the size they had been, and shredding the life right out of me. Somebody was screaming again. This time it was me.

All of a sudden the biting stopped, and the biggest dog I'd ever seen was standing over me. Its huge black head dipped until I had to stare into its blazing red eyes, and its fangs gnashed as drool dripped across my face.

I started to shake.

This thing had come to tear out my throat.

"Off!" Levi bellowed. "Cain. Off now!"

The black monster snapped its jaws at my face one more time, then, glaring and growling, it leaped away from me.

The next thing I knew, I was moving, up away from the monster dog and the rest of the howling hounds. Electricity ripped through me as Levi held me to his chest and carried me out of his pack of hunting dogs, squeezing me close, pressing me tighter against him until his clothes caught fire and his skin started to burn.

"Easy now," he said in a low chant. "Easy. You be easy." Each time he spoke, my pain lessened—but his had to be awful.

"Put me down," I said, slurring, barely audible. "I'm killing you. Put me down!"

"I'm sorry, Forest," he whispered as he eased me to the floor, propping my back against a stardust wall. "I'm so sorry."

Goose shadows flickered past in a migrating V-shape, honking softly. Levi sat down beside me, tore off some of his black shirt, and wiped blood off my cheeks until the fabric got too hot to handle.

"Easy," he kept saying, and sometimes he closed his eyes. Black fog drifted from his arms and fingertips, and my pain went away one bite at a time, one inch at a time. He was healing me.

Burned skin showed on his chest, raw and blistering, and I wished he would work some of that healing on himself. If I could have helped him, I would have.

A few dozen feet away from us, Levi's dogs circled around Decker Greenway, who was huddled against the now closed clothing room door. I got here in time. I grabbed Levi's forearms, then jerked my hands away when he winced from the shock I gave him.

"Don't take him now," I said, my voice nothing but a rasp in the now-quiet hallway. "Not yet. Just wait a few minutes. His Sally is coming."

Levi's handsome face went from worried to sad, and the blood-tattoo teardrop in the corner of his eye seemed all too real. "You almost got yourself killed for that?"

"They have to be together," I told him, my voice stronger now that I could breathe and wasn't being tortured by a thousand dog bites. I wanted to hold Levi and put my head on his shoulder and beg for Miss Sally and Decker, but I was poison to him. My touch brought Levi nothing but blisters and misery.

"It won't matter," he told me, his voice heavy with the same sadness I saw on his face. "When they cross over, they'll forget or they won't. Being together won't make any difference."

I held his gaze. "It'll make a difference to them."

Seconds passed. Then more seconds.

"Grant him asylum," I said, thinking about the irony of where we were and what I was asking Levi to consider. "Don't make him cross over until Sally finds him."

Levi closed his eyes, then opened them. "This really means so much to you?"

"It does."

"Enough to make a deal with me?"

"Don't do it," Decker shouted from next to the door. "That's a bargain with the devil, girl!"

Hounds growled and snapped, and Decker fell silent as Levi's dark eyes captured mine. He was sitting so close to me I almost couldn't stand it. "I won't hurt you. Can you trust me that much?"

I thought about it, then let out a slow breath. "Yes."

"Then here's my bargain. Decker stays and waits, and I help him cross over with Sally. You can watch to be sure I'm true to my word." Levi paused, gazing at me so intently that I wanted to look away, but also never wanted to look away. Could he mesmerize people and steal their will?

Did I care?

"For your part, you'll spend a little time with Imogene and do some learning," he said, "and we'll see if we can figure out what kind of power you have—because you definitely have some."

Once more, I thought about his words. Deals like this always had hidden meanings, didn't they? Traps to snare the idiot who made them, sure that they knew what they were doing.

I didn't have any clue what I was doing. I freely admitted that. But it didn't sound like Levi was asking for too much.

"You think I can do whatever Imogene does?" I said. "You think I'm whatever she is?"

Levi nodded. "Somebody knew about that, and tried to hide you. They must have had reasons. Whether they meant you good or evil, we have to figure that out."

"All right," I said. "One more condition, and I'll make your bargain."

Levi's brows lifted. He obviously wasn't used to people negotiating with him, but if I was handing over any part of my will or freedom, it would be on my own terms.

"Get rid of the dogs and the geese," I said. "I don't want Miss Sally's spirit scared out of its wits."

"Forest—"

I cut him off. "My way, or no deal. You can cross them over without all this." I waved at the stardust. "Low drama. Got me?"

Levi hesitated. I could tell he was truly worried about something. My safety? His own? But a few seconds later, he lowered his head and yielded with a quiet, "Okay."

"Then you have a bargain. Do we have to seal it in blood or something?"

He raised his head, his face only an inch from mine, his black eyes bright with amusement. "No. Anybody who breaks a promise to me crumbles to dust on the spot."

He was kidding.

I knew he was.

Right?

"What did you do, Forest?" Decker Greenway sounded desperate and sad. "You shouldn't have—"

He stopped talking, turning toward the hall that led to the

geriatric ward. He walked forward a step, heedless of the growling hounds.

My heart stuttered, and tears blurred my vision. There was only one thing that would get Decker's attention like that, and it was sad and magnificent, wonderful wrapped in awful. I didn't know whether to cry or shout with joy.

As I stood, the tears won out, followed by fear and shivers and a few hard seconds of talking to myself about being a grown-up and not freaking out.

Levi got to his feet in front of me and held out his hands, and the dogs and geese and stardust went away. The hallway returned to its normal tile and stone, the night lighting offering nothing but a dim yellow glow.

"Doing this your way," he said without looking at me.

From far above Lincoln Psychiatric Hospital, the bells of Tower Cottage started to ring.

Miss Sally Greenway was coming to find her husband.

CHAPTER SEVEN

She didn't come at a run.

She didn't come slowly, either.

Sally Greenway walked down the hallway toward the clothing room like a woman who meant to die on Halloween—like a woman who knew right where she was going.

Her face, the face that had been made of black marble and wrinkles, looked young and smooth and soft. She wore a short-sleeved yellow dress and she was barefoot, with her ebony hair flowing long and natural down her shoulders. She might have lived in the 1920s or the '30s or the '60s. She was timeless, and she was free, and she headed straight for Decker.

He started to cry. Then he opened his arms wide and Sally fell against him, wrapping herself around him until every part of her was touching him somewhere.

"I'm sorry," she said, but he told her she was silly, and that he loved her, and that he was the one who was sorry for getting himself dead trying to break her out of Lincoln, and they laughed, and the bells rang, and I never wanted them to have to let go of each other.

My fingers drifted to my bracelet, and I squeezed the wood and iron against my skin. Whoever gave me the bracelet—did they love me? Did they give me up to keep me safe?

Would anyone ever care about me like Decker cared about Sally?

Levi kept me about twenty feet away from the couple. Anytime I leaned closer, he held up a hand to stop me.

He kept his voice quiet as he said, "These aren't ghosts, just so you know. They're more like spooks. Maybe specters."

"What?"

Levi's mouth pressed into a straight line as he watched Sally and Decker. "Imogene's books up in the tower—she writes down everything she runs into at Lincoln. Got herself a sort of system. She says ghosts, they're just a sad bit of soul that got lost going to the other side. But up from that, there's stronger spirits. These two here, they got a touch of Madoc blood, so they're spooks at least. They can hurt you. "

I didn't say anything. I didn't even know where to start asking questions.

"They can't cross over by themselves," Levi said. "I have to help them."

I shook my head. "Leave them alone. Your idea of helping is to hunt them like animals."

Levi's smile seemed wry and sad. "I use things every soul's afraid of, that's all. It's too dangerous to leave energy like that loose on this side."

I wanted to argue with him, but thought better of it. What did I know about spirits? Exactly nada. And he'd kept his bargain with me so far. Decker and Sally were together, and they'd at least have a shot at remembering each other when they crossed.

"Let them hold hands, okay? Let them keep touching each other." I don't know why that felt important, but it did.

Levi shrugged. "If it makes you feel better."

He approached the couple slowly.

They let go of each other and turned to meet him, and heat blasted out of them, whipping past me like a sandstorm and dousing the lights in the hallway. My skin stung all over, and I blinked furiously, trying to clear the sensation of grit in my eyes.

Levi started to radiate black fog. Then he spread his arms and started talking. The bells seemed to ring louder.

"Haint," Decker said, "you can take us now. I won't fight you anymore."

"I'm not a haint," Levi said.

"You somethin'," Sally whispered, and I winced at the fear in her voice. "Even death didn't want you."

Levi shrugged. "Guess I'm unforgiven, like my grandmother."

Unforgiven.

What did that mean?

More energy crashed into me, knocking me against the wall and holding me fast. I could see, but I couldn't move or speak.

The clothing room door opened behind Decker and Sally, and I saw an endless, swirling black hole. I got dizzy so fast I would have collapsed if I hadn't been pinned to the wall.

As I stared into the whirling mass of nothingness Levi was urging Sally and Decker to approach, I thought I saw shapes. Trees and hills, big ones, rounded like ancient mountains.

Levi's voice dropped even lower, and he seemed to be chanting. Whatever held me turned me loose, and I found myself walking. All I could see was beauty in the darkness. Voices started to sing, sweet and soft and achingly haunted, and I had to get closer. I had to see the singers.

Keeping up his chant, Levi moved Sally and Decker to the edge of the darkness, which turned misty and spread into the hallway. Black fog spilled toward my feet, and when it reached me, I heard the singers more clearly.

Yes. That was right. I needed to keep walking.

Levi joined Decker's hand to Sally's. "This is for Forest," he said, and eased them into the breach together.

He followed them, palms on their shoulders.

I followed him.

Stardust blended with midnight and nothing. Obsidian mist chilled my face, and still the singers called to me. How could anyone hear that sound and not answer? I wanted to sing with them until I laughed and cried and forgot everything I had ever known. I wanted to dance until I couldn't dance another step.

Black became light, and light sizzled into blackness. I smelled pine and honey and fresh river water rushing over smooth gray rocks. I heard the daylight and the moon, smelled tomorrow, and felt yesterday's breath on my neck. My bracelet grew thorns that stabbed deep into my wrist, and the pain tasted like sunshine.

Nothing dissolved into everything, and I walked into a meadow with blue-green grass that tickled my fingertips as I bled on the soft brown earth.

Decker and Sally ran ahead of me, laughing and holding hands, until they vanished into the weeping branches of nearby willows. I had a sense of life all around me, life and death and everything in between. There was so much beauty here, and so much darkness. The grass, the dirt, the rocks, the trees—they all seemed to be aware of me.

They all seemed to be reaching for me.

"Forest!" Levi's shocked voice snaked beneath the songs in the fresh, warm air. Then he was standing in front of me. He was taller here, and too handsome to believe.

Grass wound around my ankles. Leaves drifted down from branches and landed lightly on my cheeks. Vines seemed to grow where I stood, stroking my legs and filling me with their joy. Birds and squirrels came closer, to stare at me. Deer and wolves, too, and stuff I didn't recognize.

"Forest," Levi said again.

This world seemed to know me. It was waiting for me, and had I been waiting for it? I felt completely alive and totally at peace. I didn't even care about the darkness at the edge of my vision.

I wrapped my arms around Levi's neck and held him close, feeling his warmth and his terrifying power cover every inch of my skin. He smelled better than anything. He wasn't hurting me and I wasn't burning him, not here in this perfect moment, in this perfect place.

A storm was coming. It charged toward me from far out on the edges of my awareness. I felt it, I knew it, and I didn't care. It was death, and I was life. I wouldn't allow it to touch us.

Levi cradled me like a fragile thing, binding me to him and setting me free forever, until he broke the embrace and broke my heart, pressing his lips against my ear and telling me in a voice like distant thunder, "You can't be here. It's not safe."

He pushed me away from him, away from the onrushing storm, and I fell backward.

I fell into darkness.

I fell forever.

And I landed alone in a dark stone hallway, bleeding from a dozen holes in my wrist and listening to the sound of my own sobs.

The bells were still ringing.

Leslie wept as she held my bracelet out of the way and bandaged my wrist.

It was too much for her, losing Miss Sally and me in the same night. She told me so—two or three times—and she never seemed to hear me when I said I was sorry. She kept looking at the pink slip on the bench beside me and shaking her head, saying it wasn't right. The ghosts in her braids kept smiling at me, and I tried not to look at them. The line between real and not real wasn't so clear to me yet.

I wasn't sure if it ever would be again.

Through the open door of the nurse's station, I saw the

gurney go by with its pitiful cargo, the sheet pulled tight and tucked over Miss Sally's head and feet.

"The bells rang from the time she died until the minute I found you," Leslie said. "Two solid hours. Where did you go, girl? And where you goin' now, without this job?"

"I don't know," I admitted, tears slipping down my cheeks.

Had I really dreamed about a field with singers and lovers and a handsome guy with the blackest eyes I'd ever seen?

I couldn't quite settle on my memories. They kept changing. One second, Levi's appearance and Decker Greenway's meeting up with Miss Sally seemed solid and right and real. The next, I lost the details, and everything turned to black fog and haunting songs.

"Something happened to you," Leslie said. "I know it did." She pulled me to her and kissed my forehead. "Let me take you home with me. See to you 'til you come back to yourself."

My heart leaped at this suggestion, but my bracelet tingled above the thorn wounds, and the beads started to burn.

Going with Leslie wouldn't be right, maybe not for me, or not for her—but the bracelet was giving me a clear message, so I hugged her, and I said no, and she cried.

My last night as a Lincoln employee felt like both the worst and best moment of my life.

I gave Leslie my badge and keys and left the geriatric ward without waiting for Security like I was supposed to do. I didn't travel in the normal way, though. I moved . . . to the left a bit. Somehow. I stepped to the side of what was supposed to be and what had always been, moving into the world that ran just underneath and beside the one I had grown up knowing.

Doors unlocked when I touched them. Nobody noticed that but me. And nobody even glanced in my direction when I crossed the campus to Tower Cottage, pressed my palm against the griffin door knocker, walked inside, and climbed up the stairs toward the painted sky. If I kept going up, I knew I could walk into somewhere else. But I didn't, because Levi had told me that the other side wasn't safe for me. Going there once had already changed me in ways I didn't understand. So I stopped at the bells and sat staring out at Never, Kentucky, until night went away and sunlight covered my cheeks with warmth.

Time passed, but it passed outside of me. I had no more part in it. I didn't know how or why, but I knew I was separate from time now, still human, still myself, but more . . . aware. I couldn't put it into words, but I knew that going to the other side had awakened something deep inside me, some kind of power. I couldn't describe it except to say that I was living outside everything I had ever known.

Ten hours or ten months or ten years might have passed before I came down from the tower. I hadn't changed on the outside, but other things had. I walked back to the geriatric ward, enjoying the spring flowers and budding trees. Inside, I noticed new paint and different light fixtures. The clothing room sign was gone. A new-looking white plaque read PATIENT BELONGINGS.

The doors didn't have locks anymore. Instead there were little boxes with red lights that scanned bar codes on badges to let people through. The lights turned off when I touched them, and the doors opened. Nobody paid me any attention as I made my way to where I knew I needed to be.

Leslie Hyatt was now in the room where Miss Sally Greenway had lived and died. I wondered if Leslie had asked for it. She seemed so tiny now, with hair thicker and whiter than Miss Sally's had ever been. I gently bathed Leslie and picked her out a gown of spring purple. Then I changed her sheets and made sure her room was spotless. Later that day, when I held the straw for her to drink a chocolate shake, the confusion left her eyes for a moment, and she stared at me and took my hand and whispered, "I always knew I'd see you again. You're one of those old souls, girl. I know you are."

I hugged her and kissed her cheek and took care of her until she didn't need me anymore.

Most people who die, they don't linger. It's a good thing.

He came to me the day after Leslie died, or maybe it was the next year. Time didn't matter much anymore, or at least, I didn't think it did.

I was sitting with the bells in Tower Cottage again, gazing out at the riot of fall colors spreading through Never.

Levi sat beside me, careful not to touch me, but so close his jeans brushed mine every time he took a breath. He was handsome as ever, and I wanted to slap him, and I wanted to kiss him, and that was okay for now. I was glad to see him.

And I was ready.

"At least we know for sure you're like Imogene and me," he said. "Otherwise you couldn't have gone to the other side and come back."

"So I'm . . . unforgiven," I muttered.

He snorted. "I guess, yeah. You're one of us."

One of us. That was a new one. I'd never really been part of group before. Now I was officially . . . what? A granny-woman?

Yay?

"What does it mean?" I asked him. " 'Unforgiven.' What did we do to need forgiving?"

Levi shrugged. "Nothing. Our great-greats must have been real pains, though. According to Imogene, until the good Lord decides to give us a pass and let us get old and die like normal folks, we have work to do to make up for their evils."

"Nice to know." And not something I really wanted to think about. I glanced at Levi, enjoying the way the light kissed the teardrop tattoos on his cheek. "If I take the bracelet off, can I touch you without burning you?"

"Probably. But don't." His hand twitched like he wanted to rest his fingers on my knee. I wished that he would, but I knew he couldn't. "You might need it someday, and I'd rather you be safe than sorry."

"When can I go back to the other side?"

He laughed. "Someday."

I leaned back, letting my head loll against one of the big bells. "Man, when someday *does* show up, I'm going to keep it busy."

Levi laughed again. I really enjoyed that sound.

"Imogene's waiting," he said. "She's got a bunch of lessons for you, about Madoc bloodlines and haunts and haints and shades and spooks and stuff. She's been writing definitions of every spirit she's seen at Lincoln for most of her life, and she'll teach it all to you whether you want to learn it or not."

"Tons of fun," I muttered. "Can't wait. I'm still planning to go to college, too, just so you know."

"Fine with me." Levi stood. "I like hanging around with smart girls."

I could tell he wanted to offer me his hand, but he refrained.

I pushed myself up and stood with my lips perilously close to one of his bright-red teardrops and whispered, "Have you seen Decker and Sally since they crossed over?"

He hesitated, just for a heartbeat. Then, "Yeah. I have."

I grinned. "Are they together?"

"They're together."

"And happy?"

"Yes."

"I'm waiting."

Levi rolled his eyes. Then he cleared his throat and said, "You were right, and I was wrong."

"See? I'm not the only one who can learn lessons."

"And rabbits aren't the only things I can feed my hounds."

I wiggled my fingers right in front of his nose. "Ooh. Scary. Why do you act like such a bad guy?"

His grin was wicked. "Maybe I am bad."

"Not buying it." I kept my eyes on his, and he looked away first.

"Imogene, she's all brightness, but me . . ." He shrugged. "I was pissed off and sad for a long time. I understand darkness best, I guess. I use it to do what I need to do with the spirits around Lincoln."

"You can understand darkness without being dark, Levi."

He didn't believe me, I could tell. And he was through talking, which was okay by me. I could let it go. For now.

Levi slipped around me, ducked under the bells, and stepped out of the tower, moving back to the real world through the painted sky.

I followed him down to the asylum, giving one of the bells a push as I went.

Part II
Hungry

Darius

CHAPTER EIGHT

Grandma Betty wasn't blind when she was born, but she was blind when she died in Lincoln Psychiatric Hospital. Blind, and a whole lot crazy.

Trust me, she had her reasons.

"Darius," she muttered from her bed on the geriatric ward.

I bent down, and she wrapped her knobby fingers around the pendant she gave me when I was little. It was a petrified wooden thorn, about the length of my pointer finger, black and shaped like a shark's tooth.

Sunlight streamed through the little windows at the top of the stone walls. It spread through the room, warming everything except Grandma. She was so cold that she could never get warm again, and I took hold of one of her hands. With the one holding the pendant, she used the thorn's leather cord to pull me down a few inches from those scarred, white patches where her eyes used to be.

"I'm sorry," she whispered. "I'm all that's been holding him back, but now I have to go." Her voice shook, but the fire that had burned her face stole her crying, too. She didn't have any way to make tears.

Nobody but her knew how she got burned the day my grandfather died, but we did know there had been some kind of explosion. The flames cooked Eff Leer to ashes and scorched Grandma, too. Mama said it was a miracle Grandma survived. As for my grandfather—good riddance.

Grandma's mental troubles started after that fire, there were spells when she'd have nightmares and shout and try to run off, but Mama and Dad kept her at home. Good thing God saw fit to make me big. At eighteen I was pushing six foot five and weighed two-fifty, so I handled Grandma until she got sick and forgetful and took to smacking me when I tried to keep her safe.

"Don't go yet," I said, my chest aching from not wanting to lose her. "Wait for Mama. She's getting lunch."

But that was stupid. Death didn't care that I loved my grandma, or that she had taught me how to sing and shave and sew buttons on shirts even though I had giant fingers. It didn't care that she had fought her cancer and dementia three years past when doctors said she couldn't. Death smelled like mushrooms growing in dark corners, and it sounded like the rattle in Grandma's breathing.

"What I started, you got to finish," Grandma told me, so quietly I barely made out the words. That didn't make any sense, but Grandma hadn't been making sense the last two weeks. Too much of the morphine she needed to keep her from screaming with pain.

When I didn't answer, she got angry, or maybe she was scared. "Darius Hyatt. You listening?"

"Yes, ma'am." I squeezed her fingers and let her hold me by my thorn necklace.

My nose almost touched hers. Her breath smelled like ripe strawberries, probably because of the ice cream I fed her earlier. I was so close she looked blurry. For a few seconds she seemed young, and she had eyes again, and they stared straight into mine.

The thought of my blind grandmother looking at me made my heart beat funny.

"You always see the truth," she told me as the life washed out of her. "Look hard."

She took one more whistling breath. Her arm jerked, yanking my hot cheek against her cold, cold skin as she went way too still in the bed.

Then she said something else.

I swear she did.

Her dead mouth moved, and her dead voice wheezed her last words into my ear.

"This time, it'll be *hungry*."

CHAPTER NINE

Can't believe you took a job at Lincoln." Mama frowned at me, then wheeled her chair square in the middle of my bedroom door so I'd have to run over her if I wanted to leave. "Both your grandmas *died* in that hospital."

"Both my grandmas were old, and their minds had left them." I pulled on my yellow Lincoln Psychiatric Security shirt, size four-x-extra-tall, short-sleeve since it was June and ten miles past hot in Never, Kentucky. "Wasn't the hospital that killed them."

"Don't bet on that," Mama muttered. "Death treats that hell-hole like a playground."

The dark skin around her eyes tightened like she was winding up for another bunch of argument, so I cut loose with, "Tuition's up five hundred dollars at Community next semester. Got to do something better than flip burgers."

She puckered her face until her lips looked three times bigger than they ought to. "Your dad's benefits should have been enough to put you through school."

I grabbed the black ball cap that went with my new uniform, bent down to Mama, and kissed the top of her head. No reason to say anything about Dad. That was an old bunch of fussing, and nothing I could fix. Dad had been a civilian contractor over in Afghanistan, and he got killed when I was six. Civilians don't get the same benefits as soldiers, so his company paid us enough to cover his funeral, then left us on our own. Mama kept teaching at Never Elementary until diabetes took her feet two years ago. I got a few small scholarships when I graduated last month, but I needed more to pay for books, save up for spring semester, and help meet our bills.

"Can you let me out of the bedroom?" I tried to look calm so Mama would stop worrying. "I don't need to be late my first day after orientation."

She shook her head no. "You look like a big old bumblebee in all that black and yellow. No son of Lela Hyatt is going out of this house dressed up like a bug."

My grandma Betty's presence seemed to whisper through our old house, weaving through the wooden floors and the white painted walls and wrapping itself around me like a hug. The hurt from missing her made my smile twitch, but I kept it on my face. It had been two weeks since we buried her. Time to get past it. Except the older Mama got, the more she sounded like Grandma Betty, and reminded me of her, too. I just hoped Mama never . . . you know. Got loopy like Grandma.

"Move, or I'll have to scoot you out of the way," I told her. "I know you'll smack me when I do it."

Mama let out a loud sigh, then rolled back enough to let me

out of my bedroom. "Not like I could stop you. I haven't been able to pick you up since you were two."

I checked the clock on my nightstand: second shift started in half an hour. It only took ten minutes to drive to Lincoln, but I had to pick up Jessie, and I wanted time to grab some coffee.

Mama caught my hand as I moved past her, and when I looked down into her dark eyes, she got a little teary and asked, "What did Mama say to you before she died, Dare? Tell me again."

The thorn around my neck seemed to get hot enough to cook through my skin and wrap fiery roots around my heart.

Hungry.

The word echoed through my mind in my grandma's dead, raspy voice. It tried to force itself out of my mouth, too, but I wouldn't let it. I squeezed Mama's fingers gently, ignored my crazy thinking about the thorn, and repeated the same lie I'd been telling since the first time she asked.

"Grandma said to tell you she loved you."

CHAPTER TEN

Y ou sure you want to work at the nuthouse?" Jessie Sullivan leaned back in the passenger seat as my old Ford truck chewed up road between Starbucks and Lincoln. "Your family's got a lot of history with crazy. I'm just sayin'."

"Shut up." I shot a fake glare in his direction, but he was right, and so was Mama. Both of my grandmas died at Lincoln, and I had some cousins who kept getting sent to the funny farm for months at a stretch. As for my grandfather, he should have been locked in a prison cellar and fed through a hole. Electrocuted. Injected. Something.

Did everybody with a family history of crazy have to worry they'd catch it sooner or later?

Jessie fooled with his ponytail full of red hair as he snickered at me. "You got the easy job. Walking around, shining your flashlight, looking huge and pretending to keep the peace and all. I got stuck with direct care. Going on the wards, getting folks to eat and stay dressed and act right."

"You hate it so bad, stroll your tall self back to Mickey D's and make two dollars an hour less than me."

This time Jessie laughed. He needed money even more than I did, because he didn't have any scholarships and hadn't saved enough cash for his first semester.

My cell phone played a song, drowning out the King of Mouth. I had my earpiece in, so I punched it and said, "Hey, baby."

"I'm bored up here, Dare." Trina Martinez's voice sang like music in my ear, shoving Jessie and crazy grandmas and money right out of my mind. "When are you coming to visit me?"

I kept my eyes on the road, but all I saw was her sweet curves, wrapped in faded jeans and a bright-blue University of Kentucky T-shirt. She was already up at UK in Lexington because she started during the summer semester, studying biology on a full-ride scholarship. She was that smart in science, and that good in everything else, too. I liked her mind. And her wild, curly hair and her big, dark eyes and her sweet, sweet smile. She had been my girl since our first middle-school dance.

"Maybe Sunday," I told her. "If I can swing the gas."

The happy sound she made set my heart to beating faster, and I knew I'd be digging gas money out from under couch cushions if I had to. Trina was the one thing I let bust my budget. She'd been gone for four weeks, and I missed her too much to talk about. She started telling me about her classes and going to get burgers with her friends and how everybody liked to drink way more than she did.

"Don't whiz past the turn," Jessie said, but I almost did anyway.

I hated to, but I told Trina I had to go, then punched off the earpiece and pulled it free as we drove through the gates of the hospital campus. I kept my eyes off to the side, watching the lines on the road instead of paying much attention to Tower Cottage. Lincoln Psychiatric's bell tower rose above everything in town, and I didn't like to look at it. Always seemed off to me when I was little, like the top was blurry or shaped wrong or something. My whole life, I'd heard if the bells rang, the crazies were coming to get you. If they rang at night, you better stay inside and lock your doors.

"Didn't your grandma Betty always say we had too many murders and too many disasters around here to be normal?" Jessie asked.

I shrugged as I turned into a spot and parked. "Like you keep reminding me, Grandma Betty was one of the crazies."

"That's harsh, man," he said.

"You talk too much."

He quit talking and started laughing lots of different crazy-folk laughs, trying to bug me.

I ignored him as I went toward the back entrance where we were supposed to clock in. I had done okay keeping the creepy stuff out of my head during my week of orientation, but thanks to Jessie, it was on my mind now. I was here at Lincoln, and I couldn't leave for the next eight hours. The thorn around my neck started feeling warm again, but I tugged its cord and dug at it to shift its position. It had been doing that since Grandma died, changing temperatures whenever it felt like it. Either necklaces could be haunted, or I was starting to imagine weird stuff. I probably didn't need to be taking a job at a psychiatric hospital.

It's either work at Lincoln or wait a year to start college.

Had to keep a grip on that.

But something *was* wrong at this place. Lincoln Psychiatric felt . . . prickly.

"One day, Dare, you're just gonna turn crazy, too. You know that, right?" Jessie made another stupid laugh.

"Not before you, fool." I turned the thorn loose, went through the door, and let it swing shut before he could grab it. "See?" I hollered through the glass, giving him a grin the whole time. "You're already talking to yourself."

Then I took off, walking fast to keep in front of him on my way to the time clock. When I busted into the long, windowless security hall and let that door lock Jessie out, too, it was my turn to laugh out loud at him. He fussed and cussed and finally got his key in the lock as I swept my badge through the clock and recorded my existence.

Most of the doors in the hallway were closed, and one of the big hall lights was off, plunging part of the way into shadow. The place seemed kind of empty until Jessie clattered inside, still cussing at me for locking him out. He got his badge swiped before he was late, then said, "Well, I'm outta here. I think I'm on the third floor this afternoon."

I gave him a one-finger salute. "Hope you get to change a few diapers."

"Screw you, Dare." He grinned, and then he was gone, pushing through the security door and jogging toward the elevator.

The door banged closed, and the shadowy hall got silent again. I shook my head at Jessie, then turned around to find my own assignment. When I set my eyes on the dry-erase board next to the time clock, the taped lines on it seemed to shimmer in the low lighting.

I frowned. I seriously did not have time for this crap. Why did my brain have to do this to me? Weird stuff had been happening to me since I was little. Grandma called it seeing the truth, but I figured it was just the family crazy showing up and trying to invite me to the nut club. I shook off the crawlies, put my finger on the board, and found my name.

Darius Hyatt.

And beside that, a single word.

Tunnel.

The letters flickered at me, and my insides lurched, and for a second everything blurred like the bell tower did whenever I tried to focus on the top.

A hand grabbed my shoulder and I nearly yelled.

"Tried to give you an easy first day," Captain James said from behind me in his loud drill sergeant voice.

My heart kept thumping double-fast as I turned to him . . . and his face looked wrong. Too sharp. Like skin on a skull, stretched tight enough to snap. He was grinning, which didn't help, but I made myself smile back.

I had liked the guy when I interviewed, and all during training. Why did he look so mean now?

Except he didn't.

Now he was just himself again. An old guy in a black hat and yellow shirt. Lots of freckles like Jessie, and age spots on his nose.

One breath. Two breaths. I kept smiling. I could do this. I wasn't losing it like Grandma had.

"Come on." Captain James jerked his thumb toward the door. "I'll show you the way."

Don't bet on that. The thought came in Mama's voice, but also Grandma's, sarcastic and nervous.

For one tick of the time clock, Captain James looked like skin on a skull again.

I followed him anyway.

CHAPTER ELEVEN

Each building had access to the tunnels before we started clos-ing the entrances," Captain James explained as he walked me down a long, twisty piece of pavement toward the Recreation Hall. "The main access is in the Boiler House, and the offshoots run like a warren under the whole campus. Sealing them off is like working a giant puzzle. This hole broke open when we tried to close the tunnel next to it. It's too wide to fix in a hurry, so we'll have to keep somebody posted to be sure no patients get hurt."

I fiddled with the security radio clipped to my belt and tried to sound cool when I asked, "Do the patients come around back of the Rec Hall much?"

"Aren't supposed to leave the game room without staff, but things happen." The captain walked with longer strides. Dude was old, but he was ex-military, taller than me, and he moved fast. I was starting to break a sweat. It was almost two miles from the front gate to where we were headed.

We turned a corner on the tree-lined road. A huge, rickety barn loomed on my right. It used to be painted white from what I could tell, but now the boards were peeling and part of the roof had collapsed. On my left was a newer-looking stone building with the word RECREATION in big letters over the door.

Captain James led us around the corner of the stone building, his bald head gleaming white through the mesh of his ball cap. Behind the Rec Hall, a field about the length and width of a Walmart parking lot stretched toward thick woods. There was a basketball court, two volleyball nets, and a sandpit with a stake. Oversized plastic horseshoes were scattered everywhere, red and blue and yellow and green, mixed in with chunks of stone and brick and mortar and a bunch of hunks of dirt, too.

The captain stopped walking and gestured toward the building. "Here's the mess."

I turned and winced at the gaping hole on the right side of the Rec Hall. It was big and rounded, with mounds of plaster and stone lumped inside where walls had fallen in. There was nothing but a dark pit where the floor should have been, and I could tell that the earth sloped down, straight into that warren of tunnels the captain had described.

No wonder somebody had to stand back here. A marching band could fall into that hole. With those snaggly bricks and the black empty bottom, the opening looked like a mouth.

The radio on my belt squawked, and Grandma Betty's voice whispered, *Hungry!*

My heart thumped once, hard and painful. My gaze jerked to Captain James, but he didn't show any sign of hearing what I had heard. He just gestured to a guy in Security colors sitting on a folding chair at a card table with a little red cooler near the mouth—the hole—and said, "That's your station. There's some water bottles in the Igloo."

The guy at the table stood and gave us a wave.

The captain waved back, and the guy trotted away toward the main section of campus, leaving the chair empty and waiting for me.

"Radio if you need a bio break," Captain James said. "I'll send you relief for dinner around seventeen hundred."

I couldn't swallow, much less get a word out, so I nodded. My gaze popped back to the hole in the wall, and I turned the volume down on the radio to hush the bursts of static and Security chatter. It was hotter than it should have been. Sweat dripped down my face, stinging my eyes until they watered.

"I knew him, you know." The captain sounded matter-of-fact, and it took a long second for his words to sink all the way into my brain.

"Him," I repeated. My lips felt numb. I couldn't look at the captain. I couldn't *not* look at that hole. I knew who he was talking about, and I was pretty sure I didn't want to hear the rest of what Captain James had to say.

"I was just a boy." He paused. Cleared his throat. "He drove the ice-cream truck in my neighborhood." Another pause. A nervous-sounding laugh. "Never will forget that music. Kids' songs, you know? It's how he snagged his victims. The children he killed."

I didn't move. Not even a twitch. The hole in front of my

frozen eyes radiated its darkness, and the radio spit out static in voices I couldn't understand.

The captain clapped his hand against my shoulder and I jumped, but I still didn't look at him.

"Sorry," he said. "Must have been hard, growing up in that bastard's shadow."

When I still didn't answer—couldn't answer—he added, "I wouldn't worry, son. You're nothing like him."

Then Captain James walked away and left me standing there like a big idiot, not sure if I should spit or piss or run back home again.

It took me a full five minutes to get my brain together enough to walk over to the sunlit table and sit down in the chair. It strained like it was going to collapse under my big butt, but it held, and I sat there staring into the hole.

A minute passed.

Maybe this job *was* a bad idea.

The thorn around my neck caught the full afternoon sun and got hot under my yellow shirt.

Another minute passed.

More sweat gathered under my black hat.

Maybe this job was a *really* bad idea.

Three minutes, then four, then five.

Then the music started, soft and faraway, from somewhere way down in that black mouth with the brick teeth.

"Pop Goes the Weasel," slow-like and tinkly, as if it came from a big music box, or from the speakers on an old-fashioned ice-cream truck.

CHAPTER TWELVE

It's not something I want to discuss." Mama squinted at me as she gripped the arms of her wheelchair. She looked all rumpled in her gown, with her black-and-silver hair going in every direction. "Especially not at two in the morning."

"Mama."

She turned her face away from me and stared at the far wall of her bedroom. "We will *not* be doing this, Darius Hyatt. That man is dead. Let him stay buried."

I sat in the wing chair across from her bed and remembered what Captain James said, about growing up in Eff Leer's shadow. I'd taken a little teasing about my monster of a grandfather, but it pretty much stopped when I hit six feet tall in eighth grade. What had Mama gone through at school? At church? At home in her neighborhood? I didn't even want to think about it.

"I'm sorry, and I know it's late." I studied the back of my knuckles for a few seconds before I caught Mama's eye and gave it another try. "I've tried to find out what I need to know online.

There's hardly anything. And at the library, those years are missing from the newspaper archives."

Mama's gaze dropped to her lap, and my eyebrows lifted. Okay. Now I knew how the newspapers disappeared.

When she looked at me again, guilt dug deep in my gut. I needed to tell her the truth if I wanted her to do the same with me.

"Sometimes I hear things. Sometimes I see things, too. It's getting harder to not pay attention to them."

Mama didn't say a word back, but her eyes went bright like she was scared and mad all mixed together. I could almost hear what she was thinking. *Voices. Hallucinations. We will* not *be doing this, Darius Hyatt.*

"At Lincoln today, I heard music, like from an ice-cream truck. It was playing 'Pop Goes the Weasel.'"

Mama flinched so hard her wheelchair rattled. Then she covered her face with one hand.

I hated myself a little. I had left out the tunnel part, and how I was stationed outside the Rec Hall, sweating and listening to that freaky tune for hours until my dinner relief showed up and I pretty much ran all the way back to the Security station. I didn't tell her that the whole time the music played, I just sat there like a coward, about to piss my pants but not about to lose my job or be stupid enough to go looking for the source of that noise.

"Mama, I don't know if it was in my head, or something— you know. Like Grandma Betty's problems. It feels like things from the past, things that run underneath the present."

Mama saw stuff like that. She taught school and went to

church and tried to pray it all away, but I knew it still happened to her. Sometimes I caught her staring at the same things that caught my eye, or listening to nothing, just like me.

She kept her hand over her face. Through her fingers, she muttered, "Eff Leer died when I was nothing but a baby myself, boy, and ghosts don't exist."

"You told me the police never found his body. Just Grandma, all burned, walking down a road." Whatever had gone down that night, Grandma got locked up in Lincoln for about two years afterward. They didn't have burn units back then, so she almost died from infections in her burns. That much Mama had told me. Why wouldn't she let go of the rest of it? "How do you know for sure he got killed?"

Mama shuddered. "He's dead. Trust me on that."

"But how do you know?" I leaned forward.

Mama didn't even try to look at me. The room seemed to get all cold. The skin along my spine prickled, and when I let out a breath, I saw fog in the air. Then a whispery cloud formed beside Mama's wheelchair. It didn't have a real shape, just an outline, but I knew what it was.

"Mama," I whispered, staring at the thing in the air beside her. I should have been terrified, but I was more amazed. Maybe glad. Something was seriously wrong with me.

Mama's hand drifted back to her lap. She acted like she didn't see the cloud beside her, but I saw her shiver. "Your grandmother had a pocket full of teeth. And she was carrying an ax."

"What?" My skin was going numb from the cold, and my brain, too.

I had more than an ax, the Grandma Betty–shaped cloud whispered in a voice like snow falling on a faraway hill.

"More than an ax," I repeated, keeping my voice as steady as I could.

What I started, you got to finish, the cloud told me, and I heard disappointment, like she was sad I hadn't already taken care of business. *It's so hungry, Darius.*

Mama's mouth trembled, and a tear formed in the corner of her eye. "She had that ax. And she was carrying . . . she was carrying some of his head, too."

The cloud sighed and shifted, then dissolved away to nothing but sparkles. Had I really seen that? Had my grandma Betty's ghost been right in front of me, talking to me?

And she was carrying some of *his head*?

My full attention snapped back to Mama as the room got warmer.

"Times were different back then," Mama was saying, her shoulders slumped so far down it was hard to hear her. "Everybody knew what my father was, what he'd done. Nobody wanted your grandmother to suffer for saving all the children he would have killed. Your other grandmother—your father's mother, Leslie—was already working over at Lincoln, and she helped us and the police and the judge work it out."

It took all my strength, but I kept my face still and nodded my head when Mama looked at me. I even got up and hugged her and thanked her and helped her back to bed.

"There's a book," she said as I tucked her in. The light on her bedside table was on, so I could see she was crying. "It's in my bottom dresser drawer. I knew you'd ask me one day. I never wanted to hand you all that ugliness unless you needed it."

When I got finished helping Mama, I went to the drawer, did my best not to look at her underclothes as I pushed them aside, and pulled out a scrapbook the size of one of those picture collections people keep on living-room tables. Then I walked back to where Mama was lying, kissed the top of her head, set the brakes on her wheelchair, and turned off her light.

Then I went back to my room and read about a monster.

Mama had newspaper articles in there from fifty-two years ago, when everything had happened. There were a few police documents and pictures of the five boys the police thought Eff Leer murdered. They were all six years old. Eff had pulled out some of their baby teeth, the sharp ones on top—canines, the police report said. Grandma was carrying them in her robe pocket when they found her with that ax and the nasty piece of evidence that Eff Leer was done killing.

She was screaming and talking crazy about evil trees, and her face was burned so bad they had to ask Mama to be sure it was her. She got shipped off to Lincoln right quick and quiet. My grandfather's death made the headlines.

Child Killer Meets Justice in Fire

I had seen a couple of photos of him before, but none as good as these. He was tall like me but skinny, with a long nose and a pointy chin tipped with a tuft of beard. He reminded me of a sharp-dressed Pinocchio, all black suit and wooden parts and sharp joints. It was his eyes that really got my attention, though. Wide and dark and colder than black ice on frozen pavement. Just looking at them made me shiver, so I covered his face with my palm and kept reading.

The article said my grandfather was trying to burn trash with gasoline, and the gas ignited and killed him. The whole headless thing didn't make the paper, but the teeth did. They were recovered and given back to the parents of the dead boys. My grandmother was described as "distraught" over her husband's crimes, and "recuperating at Lincoln Psychiatric Hospital." My grandma Leslie was quoted in the article, asking people to give my family some privacy as they dealt with all the shock and tragedy.

My cell phone buzzed in my pocket. When I took it out, I saw it was close to three in the morning. It was Jessie, who never slept.

U awake?

Y, I texted back.

U ok?

Y. Lie. I was good at lying. Like my grandfather. Like my mother. Another text buzzed in.

U a dumb@z?

That dragged a smile out of me. I typed **No U R** and sent it. Then I pulled up Trina's number and sent her an **Ilovu**.

Two seconds later the phone played Trina's song, and when I answered, she said, "I was just now wanting to hear your voice."

And I just now found out my grandmother took an ax to my grandfather's head, then set him on fire. I needed to talk about it, but like Mama said, I didn't want to hand all that ugliness to Trina. There are some things you just don't say to people, even if they're true.

"You coming up this weekend?" she asked.

"I'm supposed to work Saturday." *My evil, dead, murdering grandfather might be haunting a tunnel at Lincoln Psychiatric.* "I'll try to come Sunday."

If I'm not locked away forever in Loony Land.

It would hurt Trina if I lost my mind, so I couldn't let that happen, right?

"I'll be waiting, Dare."

Like the ghost-cloud of my grandmother and "Pop Goes the Weasel," down in hell.

I closed my eyes. "I like hearing that, baby. I'll see you Sunday."

CHAPTER THIRTEEN

Sometime after I talked to Trina and before I woke up on Friday morning, a child went missing.

The guy on the news said he was six years old, his name was Jonas Brown, and the FBI and the National Guard were organizing a search. It took the local reporters ten minutes to bring up my grandfather. It took the national anchors five.

I made breakfast, put Mama in the car, and took her to spend the day helping clean our church, just in case reporters figured out we were what was left of Eff Leer's family and showed up at our door. I didn't want Mama bothered, especially if I wasn't there to look after her. I talked to Trina again before she went to class, and she gave me her love. I went by Starbucks and hassled Jessie while he played his online game. He gave me the finger. He also gave me a long lecture about the fact my grandfather was dead, and nobody was carrying on his evil. The kid probably got lost. They'd find him farting around some lake or clubhouse, and everything would be fine.

I wanted to believe that. I really, really did.

That afternoon, I went to work. When I got to Lincoln and found *Tunnel* next to my name on the assignment board, I wasn't surprised. Jessie wasn't on the schedule until Sunday, and there was no sign of Captain James, so I was on my own.

A bunch of security officers got to the time clock at the same second as me, so I waited my turn, swiped my badge, and headed out of the main building for the long walk to my post. They didn't stare at me or start whispering behind my back as I went, so I figured everything was okay, at least for now.

It wasn't sunny and hot like the day before. It was cloudy and dark and hot—the kind of day where the sky turns to metal and the air stinks like scummy puddles. By the time I got to the back section of the Rec Hall, sweat stung my eyes, and I wanted a water from the cooler on the card table in the worst way.

The guy stationed at the table saw me coming, gave me a pretend salute, and ambled away as I huffed the last few yards to the chair. When I opened the cooler, I found a half-empty bottle of water. Great. Whoever that guy was, I hoped he didn't have typhoid, and I killed what was left in a few gulps. Then I loaded some ice into the bottle and set it on the table to melt.

I sat down and checked out the area. Somebody had picked up the plastic horseshoes and stacked them near the metal stake in the sandpit. Otherwise, it looked pretty much the same as the last time I was here, with the big field bordered by woods, the basketball court, and the two volleyball nets. Everything had a steely gray coloring because of the weather, and the thick-feeling air made the silence seem too loud.

I glanced at the hole in the Rec Hall wall that led down into the tunnels. Still taped—wait. Did something just move in there?

I hit my feet so fast the ice bottle tumbled off the table. Something *was* moving. Walking up through the darkness from the warren underneath Lincoln. Pain stabbed through my ribs. I grabbed at my chest, catching the thorn pendant in my fist. Could guys my age have heart attacks? 'Cause—

Wait a minute.

As the thing in the shadows came closer, I could make out the yellow shirt and black pants and ball cap that matched what I was wearing.

Captain James hurried around the edges of the tape, his shoulder to me, then his back. He didn't wave or slow down or anything, just kept walking. Man, but he didn't look right. Too thin. Too tall. I almost couldn't tell the color of his skin. For a few seconds it seemed as dark as mine, then lighter, then too light, like if I squinted, I could see right through him.

My breath hitched. I thought about running.

As if he could feel me staring holes through his shoulder blades, Captain James stopped at the corner of the Rec Hall. He turned toward me slow, like he was trying to decide what he was going to do if somebody was watching him. Never mind how hot it was, I turned completely cold as he looked at me, smirked, and lifted his hand in greeting.

I let go of the thorn and lifted mine in answer.

I was waving to skin on a skull—a skull missing two teeth in the front. The pointy ones on top.

It's in my head. It's not real.

I wanted to yell, but my throat was dry, my voice not working. Air whistled out between my open lips.

Captain James didn't stand around long enough to turn normal again. He left me with my hand in the air like a fool. My fingers curled into a fist. I kept my eyes on the spot where I thought I had seen the skull thing dressed in the Captain James suit. Had it really been there? Was it all in my head?

I lowered my arm and counted under my breath until I got to one hundred. That always helped me not to be afraid of weird stuff when I was little. This time, it just helped me feel stupid. I pulled my cell phone out of my pocket and touched Trina's contact picture. We weren't supposed to use cell phones when we were around patients, but the only crazy person out back of the Rec Hall was me.

It rang three times, then went to voice mail. She was still in class. I listened to her sweet voice tell me she wasn't able to take my call, and that I should leave a message. I didn't trust myself to make sense, so I hung up instead of talking to her. Then I called Jessie and asked him to snag me some waters and a bag of ice and some grub and drive them to my station.

Half an hour later, when I saw him jog around the building toward me, I started breathing normal again.

"Dude!" Jessie said when he saw the hole I was guarding. "That's ginormous." He handed me the heavy bag of water and ice. "Think I'll get in trouble for being on campus when I'm not on the clock?"

"Not if you're bringing me lunch." I put the bag on the table.

It was totally stupid, but I had a sense that the tunnel—or maybe whatever was down inside it—was behaving because Jessie was here. No more weird pretend security captains crawling to the surface, no repeat of the creepy ice-cream truck music from yesterday, no vortex sucking me down to Hades. Nothing. It just sat there, all innocent. It might as well be smiling at me.

Jessie started loading the ice and waters into the cooler, and I just kept staring at the opening to the tunnel. "My grandmother whacked my grandfather."

"No joke?" He didn't even slow down on arranging the ice. That was the thing about Jessie. He could be completely annoying, but he had no mean judgment in him anywhere.

I sat in the folding chair, pawed through the snack bags and sandwiches Jessie had brought, and grabbed myself a roast beef and cheddar with sour cream and onion chips.

Jessie plopped down on the ground beside the table, found himself a sandwich, and picked a bag of cheese puffs. After we had eaten for a minute, both of us keeping our gazes fixed on the tunnel opening, I said, "I got on Mama last night and finally made her talk. My grandmother took an ax to the murderer, then set him on fire."

A small laugh popped out of Jessie, almost like a cough. A few flecks of cheese puff hit the grass in front of him, looking redder than his hair. "Go, Grandma Betty." He wiped his mouth with the back of his hand. "Bet she saved a lot of kids—but that must have been hard for her."

I told him everything Mama had finally shared, even the part about Grandma carrying some of my grandfather's head. He didn't vomit or anything. He also didn't take his eyes off the tunnel.

"When she was dying," I went on, trying to crank out what was worrying my brain, "she said something I thought was crazy talk like always, but now I'm wondering."

Jessie didn't say anything. He was waiting, letting me get everything out in one big wheeze. That was good, because if he interrupted me, I would stop talking.

I put down the last piece of my sandwich. "She said, 'What I started, you got to finish.'"

Now it was my turn to wait. Jessie stopped eating his cheese puffs and finally tore his eyes off the tunnel long enough to glance in my direction. After another few seconds, he shrugged. "If she cut off his head and burned his body, I'm pretty sure she finished what she started."

"Yeah. I kinda thought that, too." *But that tunnel plays ice-cream truck music when you're not around to make it behave, and Grandma Betty's ghost showed up to shame me last night, and now a kid's gone missing.*

I had to be losing my mind. No other explanation for how crazy I was thinking. Something like sadness crawled into my chest, mostly because I knew better than to lay the really nutty stuff in Jessie's lap. I shared everything with him and Trina. Almost.

"Your grandmother was probably all confused and scared that monster was coming to get her," Jessie said, turning his attention back to his cheese puffs and the tunnel. "That Jonas Brown kid—no ghost took him. I'm telling you, he just got lost or something."

"Everybody in Never probably thinks my grandfather's back." I shook my head. "Nothing like being the bogeyman's grandson."

"Sucks to be you." Jessie kept eating until rain started to fall. Nothing heavy. Mostly random spatters, but it was enough to get Jessie scrambling to his feet.

He helped me stow the few remaining bags of chips and pieces of sandwich in the bag, scrape out enough cooler ice to stow it in the Igloo, and lock the lid down before he took off jogging back to his half-wrecked Mustang. He said he was parked close and wouldn't get too wet. That was more than I could say for myself.

I made sure the communications radio was fastened into its leather case, pulled my ball cap tighter over my eyes, and got ready to ride out the wet. No way was I taking shelter at the edges of that tunnel.

Jessie hadn't been gone five minutes when the ice-cream truck music started. "Pop Goes the Weasel," just like before. I glared at the tunnel opening, more pissed than anything, but I could feel . . . something. Pulling at me. Teasing me. Almost daring me.

"You can knock it off," I said, refusing to think about who or what I was really talking to. "I won't be falling for that mess."

The music hesitated.

My heart nearly stopped beating in the silence.

Then the creepy tune started right back again, slower. My brain filled in each word as the notes played.

All . . . around . . . the mulberry bush . . .

"Not working. I'm not coming down there."

Seconds passed between each note, like the tunnel was mocking me.

The monkey . . . chased . . . the . . . weasel . . .

"You're dead, and you're staying dead."

And I refuse to lose my mind.

My whole body was shaking.

I forced myself to look away, running my gaze along the Rec Hall wall. I didn't have to look straight at it to save patients, right? I could glance all around the hole to be sure nobody was getting close.

Maybe if I didn't stare directly into that darkness—

The mon-key . . . thought . . . it was . . . all . . . in . . . fun . . .

POP! goes the weasel.

The last notes rushed together, loud and off-key. I winced and covered my ears.

When I finally pulled my hands away from my face, I heard something different rising from the earth below Lincoln Psychiatric.

Tiny, halting sniffles. Little choking sobs.

Oh God.

It was the sound of a little kid crying.

CHAPTER FOURTEEN

I didn't slow as I crashed through the yellow tape. My fingers fumbled with the flashlight on my belt, and as I ran down under the floor of the Rec Hall, under Lincoln Psychiatric, I managed to keep the thin beam shining ahead of me.

The floor was brick. The walls were brick. Old, dark red. Stained. I didn't want to think about it. Everything was arched and rounded, about the size of a train tunnel. The air was hot, then got cooler as I outran the gray glow from the world above me. The flashlight's beam seemed to get smaller. The air smelled like dirt, then stinky water. The walls were getting closer.

Old bulbs lined the ceiling, long and broken. My breathing sounded too loud, and the echoes of my running footsteps ricocheted on the brick. I felt like I was crushing the noise I was trying to find—the cries of a kid.

Please don't let this be happening.

The kid might be Jonas Brown. This might be real. Or I

might be crazy. But if there was even a tiny chance the kid had found his way down into the tunnel, I couldn't let him die. My blood, my family—if I had to die to save a little boy, I'd be paying a debt we owed.

My heart thumped as darkness crowded in on me. My flashlight punched at shadows too dark to light up, and the crying echoed ahead of me. The floor slanted down, and the walls got even closer. I wished I could run faster. I wanted to bellow and make all the stone drop away until I came face-to-face with the kid.

The notes of "Pop Goes the Weasel" started plinking like somebody had opened a demented music box. If I got my hands on whoever was playing that junk, I'd choke them. Made it hard for me to hear the kid, but there was only one way to run— straight ahead and down. It was cold now. My teeth started to chatter. I swept the flashlight left, then right, then left again. If I held out my arms, I'd hit the brick walls to either side of me. The tunnel was getting narrower and narrower.

The crying got louder. The kid sounded scared.

I growled and ran faster, the flashlight beam barely picking out fallen chunks of brick before I tripped over them. A chicken voice in the back of my head wondered how many kids heard that same music from my grandfather's ice-cream truck right before they died.

What was *wrong* with somebody that would make them kill little children? Or chop up their husband with an ax? What kind of diseased genes did I have, anyway? Had to be why I was crazy.

Had to be why I was hearing things now, but there was nothing I could do except run down that tunnel, because it was real. I didn't care what anyone thought, because it was *happening*.

My fists tightened as my arms pumped, making the flashlight jerk up and down. Twisted shadows dangled toward me. Snakes?

I dodged.

The shadows got bigger, and the space got so tight I had to slow down. Soon I was walking with my shoulders hunched forward so I'd fit through the tunnel, my elbows barely missing bricks. I was burning up and sweating even though it was frigid. The giant snakes weren't snakes at all. I could see that now, having managed to shine the flashlight high enough. I was looking at tree roots, and stumbling over the bricks and mortar the roots had dislodged.

I tried to tell myself the roots came from the real world—but they didn't look like any roots I'd ever seen. They reminded me of huge, gnarly fingers with dirty nails. The thorn around my neck had to be branding my skin, it was so hot against my chest. These roots were black like that thorn. They went on forever, and I couldn't imagine the size of the tree they were meant to feed.

Hungry, my grandmother's voice whispered just as the crying kid let out a shriek, and I jammed on the brakes because a brick wall sealed the path in front of me.

"Damn," I wheezed, bouncing the flashlight all around the bricks. A solid wall, from the looks of it. Again I heard my grandmother's words, the ones she spoke before she died. *You always see the truth . . . Look hard.*

I narrowed my eyes like I did when I wanted to see through something, see around it and into it, catch what most people missed. Nothing but dark, stained brick and those awful roots. I tapped at a place where the mortar looked loose. A few crumbles fell away, but the wall felt solid everywhere else I punched and poked.

Look hard.

Grateful that the stupid music hadn't started again, I stared to my left, running the flashlight up and down the seams of the corner. Nothing there but more roots, spilling down the brick and biting into the floor. I turned as much as I could in the little space and shined my light on the right wall.

Part of it moved—only it wasn't the wall. It was a solid coating of bugs.

"Jesus." I stepped back, banging into the roots, and my insides lurched from the dirty, poking touch of the cold wood. My skin crawled like those roaches were climbing toward my head. Somebody was swearing, and I guess it was me as I crammed my jeans into my socks so nothing could run up my pants. Couldn't do anything about closing my sleeves or collar, though. If they got on me and got that high, I'd probably piss myself and fall over dead, anyway.

I flashed the light in that corner over and over so the nasty little things would stay away, and that's when I caught . . . something. A shimmer. A strange, darker darkness at the wall seam. I looked hard, just like Grandma told me to. The air in the right-hand corner of the tunnel had an oily sparkle, like it wasn't solid, like it didn't have bricks behind it, except it did. I could see them. Sort of. They seemed lighter than the bricks on the left, or those in the wall in front of me.

I focused on the kid's pitiful crying and made myself inch forward. The whole time my eyes kept yanking to the side, checking for that moving curtain of roaches.

Man, I didn't want to, but I had to keep moving, jamming my bulk right up in that corner until my cheeks touched the chilled bricks and the scent of dirt and a billion rotten bug parts flooded my nose. I pushed forward into that greasy-looking black and thought I felt ten thousand roach legs scratching my skin, and—

I stepped through the wall, scraping my elbows on both sides, dropping my flashlight and stumbling and stomping to get my balance, jerking air into my lungs and hoping I didn't breathe in any roaches. I stood straight up in a big basement room, maybe as big as the field stretching from the Rec Hall to the woods surrounding Lincoln Psychiatric.

It was old. The walls—when there had been walls—had been made from wood, like the floor. All of it was rotten now, with plants growing through the boards, and bugs . . .

Yeah, there were bugs. Probably rats and mice and all kinds of other stuff I didn't want to see, too.

The thorn around my neck burned me so fast and hard I had to grab it. My eyes hurt from the weird red light that filled the place. It was coming from the base of a tree in the middle of the room that had to be the size of a whole building. Thirty feet across, maybe, and at least as deep, with hundreds of scrubby branches winding together and tangling all over each other. It had huge thorns and clumps of weird white flowers that gave off a sweet stink, like something that died in the sun.

The top of the tree reached high into the darkness at the basement's ceiling.

At least now I knew what those disgusting, twisty roots attached to. And where the crying was coming from.

Huddled against one of the biggest, fattest roots was a little kid with dark brown hair and dirt all over his bare feet and arms. He was wearing jeans and a striped shirt, and he looked just like a messy version of the kid I saw on the news this morning.

"Hey," I said to him. "Jonas. Come here. I'll get you out of this place."

His sniffles choked away to nothing, and the kid twitched, but he didn't unlock his hands from around his knees.

"Jonas," I said. "I don't know how you got down here, but I'm with Security at Lincoln. I'll take you to your mom and dad."

The red glow coming from the tree flickered as a cold breeze swept through the chamber. The kid whimpered and huddled into a smaller ball.

Okay, fine. That's why God made big people big and little people little. I didn't want to scare the kid, but I needed to pick him up and get him out of this nightmare place. Refusing to look around too much or think more than I had to, I strode forward, bent down, and grabbed Jonas.

He didn't struggle as I lifted him, but he didn't grab me back, either. He just kept his arms wrapped around his own legs like if he let go, he'd disappear forever.

I couldn't make myself turn my back on that tree, so I inched away from it, trying to aim for the weird corner in the solid wall that hadn't been so solid after all. The red light flickered again, and another burst of cold air whipped through the giant chamber. Gooseflesh broke out across my neck, and Jonas let out a low whimper. I kept backing up.

The wall shouldn't be so far away. I hadn't walked that far to pick up the kid. I glanced over my shoulder. The wall was a few feet behind me.

When I looked back at the tree, there was a man standing beside it.

My breath hitched so suddenly my ribs hurt, and I stopped moving.

The man was wearing a tuxedo with tails, like people at prom who want to look badass. He was tall, with dark skin and long legs and knobby, puppet joints. I couldn't tell much about his nose or chin, because the left side of his face was missing. Part of his left arm was gone, too.

A horror like that couldn't be standing up, much less be alive. It definitely couldn't take a step toward me, or whistle "Pop Goes the Weasel."

But it did.

I squeezed Jonas to my chest so hard I made him cry.

The thing that had been my grandfather laughed, and my skin crawled like all those roaches had jumped on me at the same time. Red light danced off pulpy parts of the horror's face as it said, "Darius. It's about time we got to meet you."

We?

What the hell was it talking about, "we"?

The thing rested its good hand on the trunk of that monstrous tree, and something in the center of the tangled mass of branches shifted. It moved slow, like a piece of wood sliding or rolling or pulling upward.

The little boy in my arms screamed.

As the tree's single eye opened and blazed a bloody, hot red, I screamed, too.

CHAPTER FIFTEEN

I stumbled and smashed backward into the brick wall. Jonas writhed in my grip and screamed again.

My grandfather moved toward us. His feet didn't touch the floor. He flew straight at me, his half mouth open in a snarl.

If I had looked at the wall, I might have seen the opening, but I couldn't take my eyes off the thing streaking across the chamber, or that tree—my God. That eye! More bark shifted, and a mouth opened. It let out a creaking bellow that shook the walls and rattled my skull and made my bones ache.

It sounded desperate. It sounded insane.

Hungry . . .

I spun toward the wall, squinting and sweating and weeping and shaking so bad that nothing made straight lines.

"Darius." My grandfather's hot breath snaked across the back of my neck. "You got my blood in you, boy. I can smell it."

I stared at the wall in front of me. I looked hard, but I saw only brick.

Fingers closed on my shoulder, and thick yellow nails dug into my skin. "Your mama came out weak, but you got what it takes."

Jonas screamed and screamed and kept on screaming. My mouth hung open. I yelled but no sound came out as I jerked away from the thing trying to claim me. Jonas and I reeled sideways—and suddenly fell forward out of the rotten basement into the tunnel.

Darkness shrouded us, but I ran. Things scuttled across the walls. Roots stabbed through the bricks, cracking and groaning as they twisted. I didn't know where my grandfather was, if he was following, if he *could* follow. The thought of that half a face flying toward me made me run harder. Crumbling bricks and dirt exploded beneath my big feet. All I could see was black. All I could hear were Jonas's shrieks and my own cowardly yells. Some part of my mind registered the walls getting farther and farther apart.

Power rippled up the tunnel after us, cold and sharp and hateful. It chewed into my skin. It smelled like death. It felt like rage and starvation.

It whispered, *Mine . . .*

I ran.

Up ahead, I didn't see much light. Was it dark outside? How was that possible? I had only been in the tunnel for a few minutes. It was still afternoon.

Whatever.

If I could just get the boy to the entrance—if I could just get us outside, I could save Jonas. A hundred feet to go. Fifty. I could see the yellow tape now, crisscrossing over the entrance.

The tape I tore to get in here?

Something rough bit into my ankle and yanked me off my feet. I went down hard, throwing Jonas ahead of me so I didn't crush him. Ribs cracked as I smashed into the brick. I heard them but didn't feel them.

"Run!" I yelled at the kid, who was scrabbling forward on his hands and knees. He glanced back at me. His face was bleeding. Blood from his mouth coated his neck and shirt.

"Run!" I tried to shout again, but couldn't manage anything but a wheeze. I kicked at whatever had my ankle. I didn't want to look. I didn't want to know what it was. My bladder turned loose as roots wrapped around me, dragging me backward, down into the darkness and the roaches.

"Monster!" Jonas screamed. He got to his feet. His knees almost buckled, but he took a step toward the tape. Another. And another. Then he started to run, shouting, "Monster! Monster! Monster!"

The roots slithered across my throat. They poked at my ears and scraped my eyes. They clawed my arms and my legs and slipped in and out of my jeans pockets.

From way down in the hell of a basement, I heard my grandfather laughing.

Then I heard voices, a lot of them. Flashlight beams stabbed into the darkness. The roots flinched away from the lights and turned me loose, sizzling as they curled away down the tunnel.

I tried to suck in a breath, but my ribs hurt so bad I couldn't. The world got fuzzy. When hands grabbed me and turned me over, I swore.

Captain James's skull-face loomed over me, frowning. A

couple of other guys in black hats and yellow shirts stared down at me.

"You were right," one of them said to the captain. "He had the kid all along."

That didn't compute. Not at all.

"Blood will out," Captain James said. "People like him need to be shot at dawn. Why waste money on a trial?"

I stared up at him, trying to make sense of what was happening as new faces came into view. Bigger flashlights. Police uniforms. One of the policemen called for an ambulance on his radio. Another knelt beside me. He looked into my eyes and frowned as he took in the blood on my shirt. He pulled on latex gloves and cut off a piece of the fabric, slipping it into a plastic bag.

Wait, I wanted to tell him, but I couldn't talk. My breath whistled in and out, in and out, but it didn't feel like enough. I started seeing spots. I needed to explain. I needed to tell him—

What?

How I heard Jonas crying and ran down the tunnel and found a rotten basement with my zombie mass-murdering grandfather and an insane giant tree?

A tree with an eye. A tree with a mouth.

A tree that was hungry.

"Tree," I choked out. "The tree did it."

The officer checked my pockets. I had a little change in there, my keys, and my phone, but that's not what he pulled out first.

His frown got bigger as he shined his flashlight on his palm, and he tilted his hand to show me.

Two little white teeth, pointy on the ends.

CHAPTER SIXTEEN

Wake him up.
Levi. Be nice.
I don't do nice, Forest.
But it makes me happy.
. . .
. . .
Fine. I'll be nice for you.

That girl could be Trina. That guy could be me. For Trina, I'd try anything. If she were here, I'd pull her close. She'd smell like flowers, and she'd tell me I hadn't seen my dead grandfather or a tree with a bloody eyeball and a gaping mouth.

She'd tell me I hadn't hurt a child.

I imagined Trina's head on my shoulder and lifted my arm to hug her. Metal clanked against plastic. I jerked my hand but couldn't move it any farther. Handcuffed. I was shackled to a hospital bed—both wrists and both ankles, too. My body throbbed from a dozen cuts and busted ribs and the place where the doctor had stuck in a tube to reinflate my lung. My chest hurt because my life was over.

My family crazy had mugged me just when I thought I was safe. I didn't even want to open my eyes. If I did, I might see my mama crying. I'd definitely see the two policemen outside my room, standing guard over Never's newest monster.

From the far right corner of the room came soft snores and snorts, and I knew Mama was sleeping in her wheelchair.

When I finally did open my eyes, I stared at the day and date on the dry-erase board in front of me, and then at the ceiling. How could it be Tuesday when I went down in that tunnel Friday afternoon? Friday night, all of Saturday, all of Sunday, and Monday until around midnight when I popped out with Jonas—gone.

Was Jonas okay?

Had he tried to tell anybody about what was haunting the tunnels of Lincoln Psychiatric?

I counted the dots in the hospital ceiling tiles.

It wouldn't matter what Jonas said. He was just a little kid. If he told stories about evil freaks trying to kill him, the police would figure he was talking about me.

And what was the truth?

I had no idea what I had been doing down in that tunnel for three days, when it felt like only three minutes. Okay, half an hour, tops—

Three days.

And I had the kid's teeth in my pocket.

Somebody pulled them right out of his head.

I shut my eyes. Images of ceiling dots played on my lids. The police had searched all up in that tunnel. If they had found biting, snaky roots or a nasty basement with my undead grandfather and a man-eating tree, they would have taken the chains off my wrists and ankles.

I didn't pull that kid's teeth.

My grandfather must have done it—but was he even real? Maybe I was playing games in my own head so I wouldn't know I was crazy and doing awful things to a kid.

There in the hospital, in the dark of my own mind and chained like an animal, I searched my heart. I didn't *feel* any meanness inside it. It thumped along, powered by the blood of a serial killer.

You got what it takes.

That's what Eff Leer had told me.

"When you open your eyes again," a girl's voice said, "don't yell."

My lids flew up and my head turned toward the sound. There *was* a girl in my room! She was my age, but kinda small, wearing jeans and a yellow blouse. She had tan-looking skin and dark curls dropping over both shoulders. Her eyes tilted toward her nose, making them look bigger and brighter than they already were.

The police outside my room didn't seem to notice her. My snoring mama didn't even twitch when the girl spoke.

Great.

I was getting crazier by the second.

"You're not imagining me," the girl said. "I'm really here. My name is Forest."

Forest? Like from my dream before I woke up in this nightmare? But if Forest was real, then Levi—

"We should go," said a guy.

My head whipped to the left.

Okay.

Yeah.

I jerked my arms against the bedrails, hating the handcuffs twice as bad. I was trapped and completely helpless. The guy had on black jeans and a black T-shirt. Red tattoos marked the pale skin under one eye. His eyes were blacker than a midnight with no moon, and when I stared into them, I knew he wasn't right in the head.

My breathing got fast. I yanked against the cuffs one more time.

Dogs howled in the distance, like the kind people hunt with, and even the close-shaved hairs on my head stuck straight up in the air. I ground my teeth, and somewhere far away, bells started to ring.

Jesus.

Those were the Lincoln bells.

I had to get out of the damned bed—but all I could do was thrash and rattle and clink.

"Knock it off, Levi." The girl, Forest, sounded ticked. "We didn't come here to upset him."

"You're right," said Dracula's brother. He had a Southern

accent, but not a strong one. "We came here to fetch him, so let's go. Now."

Forest sighed. "You can't just barge into hospital rooms and snatch folks out of bed. He's hurt, and you'll upset his mother."

Levi stretched his hand toward my shoulder. I tried to get away from him, but the cuffs held firm. Something like black fog came out of his fingertips and shocked my entire body. My mouth came open and I shouted, but no sound came out at all. Sweat beaded on my face and arms and legs, and the blazing agony in my chest made my eyes water. I was burning. I knew I was on fire. My mouth opened wider and my eyes bugged. Needed to breathe and the heat had to stop and—

And it did.

Just like that.

Gone.

I sucked air so loud both officers at my door turned to glance inside, and Mama let out some extra snorts as she shifted in her wheelchair. The policemen gazed at me, then turned back to the hall, oblivious to Forest and the guy who had just tried to kill me. But I was breathing a lot better now. I didn't have pain anywhere. No cuts or bruises, either, and my ribs felt pretty normal.

Levi looked like he was hurting, but only for a second. He let out a slow breath, then brushed his fingertips across the shackles.

More black fog came from nowhere, and the handcuffs made hissing noises, then fell off. Levi caught the one on his side before it hit the floor and laid it on the bed. The sight of all that metal falling off me, the sudden freedom after being tied to the bed—it made me light inside. My nerves settled in spite of the situation. I flexed my legs and arms before sitting up. Then I pulled the sheet over the broken cuffs so the guards wouldn't be able to see that I wasn't chained.

"There," Levi said to the girl. "He's not hurt anymore. Now can we go?"

Forest frowned at him, but I could tell she wasn't that unhappy. Trina looked at me like that sometimes. She usually kissed me right after. Or slapped me. Depended on the situation.

As for Levi, when he looked at Forest, I could see right through his big bad act. He was our age, or close to it, and something about him seemed jumpy. This girl Forest, she was his kryptonite or garlic or whatever controls freaky dudes with vampire skin and bloody teardrop tattoos.

"Please excuse him," Forest said to me, gesturing to Levi. "He had a hard life, and some bad stuff happened to him. He's a little low on the social skills, but I'm working on it."

I was trying to pull myself up in the bed, and he reached down to grab my arm. I thought he meant to help me, but a frigid wind knocked him sideways before he got hold of me.

Don't you touch him!

Women's voices—two of them, and I knew them both. My grandmother Betty, and my grandmother Leslie, too. The sounds came from my head and from the air, from nowhere and everywhere all at once. Mama woke with a grunt and sat up straight in her wheelchair.

I jumped when I heard the whispers. So did Forest and Levi, but out in the hall, the policemen didn't twitch. Whatever this new crazy was, it was only happening in my room.

"Grandma Betty?" I whispered as a misty shape formed between my bed and Levi, and he and Forest and Mama could only gape at the foggy image. A second image flickered beside the first one, and this one was even more clear. "Grandma Leslie—" I started, but Forest cut me off with a little cry.

"Leslie Hyatt," Forest whispered, shocking me almost as much as what I was seeing. Her eyes had gone wide. She walked around the mist like she was taking in all the details. "Leslie," she said again, as if she were talking to her best friend, even though there was no way she could know a woman who had died when I was just a little kid.

"I thought you said only people with Madoc blood could turn into spooks and haunts," Forest said to Levi, never taking her eyes off the cloud that was Grandma Leslie. "Like Decker and Miss Sally."

"I thought—well." Levi edged closer to my grandma Betty. "Maybe these two have a touch of it."

"She didn't," Forest said, reaching her fingers toward the image of Grandma Leslie.

As Forest's fingertips passed through the edge of the woman-shaped cloud, Grandma Leslie smiled.

You look good, girl, Grandma Leslie told Forest in a voice like a summer breeze.

Forest lowered her head and covered her mouth.

I felt my grandmothers like a force in my heart, angry and determined and scared. I glanced at Mama, who was shifting focus from the ghosts to the girl to the guy, her eyebrows lifted so high I couldn't see them under her messed-up hair. The lines on her face got deeper by the second, and I knew she was probably scared—but she was seeing everything that I did. Maybe I hadn't lost my mind. Maybe I didn't pull some kid's teeth out of his head and hold him hostage in the tunnels under Lincoln Psychiatric for three days.

Relief hit me so hard I almost put my face in my hands and sobbed.

Forest got hold of herself, straightened up, and smiled at Levi. "Leslie Hyatt didn't have Madoc blood, and she's right here in front of me, clear and strong as a haunt. I guess you don't know *everything,* do you, Levi?"

"Imogene's gonna have to fix her books," Levi muttered. His expression got all worried for a second, then he covered it. He made a grab for me, but my grandmothers hissed at him. Mama gripped the arms of her wheelchair like she meant to get up and beat on Levi, too, but her eyes darted to the police in the hall and she kept still.

Grandma Betty raised her hand. Light flashed around her palm, and suddenly she was holding a see-through ax. She brought it down hard. Levi leaped away from her so fast I didn't see him move. The ax hit the floor with no sound. It didn't do anything—not even a chink showed in the tile. Yet I had a hunch that if that ax had hit Levi, there would have been damage.

He must have thought the same thing, because his black eyes had gone huge, and he gave Grandma Betty some space.

Grandma Leslie stood beside Forest, and I could have sworn she had a comb in her hand. *Don't touch my grandson,* she warned Levi, shaking the comb.

Don't touch him, Grandma Betty echoed.

When my grandmothers spoke, it made my soul ache. I didn't remember much about Grandma Leslie except for stories about how hard she worked, and of her long years helping folks at Lincoln Psychiatric. She sounded proud and strong, and the force in her voice reminded me of my father. As for Grandma Betty, I missed her fierceness. I missed her love. I missed everything about her so much, and she was here, but I knew I couldn't hug her. I couldn't hug either one of them. If I tried to put my hands on them, they'd be nothing but cold air, and that would hurt more than anything.

"Promise them you won't harm Darius," Forest told Levi. "Give his grandmothers your word." Her gaze shifted to Mama. "And tell his mother what she needs to hear."

Levi sighed.

Forest waited.

I wondered if all strong, smart girls studied the same playbook, because she and Trina had a whole lot in common when they wanted something.

Levi caved so fast it would have been funny, if funny was allowed in nightmares. "I promise I won't put my hands on your grandson," he told my grandmothers. To my mother, he said, "I promise I don't mean Darius any harm, and I'll do my best to protect him."

Forest smiled, covering over Levi's coldness with soft warmth. "He can't break his promises. If he even thought about it, Imogene would kick his butt."

Grandma Betty nodded. *The healer woman,* she murmured. *She helped my mama have me.*

"We need to find Darius's grandfather—" Levi started, but Grandma Betty muttered a few sentences to me, then vanished.

Grandma Leslie waved her comb at Forest. *You be good, girl. I'm watching.*

Then she vanished, too.

Levi and Forest surged to the spot where they had been standing, both of them sweeping their arms around as if they might snatch my grandmothers back from wherever it is ghosts go.

Forest turned to me. "Can you get them to appear again?"

I shook my head, glanced at the police officers, and whispered, "Grandma Leslie and Grandma Betty did what they wanted, how they wanted when they were alive. I imagine it's the same now that they're dead."

My mother still had a stern expression on her face, but she nodded and added a soft "Mm-hmm." When she blinked fast like that, I knew she was trying not to cry, trying to keep it together because I was watching, and because I needed her, and because there was nothing she could do to pretend she wasn't like me now, seeing stuff other people couldn't see. You can't stop truth any more than you can stop death.

Levi narrowed his eyes at me. "What did your grandmother Betty say before she vanished? I couldn't hear her."

I thought about blowing him off or shrugging, or just saying nothing, but that didn't feel right. He had come here and healed me and taken off my handcuffs. I wasn't sure, but I thought he and his girl, Forest, were trying to save me. So I respected the truth in the room and said, "She told me not to trust you. She said, 'Imogene's a good woman, but she screwed this up once already.'"

Levi's black eyes flashed. His tattoos surged like fresh blood on his face as his lips pulled back from his teeth. Energy played off him in black clouds, and shadows formed on the hospital-room walls, birds and dogs and other things I couldn't figure, sliding in circles like some crazy merry-go-round. Mama rolled her wheelchair a few feet away from the things.

One of them reached for her.

It was a big black dog's paw with long claws, dripping shadows that fell on the floor around her wheelchair and wriggled away. Then the rest of the giant black dog popped out of nowhere, padding into the room like it belonged with normal living things.

How Mama didn't scream, I don't know. I almost hollered, but Forest touched my arm and glared at Levi as the monster-dog came to sit beside him.

Levi was shaking and getting . . . darker, somehow. The dogs in the distance seemed a lot closer, and now I heard birds, too—honks and squawks and rushing air from powerful flapping. I saw Levi grow taller. I saw him with light and darkness inside, and he radiated fire and ice at the same time.

His dog opened its mouth and snarled.

"Stop it," Forest said to Levi. "Right now. I mean it."

He managed to shut her out, for about five seconds. Then his head drooped, and the shadows on the walls and ceiling slowed to a crawl. He rested his hand on the big black dog's head, and the thing quit growling. A second or two later, the shadows vanished, and the sounds of the dogs and birds faded away until I didn't hear anything but my heart racing and Mama's breathing and the soft *clang-clang* of the crazy bells at Lincoln, ringing to scare everybody to death.

"My grandmother Imogene sent Efnisien Leer to the other side fifty-two years ago," Levi said without looking up from where he was petting the black dog's head. "I can show you in her record books. We thought he was gone."

Forest and Levi looked at each other, and a few seconds later, Forest added, "Levi's grandmother keeps track of what goes on around Lincoln, and she tries to take care of problems."

Mama didn't seem as surprised as I was, because she didn't miss a beat. "I remember seeing Miss Imogene when I was little. The midwife, right? The one half the town called Granny back in the day?"

Levi nodded.

"I heard a rumor she was born the day that hospital opened," Mama said, "to the first woman ever admitted to Lincoln. I figured she had to have passed on, but since she's still kicking, can she tell us how my father came back from the dead?"

Levi's frown made me wish I had a sharp stake to defend myself, but his voice was calm when he answered, "He's not back from the dead. Not exactly. He just moved what's left of his energy back to this side to cause trouble. He's a shade."

I gave that some thought, then came up with my own question. "Can he be killed—again?"

Levi met my eyes. "Anything can be killed, if you're strong enough to do it."

For now, I didn't want to think too much about the fact that my grandfather wasn't only a serial killer, but a real-live monster now, too. "Bad blood" was taking on a whole new meaning for me. "If your grandmother Imogene made his spirit cross over when he died, then how did he make himself a shade?"

Something flickered across Levi's face. He twisted his fingers in the black dog's fur. "Shades either have a lot of power in them when they die, or something strong helping them get up to no good."

"Spirits usually can't move back and forth without help." Forest pushed her dark curls behind her ears. "Levi and Imogene have to do it, or me. I'm learning how. But we didn't do this."

Mama folded her hands in her lap. "So someone with some terrible power got hold of Eff Leer's energy or spirit or whatever and brought what was left of it back to this side? Who would do something that awful?"

Fresh fear crossed Levi's face. He pulled his arms low over his belly.

Forest glanced at Levi like she wanted to put her arm around his shoulders. "My guess is, somebody or something even more awful than Eff Leer. There are a lot of strange things in Imogene's records."

"Strange like the tree?" My question came out louder than I intended, and the officers outside my door turned to see what I was saying and doing.

Forest raised her palm to them and gave the air a slight push. They turned back to the hallway as if they had been hypnotized.

"There's a tree," Levi said. He wasn't asking a question, and the dread in his voice turned my insides to icicles.

"A big one." My fingers lifted on instinct, and I touched the thorn pendant I still wore. "It had roots that moved and an eyeball and a mouth, too. You know what it is?"

"That's a witch tree." Levi closed his eyes. "We need to get to Lincoln and go after it before anybody else dies." He took his hand off his dog and told it, "Cain, go."

As Forest started walking toward the hospital room door, the giant monster-dog turned and leaped straight into the air, vanishing without a sound. Meanwhile, Mama rolled her chair between Levi and me, blocking my path. "You can't do this, Darius. You're already under arrest—and whatever's in that tunnel, it meant to hurt you just like it tried to hurt that little boy."

"I know." I got to my feet, knowing that Levi and Forest would handle the police, and Mama, too, if I couldn't get her to back down. "That's why I have to go."

She opened her mouth to argue with me, but for the first time ever, I interrupted her and admitted, "I didn't tell you everything Grandma Betty said the day she died."

You always see the truth . . .

Look hard . . .

This time, it'll be hungry . . .

Mama went still in her chair, her mouth half-open, her eyes

wide and mad and sad. She waited me out until I found enough courage to tell her the rest.

"Grandma Betty told me I had to finish what she started," I said. "And I think you know what that means."

Mama shook her head once, then shook it harder and covered her ears. I caught her wrists and pulled her hands away from her face, then squatted low enough to look into her eyes. "There's no option here, Mama. If I don't do what I'm meant to do, more kids might get killed—and who knows what kind of evil will get loose in the world?"

"Darius," Mama whispered, "what if you come back wrong in the head like my mother did? What if you don't come back at all?"

I should have been scared or worried or pissed or something, but I still felt nothing much besides relief that I wasn't as crazy as I thought I was. I kissed Mama's cheek and spoke into her ear, where she had to listen to me even if she didn't want to. "I have to go to Lincoln Psychiatric, take care of that tree, and kill my grandfather for good. I'll come back any way I can."

CHAPTER SEVENTEEN

We left Mama in the hospital room, pretending to be asleep so she could plead ignorance when the police officers realized I was gone. The police never glanced in our direction, and neither did anyone else as Levi and Forest walked me out of the hospital, into the moonless darkness that had swallowed Never whole. There was no breeze. The stifling air smelled like mown grass and tar and fertilizer, everything Southern and summer and alive, even though death was sneaking around under the ground just a few miles away.

The parking-lot lights shimmered in what was left of the day's blistering heat. The farther we got from the hospital's front door, the more my nerves started getting to me. It was one thing being tough for Mama's sake. It was another to actually face my grandfather and his bloody, mangled body, never mind that awful tree.

The officers who arrested me apparently hadn't noticed my thorn pendant, but they had taken my phone. I couldn't call

Jessie or Trina to tell them anything, like that I was on the run, or that I'd try to come back, or good-bye. It shouldn't have surprised me, though, when they met us in the parking lot as we headed for what Levi and Forest said would be a shortcut to Lincoln. Trina was wearing jeans and a blue polo, and she looked good as ever when she jumped out of Jessie's car and ran toward me, and for a second, I thought I was dreaming.

Then she was in my arms and kissing my neck, and I buried my face in her thick, sweet-smelling hair and just stood there, holding her.

"I knew you didn't do anything to that kid," she murmured into my chest. "They let you go, right?"

It hurt having to push back from her, let her go, and shake my head. "No, baby. I'm sorry. I just escaped from being chained to a hospital bed."

Trina's big, dark eyes welled with tears, and she started poking her finger in my chest. "Then you turn right back around, march yourself inside, and give yourself up before you get in more trouble."

"Dude," Jessie said, nodding his head in agreement. "The police could start shooting. You have to be smart about this."

I glared at Levi and Forest and kept glaring until they let Jessie and Trina see them. I knew when it happened, because my best friend and my girl jumped at the same time and gaped at the people who seemed to have popped into existence right beside me.

"This is Levi, and this is Forest," I said. "They're going to help me get rid of my grandfather for good."

Trina didn't say a word back to that. Her pretty face seemed shadowed and hidden despite the parking-lot light right above us.

Jessie folded his scrawny arms and stared at me, his heavy red eyebrows pulled together over his freckled nose. "You need to explain," he said. "Spell it out, because that sounds totally nuts."

I gave them the short version: my grandfather was a ghost, haunting the basement and the tunnels under the hospital and getting more dangerous by the second, a crazy tree was giving him power or something, and I had to take him down like my grandmother had tried to do before me.

Jessie blinked a couple of times, but true to everything I knew about him, he shuffled through it in his head, and he believed me. "Your grandfather almost killed your grandmother, though." His frown reminded me of Mama's. "She got her eyes burned out of her head and went nuts."

"This can't be for real," Trina muttered, but she couldn't quit looking at Levi, and I knew she realized that he wasn't anything she'd ever run into in the normal world. "You're confused. Something's wrong."

Her words got softer and softer, like she was trying to convince herself and failing. I wanted to put my arms around her, but I wasn't sure she wanted me to touch her right now. The light from the lamp finally seemed to reach her, and it showed me the wild expression on her face, how she had gone from girl to terrified animal, and might bolt if I made any fast moves.

"I wish it weren't real," I said, mostly to her, but I could tell she didn't hear me. She was lost in her own head, disbelief and shock showing in the tight lines of her body. The sudden distance between us hurt me deep inside, but I couldn't blame her. This was weird and wrong, and she shouldn't have to be a part of it. Maybe Trina had always been too good for a guy like me. Even if she didn't walk away over all this, how could we have any future together? She was normal and good and sweet.

I had bad blood.

And I was suspected of trying to kill a kid.

I'd never get my life back. Not the way it had been.

I made myself shift my attention to Jessie, who was still frowning. "Grandma Betty went to fight one monster, but she found two. She never had a real chance." I pointed to Forest and Levi. "I've got help."

"We need to get moving," Levi said. "The police could figure out you're gone any second, and things'll get complicated."

"I don't want you to do this," Jessie told me.

"I have to." I risked a glance at Trina, but her expression had turned to stone. I couldn't see any feeling in her face at all, except for tears on her cheeks, glittering yellow in the glow of the parking-lot lights.

Levi urged me forward toward a huge oak tree at the edge of the parking area. I hated turning my back on Trina and Jessie, but I knew I had to go. I walked away from them, ten feet, then twenty, and as we got to the tree, Forest took my hand.

Night seemed to move around us, making wavy lines in the darkness. Energy crackled across my skin, and my nerves jumped.

"It's okay," Forest told me. "You have Madoc blood in you, so I'm going to walk you across the edge of the other side with us, to save time and to be sure the police don't stop us on the way. It won't hurt, and you won't lose but a few seconds."

I wasn't sure I believed her.

But I had to do this, so I went forward, bracing as I struck the moving darkness. It buzzed around me like a thousand bees. My thorn pendant vibrated with it, and my stomach churned.

"Darius!"

Trina's voice chased me into the humming void.

"Darius!" Closer now, like she was running toward me.

I tried to turn, to break away and go back to her, but Forest pulled me deeper into nothing.

Then, before I could do anything to stop it, Trina and my old life flamed away from me like a shooting star.

I almost fell on my butt as we dropped out of—of—what felt like living, moving, emptiness. My brain spun in circles as I staggered around, trying to breathe and get my balance and reach for Trina all at the same time. I kicked a red plastic horseshoe across the night-darkened grass, swore, and located the wavy image of Levi a few feet away from me, framed by the hole in the Rec Hall wall like some bizarre picture from a scary book.

"Forest is grabbing some stuff for us," he said, but I wasn't interested in listening.

"Take me back," I demanded. "Trina was calling for me. She wanted to say something."

He just stood there looking at me. *You can't go back*, his expression said. *That girl and that life are gone forever.*

My stomach lurched. I doubled over, vomited, coughed a bunch, then went to my knees. Everything whirled in big, gut-flipping circles. Levi came close to me, but he didn't touch me, just like he had promised my grandmother. "I'm sorry," I heard him saying. "Some people get sick when they touch the other side."

Time lost all meaning to me as I fought not to puke again and tried not to pass out. My strength left me, and I shook like a scared kid. Seconds and minutes went by, and each one felt like an hour. I couldn't stand even after I got my breath back. I felt too sad and too heavy, so I stayed on my knees and stared into the grass and dirt of the big field behind the Rec Hall.

"What are you?" I asked Levi, not expecting an answer. "A shade, like my grandfather?"

He sighed. "I'm not a shade. I died and went to the other side like he did, but all of me came back."

If he hadn't sounded so honest, if I hadn't also seen the shade of a dead serial killer walking around and a tree with an eyeball and the ghosts of my grandmothers, I would have thought he was lying.

"You're not, like, a vampire or anything, are you?" I looked up at him. "Undead, or some stupid crap like that?"

He shook his head. "Flesh and blood, and I like pizza better than burgers. Can't really eat Slim Jims and peanuts, though. They remind me of the night I died."

"How did it happen?"

"I got murdered. The guy who killed me tried to burn my body, but my grandmother fetched my spirit back from the other side and pulled me out." He touched the tears under his eyes. "But I got scars here that look like blood, and now I can do stuff like Imogene can. We don't know why."

I thought about the way Levi had changed back at the hospital when he got mad. The weird stuff on the walls. The way he had healed me. The way my handcuffs had melted. Levi came back from the dead with way more than a few bloody teardrop scars.

"So." I tried to focus. "You're alive. And so is Forest, and so is your grandmother. Right?"

Levi nodded.

"Can you die again?"

"Yeah," he said. "We can all die. Me and Forest and you, too. As for Imogene, I used to think she couldn't die, but she's . . . fading. Getting weaker every day, so I think maybe she can die. I don't think she's strong enough to bring us back if we get killed. It's because she's getting weak that bad things are happening. She's all that holds back the *really* crazy stuff trying to get out of Lincoln Psychiatric."

"What is she?" I shut my eyes for a second, trying not to think about what could be crazier than the things I'd already seen. "Who gave her the job she's doing?"

"Imogene's actually my great-great-great-grandmother, or something like that." Levi shrugged. "She took me in when my parents got killed in a car wreck. As for who set her to guarding Lincoln—God, I guess. Maybe the devil. I don't know. She always tells me she was born doing what she does."

"But you didn't get your, um, abilities until after you . . ."

"Died and got brought back. Yeah." He looked sad for a few seconds, and it made me wonder what he'd been like before he got killed. "Imogene says that when you have skills, you're supposed to use them. " He gestured in the direction of the hospital. "If you don't do what you're meant to do, then you got a good chance of ending up in a place like Lincoln."

Something in his tone gave me a case of deep shivers, and I asked my next question quickly, before I could chicken out. "Are we going to die tonight, Levi?"

He thought for a time, then shrugged again. "Maybe. I don't have psychic skills. You backing out?"

"No," I told him, more sure than I had ever been before. "I'm in."

"You okay?" Forest asked me a few minutes later, when she got back from wherever she'd gone.

I managed to nod, even though I didn't want to. "I just need to know more about what's going on. What's that you said about a witch tree?" I asked Levi.

"I read about them in Imogene's records," Levi said. "She's seen a couple. Sometimes folks do blood rituals, and they store up the bad energy in trees and call them vessels."

"So, bad energy, bad tree?" I glanced at him, but it didn't seem like he was planning to say anything else.

Levi didn't say more, but when Forest looked at him, he said, "I think your grandfather's even older than Imogene. Like, way older. From back when people made sacrifices to trees all the time. His vessel must have liked children."

I closed my eyes. "Like the evil tree in the *Sleepy Hollow* movie?"

"Yeah," Levi said. "Like that."

My brain flashed to that Tim Burton movie, to a scene with a writhing, screaming tree trunk full of skulls and blood. "Great."

"I think your grandfather and his tree were waiting for your grandmother Betty to die," Forest said. "They were afraid of her. So, now that she's gone, the tree is—"

"Hungry." I got to my feet and straightened to my full height. "So how do we kill it?"

"I don't know." Forest gave me an apologetic look as she held out a wooden handle toward me. "Levi and Imogene can't even sense it, and when Imogene crossed your grandfather over before, the tree wasn't there. It must have been hiding."

My eyes fixed on the handle, and I took a shiny, brand-new ax from her. Still had a tag from the twenty-four-hour box store where she bought it. She had one, too, and so did Levi.

I guess this made it official. I was about to follow in my grandmother's footsteps and add "deranged ax murderer" to the list of labels stamped on my soul. Without intending to, I shifted the ax in my grip and tested its heft and balance. It felt scarily natural.

My eyes drifted toward the Rec Hall and the entrance to the tunnels, and to the crisscrossed yellow police tape that reminded me of who and what I was. "So we try to chop up the witch tree. But what about my grandfather?"

"He might die when the tree does," Levi said. "Or get weak. I'll grab his spirit and cross it over."

"You can do that?" I gripped the ax a little tighter. "Snatch a soul out of a living thing and make it die?"

"Eff Leer's a shade, not a living thing," Levi said. "Without the tree, we can bust him up for good and all."

That felt like a hedge to me. I was pretty sure Levi could kill things by grabbing their soul or spirit or energy or whatever. No wonder my grandmothers didn't want him to touch me. But that was stuff to worry about later, if I lived to worry about anything at all.

"Okay, then." I raised my ax in front of me like a talisman and started walking toward the hole in the Rec Hall wall. "Let's go finish this job."

CHAPTER EIGHTEEN

We tore away the police tape and walked into the tunnels together, Levi on the left, Forest in the middle, and me on the right. Dogs appeared from nowhere and fell in behind us.

It was dark, but Levi's skin gave off a silvery light that glittered against the ax blades and lit our way. It was cold at first, then hot, then unnaturally hot, like we were walking straight into hell. The air smelled like bitter copper and dirt and wood.

My eyes darted all around the tunnels, searching for any movement or any hint of roots. Did they know we were coming?

The bricks on the tunnel walls seemed to stretch closer to us.

Down we went, silently, no jabbering about plans that would never work or strategies that wouldn't help.

The space in the tunnel got smaller. Another few steps, and I bumped shoulders with Forest. Levi had to go in front, with Forest following and me bringing up the rear.

Rustling sounds echoed through the tunnel behind us, and I whipped around, ax raised, ready for anything. Goose-like shadows tracked along the glowing brick walls, knifing forward, as quiet as the dogs. The hair on my arms prickled. I felt hunted.

"Darius," Forest whispered, and I realized I wasn't moving. I didn't want to keep my back turned on those dogs, especially Cain. Something about them reminded me of the tree roots, like they were bloodthirsty, deadly extensions of something powerful, and weren't to be trusted.

"Darius," Forest said again, and I made myself turn toward her and Levi. The world went squishy and wavy, like it wasn't solid anymore. My thorn pendant seemed to flare, then burned against my skin.

I touched the wood through the fabric of my shirt. "They know we're here."

Levi lifted his ax in a salute toward the darkness in the section of tunnel ahead of us. "And we know they're here."

That's when the music started, rusty and creaky and teasing. "Pop Goes the Weasel," slow-like and distorted and totally wrong.

The dogs behind me snarled. I snarled with them. Levi started walking again. Forest and I followed.

The brick floors and walls seemed even closer now. We were getting toward the end of the tunnel, where the chamber entrance would be, and I said so to Levi and Forest. Then I saw the snake shadows.

"Roots!" I yelled as one dropped out of the ceiling. It whipped around Forest's neck, jerking tight, and she dropped her ax and grabbed for the root.

My heart skipped. I raised my own ax, but Levi moved so fast he was nothing but a black-and-silver blur. His ax whistled through the hot air and cleaved the root in one blow. The part choking Forest went limp and fell away from her. The other half snapped back into the ceiling like a live wire, spraying blackish gore as it went. Droplets spattered across my face and arms, each one burning like boiling water.

I tried not to holler from the searing pain, but I couldn't help it. The sound came out like a squeal, and Forest cried out, too. Levi pointed his finger at me and mumbled something. My skin stopped burning, and I used my shirt to wipe the rest of the stuff off my face and arms as fast as I could.

Slithering, crackling noises filled the tunnel. "Pop Goes the Weasel" got louder as the monkey chased the weasel. I squinted into the darkness as the dogs behind me yipped and whined and the geese started honking and screeching and flapping, and Forest said something loud and pounced on her ax, and I saw why.

It wasn't one root coming for us this time. It was dozens.

They burst out of the shadows like a snake army, writhing across the bricks to get at us. I swore and swung my ax at the nearest bit of gnarled wood as it tried to stab my ankle. The blade barely bit into the wood and jammed immediately.

From somewhere, my grandfather started laughing.

"Son of a—" I stomped my foot against the wiggling root and tried to pull the ax free, but it held tight. Cain pounced on my root and the other dogs jumped on others, snapping their teeth into the wood and shaking the roots like rabbits. Goose shadows covered the roots still attached to the walls, and Levi whirled by me, swinging his ax over his head in big, wide strokes.

Forest was having trouble like me, striking at roots and then having to pry out the ax blade. The hounds helped, keeping the roots busy as we worked. Then I couldn't hear anything but that stupid ice-cream truck song and barking and yelping and honking and chopping and disgusting spurting noises from the roots when we did manage to cut through them.

Levi and I never looked at each other, but our goals seemed to be the same—keep all that nasty wood off the girl, and keep walking. He took the front and I took the back, and Forest only had to worry about what got past us. Which was less and less as we got the hang of it.

My skin started burning again, but Levi made it stop with that fog from his fingers. I squinted so none of the goo could get at my eyeballs and chopped and pulled, chopped and pulled, chopped and pulled. Soon the burning in my shoulders had nothing to do with gore, and I started to laugh so crazily that my grandfather shut up.

"Bring it!" I shouted. "We can do this all day!"

Maybe we were cutting down the tree's energy a little. Maybe we were killing it by inches. I didn't care, just as long as I was hurting it, and through it, Eff Leer.

"Pop Goes the Weasel" cut off abruptly, and the roots that weren't already confetti or dog food snapped against the brick walls as they withdrew.

I listened to my own heavy breathing in the sudden silence that followed. The tree's blood glowed black all around us. My own blood raced from what felt like a victory, but Levi still had his ax raised, and so did Forest, and so did I. The air felt hotter and smelled bitter. The earth under the bricks at our feet seemed to bubble and seethe, and sharp claws of fear dug at my chest.

My grandfather had been toying with us, as playful as ancient serial killers ever got.

Now he was pissed, and the corrupted earth under the control of the dark druid was reacting to his rage. The tunnel floor started to buckle.

"Move," Levi yelled. "*Now!*"

CHAPTER NINETEEN

I ran and jumped and fell as the earth tore itself to pieces all around me. Heat blasted out of glowing rents in the ground. Nowhere to go but straight ahead. Pain seared my feet, and I thought my shoes were melting. I hit my knees in a tooth-crunching thump, then scrambled toward the spot at the tunnel's end where I remembered finding the basement the first time I came down this hole.

So hot. Hard to breathe. I didn't know brick could turn to water—or was it blood? Molten blood. I was going to melt right into it or go up like a fizzling skin torch. The stink of burned hair crowded into my nose. Dogs howled and screamed. Geese screeched. I thought I heard Levi shouting, and Forest, too, but I couldn't tell if they were ahead of me or behind me. Blazing curtains of heat turned everything orange and red.

When I couldn't walk, I crawled.

Sweat poured down my face and stung my eyes but I kept crawling, banging the blade of the ax each time my right fist smacked the bubbling earth. The ground was trying to suck me down. If it pulled me under, I'd get crushed, or my face and bones would turn to liquid. My heart pounded hard enough to burst.

Fire coated the brick walls on either side of me, biting at my arms. The light drove a solid curtain of bugs ahead of it. They swarmed over the tunnel's end, then cooked with horrible hisses and crackles, pelting my face and shoulders as they died.

My arms and legs ached as I shoved myself forward, bashing into burning dirt and pieces of brick as I tried to find the spot, the place where the tunnel turned into an old rotten basement under the asylum. Fire blasted up from the earth in gouts and geysers. This was hell, and I was going to burn.

"Darius!" Forest called to me, but I didn't stop.

"This way!" I hollered as I smashed my shoulder into more hot brick, hitting the tunnel's wall like a rabid bull. Again. Again. The opening had to be here. Smoke made me choke and cough, and tears turned my vision yellow. I smashed the wall again and my skin tingled, and I pitched forward so hard the ax went flying as I smashed into wood and dirt, rolling three or four times until I hit something solid and cracked my jaw against—

A pair of legs.

Black tuxedo pants.

My chest caught fire. Not my skin—the thorn pendant. I grabbed it as I looked up. Through my wet, blurry vision, I saw my grandfather standing in the basement, bathed in red light from his witch tree.

He looked tall. His elbows and remaining wrist and fingers

looked huge at the joints, and that face—I wanted to look away from the ruin of it, but I didn't dare. Behind him stood the tree, huge and vicious, with its bloody eye and big mouth and grabby branches covered in giant thorns and sick-smelling white flowers.

Smoke rose off my skin, drifting up to the place where the tree's crown reached the basement's rotten ceiling. Blisters covered my legs and forearms and cheeks, and I wanted to yell from the pain, and because I was down here in hell alone, Forest and Levi had probably already burned to death.

I wasn't going to do any better than Grandma Betty did against these monsters. Worst of all, I had lied to my mother. I wouldn't be coming back.

"Get up," Eff Lear told me in a voice icy enough to put out a thousand fires. He kicked me hard in the back, driving out my breath. "Die on your feet like a man."

I hauled myself away from him, jerking as my muscles screamed against that kick. I was crawling on hands and knees like a terrified baby, and I didn't care. I kept right on crawling until I got to the ax I had dropped. I snatched it off the ground and stood, holding it in front of me in both hands. My breath wheezed out between my blistered lips, and I had to squint to see through the sweat and blood running into my eyes.

Eff Leer and the tree were about ten feet from me now—too far to swing at, too close to run away.

"Who did you bring with you tonight?" My grandfather scented the air and licked his lips. "I smell blood."

I stood there with the ax, wishing I had the guts to start swinging.

My grandfather stretched out his one whole arm. The knobby fingers seemed skeletal, and they cast giant shadows on the far chamber wall.

Something cracked.

I jumped, almost dropping the ax, but locked my elbows to hold it still.

Levi walked past me, holding his weapon at his side.

My grandfather lowered his arm. "You think you can do what your grandmother couldn't, boy?" He smiled without any humor at all. "Try it."

Was he talking to Levi or me? Both of our grandmothers had tangled with him and lost.

And where was Forest?

My eyes darted right, then left. I didn't want to give her away if she was hiding, but what if I let her burn in the tunnels? She had called out for me, and I kept crawling away. What kind of worthless piece of crap was I?

My skin was so singed I was sure it was peeling off me. Tears ran down my face, but I kept my ax raised. Cain and the dogs and geese that seemed to follow Levi were nowhere to be found.

"Efnisien Leer," Levi said. His voice made the red light in the basement flicker. "You and that witch tree are done. Come peaceful, or come in pieces. Your call."

Levi lifted his ax. From the side, his pale face seemed longer and more set, his expression all business. The red droplets under his eye sparkled like real blood.

The laugh that came out of my grandfather curdled my insides. His hand shot out, and Levi's ax twitched. My own ax tried to jump out of my grip, and I staggered sideways, trying to keep hold of it. The chamber rumbled, and the scratchy-scrabbling sound of thorny wood snaking across stone made me turn in circles, swinging out with my weapon in case roots were coming after me.

They weren't.

They were circling the chamber walls, stacking themselves one on top of the other, thick and thorny and dense.

No escape now.

"Levi," I said, but he didn't answer.

Two of the roots shot toward the back of the chamber. I heard shouts and screams coming from far away but getting closer fast, and then the roots whipped back into view.

Oh God. No.

Everything inside me withered.

Trina and Jessie.

Roots twisted around them, holding them as they hit at the wood and yelled and tried to jerk themselves free.

They must have come after me when I left the hospital and gotten to the tunnels, and now—

No, no, no!

"Levi!" When I turned back to him, he and my grandfather were circling each other. Levi struck with a quick swing of his ax.

My grandfather dodged away from the blow. "You don't have the bitch's power, boy. Give it up."

Levi swung again.

My grandfather sniffed like he was smelling the blood he was about to spill, and his eyes widened. He stopped circling Levi and backed toward the tree. His head swiveled left and right. "You found a new one," he murmured. "A *young* one. Where is she?"

He spun toward the corner of the chamber, toward the entrance, and I realized Forest had to be hiding right about in that very spot.

Levi bared his teeth and lunged, brandishing the ax in a wild blur.

My grandfather stumbled.

Branches tore away from the walls to help him, and I charged the roots holding Trina and Jessie. When my blade struck wood, it was like hitting solid stone. Sparks flared. My wrists wrenched as the hilt tore out of my grip. My ax skittered across the rotten floor toward Levi and my grandfather.

Trina let out a scream that shredded my heart.

"Coming, baby." I jumped for the ax. A branch caught it before I ever got near, and in a whirl of leaves and rotten white flowers, the ax came barreling toward my face. I dodged sideways and smacked into the tree's thorny base, just below its eyeball.

Its mouth opened. Moss-wrapped teeth ripped across my gut and snagged the waist of my jeans, jerking me off my feet.

The tree held me there in its mouth, upside down and kicking and hollering. Every part of me felt torn in half. Then I saw Trina and Jessie get lifted off the floor, too. They dangled from the roots about fifteen feet away from me, limp like dolls. Their faces had gone slack, mouths open, eyes shut.

Terror froze my pain and my blisters and my brain, and I couldn't think at all.

The branches dropped my ax and grabbed my legs, wadding me up so the witch tree could eat me. I kicked harder. Out of the corner of my eye, I saw my grandfather smash Levi in the face with his knobby fist and drop him like a prizefighter.

Then the tree turned me, and all I saw were wooden teeth and thorns and that big, nasty bloodshot eyeball rolling and rolling. I screamed and punched bark with one fist. It was going to eat me, and then it would eat Jessie and Trina. I couldn't stop it.

I grabbed the thorn pendant and tore it off my neck. It was just a thorn, burning and black like the tree itself. I couldn't stop it, but I could hurt the tree and give the others a chance.

I smashed the curved tip forward, ripping into the fleshy eyeball.

The thorn exploded in my palm. Gore blew out of the eye like a hot storm of acid, gushing into my face and chest and throwing me backward, turning everything to fire and misery and darkness. It kept coming, everything in that tree, hot blood spewing like a fountain that might never run dry.

The branches dropped me, and I smashed to the floor as the tree bellowed and shrieked. The whole chamber rocked. The floor shuddered and collapsed. I smelled burning wood and skin and hair—my skin, my hair. I screamed with the tree, rolling around but still burning to death anyway. I couldn't see anything. I couldn't think of anything but Trina and Jessie, and Levi and Forest. I listened for their screams, but all I could hear was the inferno, then my grandfather's raging shout and the sound of his footsteps as he came for me.

"What did you do?" he growled. Then, louder and completely unhinged, "What have you done?"

His fingers dug into my cooking throat, and I knew he was choking me. He was killing me. I was dead, already in darkness, and—

"He's not yours." My grandma Betty's voice whispered through the universe. For two seconds, I felt her. For another two, I smelled her, all powdery and soft like when I hugged her. "He'll never be yours."

My grandfather snarled.

Something whistled through the air. There was a wet crunch, followed by a thunk. I didn't have to be able to see to know my grandfather had finally lost what was left of his head.

"That's better," Grandma Leslie said. "You been working on your aim, Betty?"

Something like cool lips brushed across my cheek, first one pair, then another. Then Grandma Leslie said, "Wake up, Levi. Take care of my grandson like you promised—and take care of my girl Forest, too."

Way off in the distance, bells started ringing.

Cool air circled around my fried skin and the rips in my belly, easing the pain, as dogs barked and geese honked and a tree screamed. I thought I saw Levi and Cain dragging something black and glittery into a dark hole so deep it had to lead right out of this world.

A few seconds later, the pain got so bad I truly lost my mind.

Levi—

Forest, we've got to get them out of here—

Nothing.

Puking.

Screaming.

Heal him. I'll help you.

Levi grunted with pain and Forest apologized, and then the world smelled like flowers and grass and lakes after a fresh rain, and I died, and then I didn't, and—

Now his eyes.

I can't. Even Imogene couldn't pull that off anymore. She's too old.

You have to try.

Fine. But only the right one. There's nothing left of the other.

Good enough.

And I woke up seeing two worlds instead of one.

CHAPTER TWENTY

Y ou ain't Stevie Wonder, but you'll do." Imogene patted my
hand as I stood in front of a mirror in the Lincoln Psychiatric
Hospital records room, way up in the bell tower that used to
scare me to death. I was checking out the pair of shades she and
Levi and Forest had made for me, with a little help from Trina
and Jessie. They were glasses like a lot of blind folks wore.

The right side of my face was smooth and perfect, and so was
that eye, so even though the lens on that side had a dark coloring, it was just tinted glass, and I could see fine and normal—I
could see the world I grew up in, with none of the extra stuff.

The left side of my face was covered with pinkish-white scars,
and in the two months since we chopped up a tree in the basement
under Lincoln, Levi had gone to work on the edges of the dam-
aged skin, coloring and shaping like a real-world tattoo artist, only
better. The scars blended into something like a tribal sun. As for
the eye on that side, it was weird. All white and seemingly blind,
but it wasn't. It saw things. The glasses turned down the volume

on the light and colors that threatened to explode my brain whenever I focused too much on what my bad eye tried to show me.

I lifted the glasses and stared at myself and Imogene in the mirror, and then at Levi, Forest, Jessie, Trina, and Mama. In the reflection, my normal eye gazed back at me, and so did my white eye. Without the glasses, I could see Levi's mix of light and darkness, and the unbelievable yellow glow that surrounded Forest. Imogene had a glow like that, too, only hers seemed thinner and weaker.

Mama had an aura, a soft bunch of white flickers. Jessie, he looked steel-blue and steady. I always knew Jessie was a good guy, but now I could actually see it. He didn't have any scars from the battle below the nuthouse, but he had cut his crazy hair and shaved, and then signed up for karate and weight training. Forest said maybe he was going soft in the head and starting to believe he could turn into a ninja. That would be a stretch, with his worn-out jeans, Lincoln Psychiatric sweatshirt, and that bunch of stubbly red hair sticking out on both sides of his head.

Trina slipped up next to me, staring into the mirror as she took my hand. She had on jeans and a pink sweater. Her aura was different—bright silver, with a sparkly kind of lightning at the edges, especially in the corners of her beautiful eyes.

"I like the glasses," Trina said, so I put them back on, and she squeezed my hand. No scars on her, either—not on her skin, and not on her soul or emotions, either. She was still in school and planned to finish, but she was changing her major to social work and planning to take her first externship at Lincoln so she could stay close.

I hadn't sensed Grandma Betty at all since I saw her ghost at Lincoln, but I hoped she'd approve. Forest had gone looking for Grandma Leslie a few times, too, but had no luck. I thought they were both gone on to the other side to stay this time, and it made me sad, but happy, too. Maybe they were resting now, or gone to heaven, or to whatever kind of life we live next. Wherever they were, I hoped they were finally and completely at peace.

We all kept standing there, Trina and Jessie and Imogene and Forest and Levi and Mama and me. Seven of us, staring in a mirror and wondering if we really understood all that had happened, and all that was about to happen.

"Well?" Mama asked. "You people figured it out yet?"

"It was the thorn," Levi said. "Betty must have taken it from the witch tree the first time she fought with it. When Darius stabbed the tree's eye, he poisoned it with the only thing strong enough to hurt it—a piece of itself."

I studied him, trying to balance everything I could see. "And my grandfather—you're sure he's crossed over for good?"

Levi managed an expression almost like a smile, but not quite. He didn't smile much, unless Forest was involved. "Without the tree, he was weak as a pinkie mouse. He won't be back."

Mama frowned. "Unless there's another witch tree that wants to let him out."

"There isn't another tree," Forest said. "Not like that one."

We all gazed at her. It was clear down in that basement that my grandfather had recognized her power. It was rare, and strong enough to scare people—and spirits, too. I wanted to protect Forest like I wanted to protect Trina, only for different reasons.

It seemed like the right thing to do, like something the world needed—especially the little piece of the world around Lincoln Psychiatric Hospital.

Maybe Forest was destined to take up the job Imogene had been doing for way too long. We had to help her figure things out, and we had to look after her.

"It's time to go," Trina said, and I nodded.

Jessie flexed the muscles in his right arm. "Shift will be changing soon. Captain James worked second today, so he won't stay for third. We better move."

Mama frowned, but she didn't argue with us. She just flicked the brakes on her wheelchair, to make sure we knew she didn't approve, and that she'd be staying in the bell tower. She was still worried about me getting in trouble, even though I had been cleared of all charges when the police decided the real bad guy had kidnapped me and tried to set me on fire underneath Lincoln.

The police didn't know about Captain James, though. How he had been some kind of minion for my grandfather and that tree. He had Madoc blood, according to Imogene's records, and some kind of power of his own, but it was turned for evil. Imogene said he had gone rotten inside, and we couldn't let him walk around free to hurt people. I figured I was about to find out whether Levi really could kill people by tearing out their spirits or souls or whatever.

"I really don't need help with this," Levi said, but nobody even looked in his direction as we filed down the bell-tower steps. "I can go with Imogene. We've always done this stuff alone."

"The time for working alone has passed, Levi," Imogene told her grandson. She was right in front of me at the back of the line, walking faster on those stairs than I thought was possible for someone her age. "When the good Lord sends you help, you take it."

It seemed weird to hear her talk about God, so before we got to the door in the main hallway of the bell tower, I said, "You talk about the good Lord, but I thought you were a witch, Imogene."

Everybody stopped walking when I said that. Levi glared at me, but Imogene only laughed.

"I been called worse than that, lots of times." She held out her hand and gave me a slip of paper. Then she gave other slips to Trina, Forest, Jessie, and Levi. "There, now. Put those in your mouths."

Nobody hesitated but me. After a few seconds, I lifted the paper and put it onto my tongue like everybody else did. It bubbled a little and then dissolved, tasting like peppermint.

"What was that?" I asked.

Imogene's grin freaked me out sometimes, because it made her look both older and younger at the same time. Her wrinkly eyes glittered at me as she said, "Nothing poison, just a bit of Scripture with a drop of mint oil."

From the witch. She didn't say it, but I saw it in the laugh lines twitching at the edges of her mouth.

"I'm not real religious," I admitted.

"Don't matter what you believe," Imogene said. "I'm the one who wrote those words to protect you tonight."

"Levi says you control spirits," Trina said, her voice quiet in the deserted tower. "That you keep records of all the different types of ghosts you've seen at Lincoln."

"Used to. I'm old now, like I keep saying." Imogene glanced at Levi. "And like everybody keeps tellin' me. But Levi's a good boy, and Forest is strong, and you three are, too."

"Are we going to need strength?" Trina asked.

"Around this old asylum, strong's always good." Imogene started walking toward the tower door.

I followed after her. "Why?"

"This place has got troubles," she said. Then she opened the big wooden door like it didn't weigh anything, and held it open for us to walk outside into the cold January night. "They have to be seen to, or terrible things can happen."

I motioned for Trina and Jessie to go on outside. "Troubles— you mean the crazy folks?"

"What looks crazy now might be sane later." Imogene shook her head, making her thick white braid bob back and forth. "You know they used to lock girls up here for having boyfriends out of wedlock? They sent 'em all here—wet-brains and feeble-minded children and teenagers who mouthed back to their parents and sick people dying from consumption or the ague. Anybody who was different or made folks angry, they got locked up here until they died. Truly, crazy's always been the least of it."

Trina stepped onto the porch and turned around to face Imogene, hugging herself to keep warm. "What's wrong with Lincoln? You were here when it was built, so you have to know."

Imogene reached up and switched off the tower's porch light

as Levi and Jessie and Forest crowded behind Trina in the sudden darkness, waiting for the answer.

"I always figured this place was a lot like me." Imogene let go of the light switch and ran her knotty fingers up and down the edge of the door. "Lincoln's got some Madoc blood flowing in all this stone and wood. It lives in both worlds."

When Imogene looked at me, her eyes seemed so old and haunted that I got to wondering if maybe she *was* the hospital come to life somehow—or if the hospital was keeping her alive. But that was seriously nutty thinking, so I didn't say it out loud.

"If a strange thing exists," Imogene went on, "or if it ever did exist, you'll see it here at Lincoln sooner or later. Crazy, oh, yes. And so many ghosts the air buzzes with 'em. They aren't all bad, but they aren't all good, either."

"The witch tree wasn't good." I let out a breath, feeling its warmth on my cheeks. "My grandfather was worse."

Imogene stepped outside, caught my wrist, and tugged me out of the bell tower with her as the door closed behind us. "Just remember, not everything that's bad around this place is dead. Keep your wits about you all the time, and keep both of those eyes open. You'll need 'em."

We all moved forward, except for Levi. He was standing on the top step, facing the nature trails and acres of woods on our right. Even in the dark, I could tell he was frowning.

"Do you smell something?" he asked in a voice so quiet and deadly it made me go absolutely still.

Then I smelled it, too. I lifted my glasses, and my bad eye picked out the thin gray wisps drifting past us.

Smoke.

Smoke with a sweet, wrong scent that made me start to shake way down inside. I lifted my fingers to my scarred face as Levi clenched his fists.

"Yea, though I walk through the valley of the shadow of death," Imogene said as she hobbled past us and started down the front stairs, "I will fear no evil . . ."

But I was fearing evil, fearing it bad, and I didn't want to walk out into that valley of the shadow of death.

Somewhere out in the cold night, someone was on fire.

We found the pyre on a piece of ground that seemed like it belonged more to an ancient forest than the woods separating the asylum from Never. It was a perfect spot, just remote enough that normal folks would never have seen a thing—or smelled it.

I held Trina's hand as we faced the embers with Jessie and tried not to notice the eerie outline of the bell tower in the distance, blacking out the stars and moon.

"Who did this?" Levi asked without looking away from what was left of the burning body. The corpse's fingers curled into strips, then crumbled in the flames.

"Same one as killed you, boy," Imogene said. "Same one as been at it for years. He's got something against Madocs. Maybe he fancies himself doing our work better than we can."

"He?" Trina asked, her voice flat and colder than the winter air.

"It's a man." Imogene sighed. "And before you go askin', that's all I know."

Forest stepped out of the trees nearest the fire. She had been trying to sense the spirit of the murdered man, to find it and cross it over if it hadn't already gone on its own. "The dead guy—it was Captain James, Imogene. You were right. I got him across. Do we need to go after the one who killed him?"

Imogene shook her head. "No. There's been enough dying tonight."

"Are we calling the police?" Jessie asked.

I didn't need to see Imogene shake her head to know the answer to that. "Let them find what they find, when they find it. I'm not sure anyone will be lookin' for the likes of this one."

"You came looking for me," Levi said. No emotion in the words, and yet every emotion in the world.

Trina's fingers squeezed mine so hard my knuckles cracked.

"What's this freak's body count, if he's been at it for years?" I asked. "Twenty? Thirty?"

Imogene didn't answer, and I had a horrible feeling it was way more than that.

"Another serial killer," Jessie said. "Unbelievable. Welcome to Never."

"Maybe he thinks he's getting rid of evil things that laws can't control, the way we were planning to do," Trina said in a shaky voice. "Maybe he's trying to do the right thing. How can we judge him without judging ourselves?"

"But whoever this killer is, he makes mistakes," Forest said as she came to stand beside Levi.

"And you never have?" Trina asked Imogene. She shifted her gaze to Levi. "You've never gone after some criminal who was using his Madoc blood to do bad things and figured out later that you got the wrong person?"

"Easy, baby." I pulled her close to me and held her. She trembled in my arms, breathing too fast. "This is too much. Let's get Mama and go home."

She finally put her arms around me and hugged me back, and after a few seconds, she nodded. We were all staying together at my house, Mama and Jessie and me, Forest and Levi, too. Trina was planning to move in with us—with me—just as soon as she spoke to her father.

As for Imogene, her home was an apartment near the top of the bell tower. She didn't leave the campus. I didn't even know if she could. After seeing this burning mess in the woods, I wasn't sure I wanted her to.

Lincoln Psychiatric needed watching. Maybe all of Never did, too.

"Come on," I said to Trina, leading her away from the fire. "This isn't anything we can fix tonight."

Trina followed me into the woods, and everyone else straggled along behind us. I was glad nobody said the rest of what I was thinking out loud.

This isn't anything we can fix at all.

Maybe we couldn't.

But maybe the bunch of us were strong enough—and stupid enough—to stay right here and try.

Part III
The Scream at the End of the Hall

Trina

CHAPTER TWENTY-ONE

W*itch.*

It was such an ugly word. I couldn't get it out of my head, but I couldn't ignore it, either. Not anymore.

"Why do you want to go to the store, Trina?" my father asked without looking up from the book in his lap. "Addie doesn't need your help."

I sat across from Never's best-known preacher two hours after his Sunday afternoon prayer service, imagining a body burning on a pyre deep in the woods near Lincoln.

Witch.

My father would slap me if I called him that.

Murderer.

He'd do more than slap me if that word came out of my mouth.

The dead man in the woods—Captain James—*had* been wrong inside. He had been evil. If my father did kill him, was that so bad?

"I missed Addie while I was at school," I told him. That wasn't a lie. I had to clench my hands together to keep from fiddling with the wax plugs in my nose. I opened my lips just enough to get air, but I made sure my father didn't notice. Or I thought I did. With my father, it was hard to know what he caught or didn't catch until it was too late.

And I will cut off witchcrafts out of thine hand; and thou shalt have no more soothsayers, my brain recited. The line was from the Bible, from the book of Micah. My father liked quoting Scripture. He just wasn't so good at living by it.

"Mmm," he said, keeping his eyes on his book. He was tall, with lean muscles and hands big enough to squeeze skulls until they exploded. He had gone bald when I was barely old enough to remember him having hair, but otherwise he hadn't aged. His skin was so smooth and dark the only thing I ever saw to rival it was a dahlia somebody gave him as a gift one Easter. He always wore suits without jackets, and his coal-black eyes had a sharp gleam. He missed nothing, and he wanted an accounting for every action, every second spent out of his sight.

"Seems like a waste of time to me, Trina. You could be studying."

Sweat gathered at the back of my neck. I should have run back to Lexington, Kentucky, after we found that body burning in the woods. I should have gone back to college, back to a future that didn't include Pastor Martinez sitting in his overstuffed recliner, controlling every minute of my time and passing judgment on every breath I took.

His fingers brushed across the cover of his book. It looked like leather, but I knew what it really was.

Skin.

His second wife, Adelaide—Addie to me from the day I met her—slipped out of the kitchen and came to stand behind his chair as he read the old spell book he had taken from somebody in Never. Somebody with Madoc blood. Somebody evil—or that he had decided was evil.

Another body, burning in the night.

"I haven't seen Trina much this visit, Xavier." Addie's voice sounded matter-of-fact. "Let us have some girl time."

My muscles tensed, but I worked to keep still. No expression on my face. No hint of anything. The air in the room seemed too hot and too still. Even with the nose plugs firmly in place, the scent of Addie's pot roast seeped into my awareness. She was cooking that on purpose, because we needed the smell of the meat.

"What are you buying?" my father asked her.

Addie placed a glass of iced tea on the table next to my father. "Salt and bay leaves," she said. The elbow he couldn't see, the one behind the chair, bent as she reached into the pocket of her blue apron and pulled out a dead man's hand.

It was all withered and pickled. Each finger had been dipped in tallow rendered from the dead man's fat. He was a truck driver, shot to death by police in another state, then shipped home for burial. At Johnson and Sons Mortuary, where Addie worked, she had been able to take the hand—the one that held the knife that the truck driver had used to hack a prostitute to pieces—with nobody the wiser. She stole enough fat from the murderer's gut to finish the job, and we had what we needed to get us a little breathing room when we needed it.

Addie moved quietly behind my father, lit the thumb of the Hand of Glory on fire, and slid it under his chair.

I imagined I could see the sick-sweet scent of the burning tallow as it eased into the room and wrapped itself around the smell of pot roast.

My father shifted. Addie flinched, and I jerked on the couch in spite of trying harder than hard to stay motionless. My heart beat faster, and faster again when he yawned.

"All right, then," he said. "You have half an hour."

Addie headed back into the kitchen without daring to look at me.

My father reached for his tea, yawned again, then put the glass back on the table. His head turned in my direction, and my pulse hammered until my eyes watered.

His lids fluttered, then lowered.

He leaned his tall frame back in his chair and rested his hand on top of the confiscated book of spells he had been studying. A few seconds later, my father started to snore.

The kitchen door swung open again, and Addie motioned for me. I moved in a hurry, heading straight for the door to the basement.

Spelled like he was, my father just grunted instead of spouting rules or reducing the time he had allowed us. He wouldn't sleep much longer than an hour, I was sure of it. No spell worked against my father for very long, but at least this one would keep him from casting his own spells to track us or listen in on what we were saying. If we were really, really lucky, he wouldn't catch on to what we had done.

If we weren't lucky . . . no. I didn't want to think about bad things and tempt them to happen.

Addie and I slipped out through the basement door, hurried down the steps, and out to the driveway. Then we ran all the way to the car.

CHAPTER TWENTY-TWO

I pulled the plugs out of my nose and pocketed them as Addie drove away from the house.

Somebody honked at us and I jumped. Was that Dad's truck, already fired up and ready to chase after us? Had my father woken from his sleep despite the Hand of Glory sputtering and smoking under his chair?

My fists clenched, but I made myself relax my fingers. What was I thinking? It's not like I would try to hit my own father, no matter how much he freaked me out.

"Trina." My stepmother eyed me in that funny way, part friend and part parent like she had been since the day my father brought home his new young wife. I had been five, she, eighteen; I'm not sure my father had understood that he was giving me an ally, not a babysitter. As for my real mother, she was long gone, probably as far away from my father as she could get. I had never gotten so much as a letter from her.

"I'm not going back to Lexington," I told Addie, fixing my

gaze straight ahead at the road. "I applied for an externship this semester, and I start Monday. After that, I may finish at South College, if my transfer gets approved."

In the reflection on the car's front window, I watched as Addie grimaced. "He'll have a fit. He doesn't want you to stay in Never."

I tried to shrug and act like I didn't care. Addie said, "I'll do what I can, but I know you didn't have me knock your father out to keep him from hearing about your school decisions."

That made me twitch. Addie didn't use spells to pry into my thoughts or the future. She didn't have to. It was as though she could read everything in my heart just by glancing at my face.

"I won't be living at home," I told her.

This made her sigh and nod. "You're moving in with Darius."

The *he'll have a fit* went without saying. A little while ago, Darius had gotten himself accused of murder and arrested. It was all cleared up now, but still. That kind of thing didn't impress fathers, especially fathers as overprotective as mine.

As for the rest of the story, I couldn't bring myself to say it yet, so I went for, "I'll have my own room," like that would make a difference.

"What aren't you telling me?" Addie asked, slowing as we pulled into the grocery-store parking lot.

The energy in the car seemed to crackle, and my insides clutched. I wondered if my father had some spell at work, creeping around the edges of our conversation, looking for a crack to seep through and soak up all my secrets.

"A few weeks ago, I got into some things over at Lincoln

Psychiatric," I said. My pulse jumped, and I glanced in the rear-view mirror.

There was no truck behind us. I was just expecting it to be there.

"Lincoln? Are you out of your mind?" Addie sounded more exasperated than mad, but I understood.

My father had always made it clear that Lincoln Psychiatric was off-limits to me. It was the one place in Never, Kentucky—other than cemeteries—I was never allowed to go, no matter what. Lincoln was a dangerous place. It was bad because a lot of *them* ended up there—the strange folks with Madoc blood. The evil things my father eradicated.

Addie was still talking, muttering instead of yelling like I knew she wanted to. "You know he'll go on and on about Lincoln Psychiatric. It's a hotbed. It's a—"

"Cess-a-pool," I finished in a bad imitation of his deep voice, with the way-South but slightly French accent he got from his Creole mother. "I know there are bad things at Lincoln, Addie. I helped kill one of them."

Addie's frown turned her soft face hard, and the light in her eyes seemed to flicker, then go dull. She had never wanted me to be part of the killing. She parked the car, shut off the engine, and bowed her head, showing me her perfectly cropped hair, the tiny curls so tight I couldn't have stuck a pin in them. She had protected me, even using spells that might bring my father's wrath straight down on her head—and I had gone and gotten myself involved in the war my father never stopped fighting anyway.

"They know about us—some of the people who can . . . you

know. Do special things." My frown matched hers. "They know for sure somebody's killing them off."

"Then we have to get ready, and I have to warn Xavier." Addie moved to start the car again, but I grabbed her arm.

"You don't have to tell him anything." An image of Darius shoved its way into my mind, with his dopey grin and stubbly cheeks—and that white, burned-out eye that saw things it shouldn't. "They aren't coming to fight us."

"They will," Addie said, shaking off my grip, but not starting the car. "They always do. Look at your history."

My history. She meant my father's ledgers. How many Madocs he had killed, and how many so-called normal people in Never had died mysterious deaths. Murders and disappearances and mysterious goings-on, he recorded it all, and always assumed the Madocs did it.

It was Satan who set evil like the Madocs free on earth, my father liked to say, *and God who tasked men like me with destroying it.*

I opened the car door and got out, hoping Addie would do the same. After a few seconds, she did, and we stood facing each other over the white hood of her Oldsmobile.

"He's wrong, Addie. Not everybody with power is evil. *We* aren't bad people, right?"

She folded her arms, frowning deeply. "We don't have power. We just know how to tap the power in other things. It's different when you have it inside you, in your blood. Then it tears up your mind and soul and makes you just like those demons Xavier hunts."

An image of the burning body flickered behind my eyes, and I had to squeeze them shut and count to three. I'd always known what my father did, or said he did, to keep us safe, but I'd never seen him at it, and I'd never seen what was left over when he finished.

The body in the woods had just looked like a dead man. Nothing huge or wicked or scary. It had been pathetic.

Was my father the one who tried to kill Levi?

I pushed that right out of my mind.

"I met some people who can do special things," I told Addie. "And I don't think they're bad."

Addie's shoulders twitched, and her frown melted into an expression of horror. "Honey, creatures like that lie to you. They can fool you into thinking whatever they want you to. That's what the devil's minions do."

"They aren't the devil's minions." I shook my head, feeling a hot splash of desperation in my guts. "They're just people, like me and you."

Addie stared at me with both her eyebrows raised so high she looked like a cartoon. "Who are these folks?"

I shrugged. No way was I giving her names, and she knew it. After a few seconds, she gave up and gestured to the store. "Come on. Salt and bay leaves. He might not notice we've been gone longer than we should have been, but he'll notice if we don't bring what we went out for."

The rest of our shopping trip and the ride home had been quiet, because I had no guts.

When Addie and I got out of the car at the house, both of

us studied the basement door, then the living room window. We were eighteen minutes past the limit my father had given us. The Hand of Glory had probably gone out, but it wouldn't leave behind any wax or ashes. He'd never know we used it, unless he found it burning. We had about an even chance of getting away with our extra time and privacy. If he was awake, he'd be pissed, and he'd keep us both at home for weeks—unless I abandoned Darius and went back to school.

Addie started for the house, but I caught up with her. "Wait. Just one more minute." If I couldn't make Addie understand this, I had no hope of ever making my father hear me. "Some of the folks who have power could help us, and we could help them. They really aren't evil, not all of them."

Addie's mouth opened, then closed. She gripped the plastic shopping bag and shook her head as if she were trying to line up jagged thoughts that wouldn't smooth together.

"One of them, this girl Forest," I kept going in a rush, "you can feel the specialness dripping off of her. Darius can see how good she is with his bad eye, but we don't know who she is, not really. The bunch of us took out a serial killer under the asylum, and a tree that was, I don't know, too alive or something. It had a mouth and teeth."

Addie said nothing at all. She just stared at me. I thought she was listening. I thought she was hearing me.

"My father has been right all along about some things," I admitted. "There *is* a war going on, only not the one he thinks. That's why I have to work at Lincoln for a while, to keep another pair of eyes on what's happening, and to help."

Addie caught hold of my elbow and slowly walked me toward the basement. I didn't fight her as she pulled me inside, closing and locking the door behind us. Once we were there in the quiet within the walls, she gazed deep into my eyes, and the tightness that had been building in my chest eased a little. I got everything said. And Addie was listening. She was always with me and for me. She would understand, and she would help me convince my father that we had to help good people—whether they had power or not—fight the real evils when they showed up.

"Darius," Addie said. "When did you find out?"

I blinked, not understanding her question.

She let out a long, slow breath, the way she did when she was sad. "When did you find out Darius Hyatt had Madoc blood?"

"What?" Frost hardened across my thoughts, then dropped lower to dust my heart. I hadn't said anything about Darius having power. That was the one secret I wouldn't share, because my father—oh. His eye. I had mentioned Darius's eye.

"It must not be strong in him, or your father would have sensed it long ago." Addie dropped the bag with the bay leaves and salt and put her arms around me. When she pulled me close to her, she held me tight. "I'm sorry, honey. I'm so sorry."

"There's nothing wrong with Darius, he's just—" I started to say as I put my face on her shoulder, but then I caught sight of my father standing in the doorway at the top of the basement steps.

His mouth made a straight line, and his expression was flat and merciless. All of my blood turned to ice, and I pushed against Addie, trying to get free.

"Don't, Trina," she whispered in my ear. "He knows you love the boy. He'll make it quick. Darius won't feel any pain."

I shoved her away from me. She stumbled backward, kicking the grocery bag as she went. My father's face had become a mask of judgment and purpose. He looked like death walking, and I knew what would happen next.

My father turned and stalked away from the basement doorway.

I charged after him, screaming as I stormed up the steps.

CHAPTER TWENTY-THREE

I was still screaming as my father went to the hall closet to get the bag he always took when he went hunting. I pushed around him, and my screams cut off as if something had hit my throat. Not breathing, not thinking, I wheeled on him, blocking the way out of the hall. He could go to the bedrooms or the basement, but he couldn't get to the front door or the kitchen door without going through me.

Scared wasn't part of the equation now. I was mad. My chest heaved from running and yelling. My arms stuck out to the sides. Not much of a fighting stance. I had no ninja training or years of experience killing things like my father did, but I'd do something. I'd find a way.

He turned toward me, gripping the brown leather satchel that held knives and axes and iron spikes and herbs and potions and whatever else he needed to take down his prey. He looked like a professor in his black slacks and pressed white shirt, with his perfect skin and clipped hair, but I knew what he really was: a death machine, with a bunch of wrong ideas.

"No," I growled through clenched teeth, startled by the loudness of my voice. *This is your father. Are you crazy? He'll swat you like a fly. You're threatening your* father.

The air stank of tallow and burned human flesh. The Hand of Glory had done all it could but failed, and now its stench was trying to choke me. I coughed and my eyes watered, but I didn't move at all. I couldn't. It was this, or Darius would be dead within minutes.

Addie made it up the basement stairs and stood behind my father, gaping. When he glared at me and went to move, she grabbed his elbow. "Xavier, don't you dare touch that child."

Her voice had such a high pitch. She was scared. I could see the fear torturing her, streaks of wild yellow lightning crackling across her smooth brown skin. The color on my father was darker, like blue-black ink. He didn't suffer from his darkness—he welcomed it. It was his armor of hatred.

The colors I saw weren't in my head. They were real. When I got really upset or scared or stressed, all the power I had ever been exposed to seemed to pull into me and come through me, and I saw colors and could do things—but not on purpose. It was all random. I had no say in it, no control over it; but right now I didn't care. This wasn't something I had ever shared with Addie or my father. Let them find out the hard way.

"I don't want to hurt you," I said, my voice still too loud. I sounded mean and serious. I sounded like Xavier Martinez.

His left eyebrow lifted, but otherwise his face stayed still as black alabaster. His gaze flicked from one of my twiggy arms to the other. "You planning to slap me to death?"

I didn't answer him.

"I asked you a question, little girl."

I didn't feel like a little girl, and for the first time, his tone wasn't working on me. Fresh rage kindled on his face. Colors darker than black seeped out of him, and he took a step toward me.

Addie yanked on his arm, but he pulled away from her. She let out a sob and turned to run back down into the basement.

My heart squeezed, then sank.

I was on my own.

"Don't you raise your hand against me, Trina," my father said. "The eye that mocketh at his father—"

"The ravens of the valley shall pick it out, and the young eagles shall eat it," I finished for him. The verse was from Proverbs.

His eyes widened just enough to let me know I had surprised him. I'd never done well with his Bible lessons, so he probably figured I hadn't been listening. He took another step, coming within arm's length from me now. I was going to have to hit him or push him or kick him or something. The thought made me sick.

"And he that smiteth his father, or his mother," he said, "shall be surely put to death."

"So you're going to kill me now?" I shot back. "I guess I shouldn't be surprised."

"You will not disrespect me," my father said, so matter-of-fact it gave me cold shivers. "Get out of my way, Trina. I'm only going to tell you once."

He shifted his killing bag to his left hand, freeing his right to deal with me. My heart crashed against my ribs. I hated that I was shaking, and I wished I could punch him or shove him and feel nothing at all, because I didn't think he'd feel anything when he hurt me.

And he *was* going to hurt me.

I saw it all over him, the barely bottled rage. It wasn't my fault, but that wouldn't matter when he hit me. His darkness would strike me down. It would destroy anything that got in his way, and then it would destroy Darius.

My father came closer and filled up my world. I couldn't see anything but his angry eyes, and the way his white teeth flashed when his mouth twisted into a sneer.

"What happened to you?" he asked.

My stomach clenched, because that was the thing I had always wanted to know about him—what had happened to fill him with so much violence?

He raised his open hand, knuckles toward me, and I knew he meant to knock me to my knees. I had to hit him first.

My muscles quivered. I clenched both fists, but didn't swing.

"Don't," I begged him, and I sounded and felt like a scared little kid as I stared into those dark eyes and tried to find some emotion or concern—anything but rage.

There was nothing.

But no matter how mad I got, I couldn't hit my father.

I wasn't going to save Darius or my new friends or anyone else.

Coward. Worthless child.

My arms sagged to my sides, and I closed my eyes.

I felt the *thunk* in my teeth and my bones, but no pain followed. I didn't stagger, and I didn't fall.

The thump and clatter of a heavy weight hitting the floor made my eyes fly open.

I hadn't been hit at all. It wasn't me collapsing to the floor, unconscious from a blow to the head. My father lay in a heap at my feet, blood oozing from the right side of his face.

Addie stood over him, the frying pan she clutched still raised like a baseball bat. Her expression was full of pain and horror, and the colors coursing over her skin defied labels.

"Addie," I whispered, stunned, then suddenly terrified for her and for my father, too. I reached for her, but she shrieked and stepped back from me, her eyes wild.

She kept the frying pan raised as she shifted her gaze from me to my father. She said something about healing herbs and spells to make sure his brain didn't swell, but I didn't know for sure whether he was alive.

Neither of us seemed able to check.

I didn't want to touch him. I also didn't want to take my eyes off Addie, because she seemed to be coming apart.

Seconds passed. More seconds.

My father didn't move.

Addie wouldn't lower the frying pan, and she wouldn't let me come close. She backed away until I would have had to step over my father to get to her. She muttered a healing spell, and it slammed into me like so many electric tingles. Every cut and bruise on my whole body fixed itself at once, and it hurt.

Maybe the spell hit my father, too. It might have hit the neighbors or people three miles away. Addie was using raw power, no talismans or potions or powders to call it or control it. I was pretty sure my father didn't know she could do that. Unchanneled power was as dangerous as a flood or a thunderstorm. Like an act of God or a natural disaster, it ran its course until it finished.

Addie's hair stuck out wildly, and her smooth apron had gotten puckered and wrinkled. Her brown eyes had gone dim, and her skin was all dusky and dull. Whatever she had just done had drained her near to nothing inside.

"Addie," I tried again, and her gaze snapped to mine.

I saw clarity. And agony. And betrayal.

"Get out," she said, her voice like a dozen demons trapped in a well.

We stood in the hallway together, gulping air that smelled like blood and the ashes of a dead man's hand. My skin crawled with the uncontrolled power in the air, and my heart raced.

Then I turned and ran.

CHAPTER TWENTY-FOUR

I have to go back and see how he is." My chest hurt, my hands ached, and my eyes burned so from tears that I could barely make out the faces in front of me.

"You know you can't." Darius's voice was soft, but it wasn't enough to make me calm down. "Sounds like you barely got out of that house in one piece."

I shook my head and tried to pretend my father hadn't been about to do . . . I don't know what to me because I defied him. I just kept seeing him lying in the hallway of our house, bleeding.

What if he died? What if he was already dead?

Levi eased toward me.

I backed up, and my shoulders hit Darius's front door. "Stop," I warned, raising my fists. My voice sounded crazy.

"You wouldn't hit a murderer," Levi muttered. "You won't hit me."

Forest had him dressed in jeans and a black T-shirt with silver Aerosmith wings, but it didn't make him look any less scary.

His long black hair was pulled into a ponytail, and his pale face seemed twice as white. The air around him glittered silver and black, dark and light, and shadows moved on the walls and ceilings.

They didn't scare me. Not even when they howled and honked and started to pull out of the paint and turn into dogs and birds. One of the dogs bristled as it got between Levi and me. My eyes saw it as a beagle, but it was wrong, somehow. The angles were off, like any second it might explode into something huge and slobbering, ready to eat me.

"My father's no more a murderer than you are." I shook a fist at Levi and his pet hunting dog, suddenly glad I was blocking the door so nobody could go charging toward my house. "I can't believe I betrayed my family for *you!*"

Darius blocked Levi by stepping into his path. "Uh-uh, man. That's my girl. You stay put."

"He's got a right to be mad," Forest said. "Xavier Martinez killed Levi. Don't you get that? He murdered him and threw his body on a pile of wood for burning. That man's as crazy as anybody locked up in the asylum."

I shook my head. "It's not like that. My father thinks he's saving the world—and you *know* there are bad things at Lincoln."

Please don't let him be dead.

Levi pointed his finger at me as his biggest, meanest dog growled. "If you take his side, you're no better than he is."

Forest stepped closer to Levi, not seeming to notice the five or six hounds growling around his ankles. The tilt of her eyes and the eerie calm she always gave off made her seem like she was from some other planet. She had total control over Levi, when she chose to use it.

"That's going a little far," she told him.

He broke off glaring at me long enough to glance at her and say, "The sins of the fathers are the sins of the sons—just ask Imogene."

He sounded sure, but his eyes darted to Forest.

"That's in Exodus," I told him. "But it doesn't really say that."

"I don't care if it says that or not, it's stupid," Forest said. "Trina's not responsible for what her father did, just like Darius wasn't responsible for what Eff Leer did."

Levi's expression stayed mean for a second, then softened. The goose and hound shadows on the wall started to fade, and the real dogs at his feet disappeared like they had never been there, all but that biggest one. "But if your great-greats hurt people, you have to make up for it."

There it was again. He was trying to sound so sure and so pissed off, but he couldn't. Not when he wanted Forest to agree with him.

Forest frowned at him. "I don't buy that."

"Imogene says she's unforgiven because of them that went before her," he whispered, reaching down to pet his dog. That made him look almost normal, but I knew better. "She thinks that's why she hasn't died."

Forest shook her head. "She isn't unforgiven. None of us are. We haven't done anything bad."

When Levi still didn't back down, Forest brushed her fingers against his elbow. Darius had told me that's all they could share, quick touches and long looks, because of some weird bracelet somebody fastened on Forest when she was a baby. It lay on her wrist looking like nothing special, just carved wood and smooth beads, but it grew with her, and as long as she wore it, nobody with Madoc blood could touch her without being burned.

Levi's posture stayed tense, and Forest touched him one more time. He flinched, but something other than pain flickered across his expression.

"Trina's not her father," Forest told him. "And you can't go gunning for him, because he *is* her father."

Levi's eyes got bigger. "What if he's on his way here to kill us all?"

Forest shrugged. "If he shows up, we'll deal with him."

"He's not coming." My lower lip quivered even though I didn't want it to, and fresh tears pooled in my eyes. "I really don't know if he's even alive after Addie hit him like that."

Darius glanced at me over his shoulder. I could tell he wanted to stop guarding me and put his arms around me, and I wished he would—but I couldn't help thinking, *Darius is one of them*.

"I'll probably end up a patient in Lincoln instead of working there," I muttered. The cess-a-pool. The place I was going to help watch, to make sure nothing truly evil found its way out into the world. "I don't even have clothes to start my externship tomorrow."

"Mama will take you to the store," Darius said. "We'll get you set for a few days, until we sort this out."

I hugged myself and tried not to shake. "How are we going to sort out my father?"

"Levi and I will go to your house and check on him," Forest said, "and do what we can to help with his healing."

"You can't." I shook my head, feeling terror rise like heat to my face. "It's not safe."

Forest looked confused. "You said he wasn't conscious."

"The house and yard are protected—warded. And Addie's conscious, and she's not herself. I'm afraid she'd kill you faster than my father would."

Addie in her rumpled apron, spent and brittle from the power she had used . . . I didn't want to think about it, but the image jammed itself into my head.

"And how's she supposed to hurt us?" Levi asked. "She got her own knives or something?"

"She's not Madoc, but she can use power." I sighed. "If Addie threw an unchecked spell at you, it could go off like a warhead and take out half the neighborhood."

"Spell. You mean like a witch's spell?" On anybody else, Levi's expression would have been a sneer. On him, it was more like normal. "I don't suppose you'd care to show me one, would you?"

"I can't." I let go of myself and shook my arms to get the blood flowing through my hands again. "I have to use talismans and potions and powders—you know, props. But the supplies are at my house. All I've got is my willow charm."

I slipped a hand into my jeans pocket and took out a piece of woven willow that Addie made for me when I was younger. It was almost a circle, with a cross on the inside. "The only time I can work more than basic spells without props is when I'm upset, and then I can't control what happens. It's random."

"Sounds like Madoc blood to me," Forest said.

Darius pulled his glasses down, studying me with his eerie white eye. "Nope. It's something else."

Forest and Levi didn't argue, because Darius could see the truth of anyone or anything, see power in all its colors and forms.

Levi studied me for a while, then finally said, "I'll ask Imogene to go to your house."

My whole body went tight at the mention of the old woman. I didn't really know what she was, but she was tied to Lincoln and to the power my father feared and hated.

Who are the real witches, us or them?

"Imogene can leave the hospital grounds?" Forest asked.

"Yeah," Levi said. "Just not often, and not for long. And don't worry, she won't pick any fights."

My breath came out in a huge rush. I hadn't even realized I was holding it. Just knowing somebody would check on my father made me feel better.

"Meanwhile, I want to go to Lincoln and keep reading Imogene's records about the different types of spirits," Forest said. "I'd rather we know as much as we can before you spend too much time working there, Trina."

This made me feel so tired and heavy that I sat down in the armchair nearest to the door, trusting Darius to stop Levi and that freaky beagle if they charged. "How can I start work and act like everything's not totally insane?"

Darius came over to where I was sitting and got down on his knees in front of my chair. His big hands rested on my shoulders, squeezing, then moved to my cheeks to cup my face and keep me looking at him.

"You act a zif," he said as I studied my reflection in the black lenses of his glasses.

"What?"

"A-s i-f," he clarified. "As if. Until things are okay, you act as if they are." He pulled me forward and lightly touched my lips with his. Tired or not, I felt tingles spread across my shoulders, and the soothing comfort of having him so close to me.

"I'm sorry, baby," Darius said in a low, quiet voice. "Would you rather walk away from all this? Because I'll go with you, if that's your call."

For a few seconds, my heart beat faster, and the room seemed to narrow until I couldn't see anyone or anything but Darius. I thought about heading back to UK, about getting away from my father again, seeing my friends, and patching up the shredded life I had started to build. I had been doing pretty good at college—and Darius meant it. He'd go with me if I got up from here and drove straight to Lexington.

But what would happen at Lincoln then?

There was evil loose in that hospital, and it was trying to get out and kill people. It *would* kill people. Imogene and Levi and Forest, they could only do so much. And no matter what Forest said about my father's sins not being my own, my father had made everything so much harder for them.

If Darius and I walked away from Never, we'd be part of

letting terrible things happen. How terrible and where it would all end I had no idea, but it didn't bear thinking about.

"Act a zif." I let out a breath, keeping my eyes on Darius. His respect—and my conscience staying clean—seemed like a fair trade for everything I was giving up. "All right. Guess I better get busy practicing my nothing's-crazy face."

CHAPTER TWENTY-FIVE

When I took my assigned wad of keys from Ms. Miller, my supervisor at Lincoln Psychiatric Hospital, my hands shook.

Act a zif . . .

I had to get the extern hours for my future as a social worker. I needed a bachelor's degree, then a master's if I really wanted to do it right. The bonus was, I could help our little group of fighters keep an eye on what was happening at Lincoln in the process. But mostly I wanted to help Darius and keep him safe from my father. If I could just understand the real fight going on at Lincoln, maybe I could make my father understand it, too.

Time to be a good actress. I made myself smile. My new black skirt and white blouse itched. My new black flats pinched my toes. I smelled like Darius's mother, because I had used her soap. Not that my nose was good enough to tease out that scent from the vanilla and cinnamon and pumpkin and watermelon and citrus and pine scents of the air fresheners, unlit candles, and potpourri in the offices all around us.

Act a zif . . .

I couldn't whimper or shut my eyes or obsess about my father. Imogene was due to check in again in fifteen minutes.

Thunder rumbled above the giant stone building, and I twitched at the sound. I had been listening to Ms. Miller for over an hour as she told me how to clock in, where to find my assignments, how to be sure I didn't transmit infection, and how to report patient abuse if I saw it. We were sitting in her office, where the walls were painted pink. Seriously. It was pale, maybe more of a coral, but it was *pink*. And she was wearing a slightly mismatched three-piece blue pantsuit.

Why did that matter? I never cared what people wore. Ms. Miller had a big, bleached-white smile and thick bleached-blond hair, yellow on top of blue in front of pink.

I needed an aspirin. Or a nice, coma-inducing tranquilizer.

Rain splattered hard against her screened and barred window, making me jump.

Act a zif . . .

Act as if I didn't want to throw up.

Act as if I didn't want to run away from Lincoln and never look back.

Act as if I wasn't about to cry every freaking minute.

Ms. Miller kept talking, but I had no idea what she said. I caught the "You'll be starting on Unit C" part, though, and I managed to keep focus through, "It's our chronic ward. Today I just want you to observe, get to know your people."

She blinded me with another megawatt smile.

My people. Who were my people again, exactly? Surely she

couldn't mean my father, the man I left for dead. Or Addie, who had bashed her husband in the head to save me.

I held back a sigh and kept right on trying to act normal.

We left Ms. Miller's office and walked into one of the hospital's long, tiled hallways. Rainy gray light spilled from open office doors, mingling with the hall's white-blue fluorescence until the whole place seemed overcast. It reminded me of Addie's funeral home, how everyone who worked there tried to make it bright and happy, but in the end, it was what it was—a place where the dead came to be stuffed in a box.

I shivered and clutched my notebook to my chest.

Darius had been waiting right outside Ms. Miller's office door. My own personal bodyguard, all glamoured up by Forest and Levi to be invisible. I couldn't see him, but I caught the scent of his aftershave and heard the comforting whisper of his breathing. I imagined his big shoulders going square as he fell into step behind us. His handsome face would be grim and stern and he was probably checking out each of the multicolored offices in case some monster came hurtling out from behind the fake fig trees.

The farther we got away from the office area, the more the building smelled like stone and cleanser and dampness, and the grayer the floors and walls seemed to become. Thunder kept up a steady beat, and when we passed windows, hard rain was hammering against the safety glass.

Ms. Miller led me through so many locked doors that I lost count, each set seeming bigger and thicker than the ones before.

When we finally got to a door marked CAREFUL, AWOL RISK, ENTER WITH CAUTION, I felt like I was in the center of a giant maze I could never escape. I held the door long enough for Darius to get through, then moved my hand. The door slammed with a loud, metallic clang. I found myself looking back at a tiny square window, set just above eye level.

Locked in.

Didn't matter that I had keys. It still felt freaky.

When I turned and rejoined Ms. Miller a few steps down the hallway, Unit C stretched before me like a corridor into an alternate universe. The walls were cinder block, like at a school, but painted a light blue. Everything seemed dull and functional, even the chairs and tables pushed up against the walls on either side of the hallway. A few bulletin boards had cheerful fall decorations tacked to them, but they didn't help much. This felt like a quiet place. A sad place. It smelled like urine and air freshener. I didn't really want to be here.

There was one man sitting in a chair, wearing jeans and a sweatshirt. He held his face in his hands, and he was rocking.

Didn't look like he wanted to be here, either.

Ms. Miller led me to a desk at the far end of the hallway and introduced me to a short woman with black hair and loud yellow scrubs. I didn't even process her whole name, just SHARON and that she was the unit's RN, and I could ask her for help if I needed it. The nurse pointed out a table where I could be out of the way and "observe," and she told me the patients would be back from their morning groups soon. Then Ms. Miller gave me a gigantic smile and told me to return to her office at the end of the day with my notes, and we'd go over my experiences.

As she walked toward the unit elevator, I just stood there, not sure what to do. My brain kept refusing to engage.

"Table," Darius whispered, and I jumped.

Sharon, still only a few feet away from me, stared like she might need to evaluate me instead of working on her charts.

I managed something like a polite smile, walked slowly away, and seated myself in a heavy plastic chair at a plastic table. From my vantage point, I could see the doorway, the nurse at the desk, and the one patient sitting in the unit's hallway to my left. On my right were the seemingly empty chair where Darius sat and a few doors leading to bedrooms on either side of the hallway.

"Should have looked before you touched that furniture," Darius mumbled. I heard the *pat-pat* of his massive hands as he examined his own chair, then eased his big frame into it. "Probably hasn't been cleaned in a month."

Before Levi and Forest made him vanish, he had been wearing jeans and a black T-shirt with a Lincoln Psychiatric emblem. Must have gotten it during the brief time he worked here as a security guard, before he got charged with murder and lost his eye. I imagined him sitting in his chair, his dark glasses glittering in the neon lighting.

"Don't stare, baby," he said, and I thought he might be grinning. "They see you looking at nothing, they might keep you here."

I plopped my notebook on the table, careful to avoid a grape-colored stain that was probably sticky. When I opened it, I scrawled, *Not funny*. Underlined it a few times. Added exclamation marks.

Darius laughed so that only I could hear him, but five tables away, in the long part of the hallway, the man who had his face in his hands lifted his head as if the sound had startled him. His eyes traveled the room until they found me, and he fixed his gaze on my face like he was searching every thought I'd ever had. He was dark-skinned like my father, but heavier, with a slack look about him like he hadn't focused on anything in decades. His eyes, though—wide and wild and terrified—I couldn't stand it. I looked away.

Maybe I wasn't cut out for this social-work thing. At least, not here at Lincoln Psychiatric.

"Don't sweat it," Darius said as if he had just read my mind. "You want to work for Children's Services, not here. This is just field experience. Credit in a class. Treat it like those stats seminars you hated."

I wrote, *Necessary evil.*

"Yeah. That."

My body relaxed enough for me to breathe regularly, and I turned the page and began to take notes about the surroundings and the man on the unit, who had lost interest in me by then. Who was he? Why was he here when everybody else was away? I supposed people could refuse to go to groups, or oversleep. Maybe they had sick days, too. All of this got recorded as questions for Ms. Miller. No doubt she thought I was an idiot already. Asking intelligent questions might help me make a better impression— and writing down everything I noticed might give us some hint about the next bad spirit we'd have to fight. Who knew what I might see but not yet understand? Levi and Forest could sort through it all later, when they got finished reading Imogene's records.

Imogene.

Great.

Thinking about her brought me straight back to my main worry—what was happening with my father.

Darius murmured, "Don't get all tense again, now. What is it?"

My cell phone buzzed in my pocket, and I grabbed for it and punched it on without saying hello.

"Your father's up and about," Imogene said in her backwoods accent, way too loud. I could imagine her standing in my front yard, holding Darius's cell phone directly in front of her mouth, talking into it like a World War II radio. "Your stepmother's seeing to what ails him, I suppose."

Relief made me lean forward and prop my elbows on the table, sticky stains and all.

"Thank you," I said in a quiet voice.

My eyes darted up and down the hallway, checking the guy in the chair and the nurse at the desk in case I wasn't supposed to be using a phone on the unit. Ms. Miller might have said something like that, but I wasn't sure I cared.

"Your house has got some good protections," Imogene went on. "Can't get through 'em, and it's probably better I don't try."

Now I imagined Imogene, who looked a little like an overweight version of Granny from that old *Beverly Hillbillies* TV show, poking around the edges of our yard. I hoped she could go invisible like Levi and Darius and Forest. A police report about the ghost of Granny Clampett trying to break into the pastor's house would be all we needed.

Sharon glanced in my direction, then frowned and shook her head when she saw my telephone.

"I have to go," I told Imogene. "Check in again soon."

I hung up.

Thunder exploded over the hospital, and lightning flashed so brightly the hallway around me seemed to flicker. I shifted my gaze from the nurse to the door, and that's when I saw her.

She came through the door.

The *closed* door.

It was Forest. Or it was her twin, wearing faded jeans and a blue shirt, with a frightened expression and a vacant, forward-looking stare.

The air around me seemed to crackle, and when I sucked in a breath I smelled trees and oceans and flowers.

Everything about the girl seemed a little faded, but I was positive I was looking at an image of Forest, and the hall was full of that calm, fresh vibration I associated with her.

But the calming vibe wasn't working on me this time.

My pulse sped up until I could hear blood thumping in my ears. My fingers twitched over my pen and pad as I watched the girl walk—only she wasn't really walking. More like gliding. The unnatural pace and flow of her movement gave me a double case of shivers.

Was Forest projecting herself here somehow? Was this some

Madoc trick I didn't know about? Had she and Levi found something in the records they needed to tell us?

Why not just call me?

Maybe something had gone wrong in the records room, up in Lincoln's famous bell tower.

Oh God.

Was I looking at Forest's fresh-made ghost?

The nurse at the desk didn't look up, but the male patient did. He scooted back in his chair and turned his face away from Forest, like he didn't want to see her.

Neither did I, but I couldn't look away. Horror pooled like ice in my belly.

"What the hell?" Darius whispered. "Is that—but—it looks like—"

He never got to finish, because the ghostly image of Forest stopped and fixed her now glowing eyes on him. She lifted her arm, and one of her long, pale fingers pointed in his direction. She opened her mouth as thunder bashed the air again and she let out a scream.

The sound tore into my mind and my skin.

The patient covered his ears and rocked hard.

I jumped to my feet, trying to shake off what felt like burning bugs crawling over every inch of my body, shocking me with a million electric bug feet.

Forest vanished, leaving nothing but the scream at the end of the hall.

The patient rocked and rocked and rocked as the awful sound

slowly died. I scratched at invisible insects, my chest hurting like I was having a heart attack.

The nurse stared, but she wasn't staring at me.

She was watching Darius, who was bent over, his mouth opened in a silent bellow, his ears covered.

He had become completely visible.

CHAPTER TWENTY-SIX

I ran to Darius and knelt in front of him. His forehead glittered with sweat, and when I grabbed his wrists, his skin felt clammy.

"Are you okay?" My words came out in a fast wheeze, and my face twitched from the fading sensation of superheated bugs making tracks across my eyelids and lips.

Darius coughed. I couldn't see behind his dark glasses, but as he lowered his hands from his ears and let me hold them, I saw the pinched lines of his face and knew he had shut his eyes against whatever had just yelled at us.

"She was bright," he managed. "Blinded me. I can't see anything but spots."

He seemed to be shaking all over. *I* was shaking all over.

I glanced at Sharon, who wasn't at the phone calling for Security like I expected. She was with the patient, kneeling just like I was kneeling, and she spoke to the man in gentle tones until he stopped rocking. Then she stood and held out her hand. He took it and got to his feet, and she began walking him toward one of the rooms—but not before she fired a look at me that would have killed most people.

"Can you walk?" I stood and gave Darius's hands a gentle tug. "We better get out of here."

Lightning cracked outside, and the bulbs in the hallway blinked off, then back on.

Darius took a deep breath and nodded as he raised up to his full height, his face aimed at the floor like he was fighting off a big wave of dizziness. "You'll have to lead. Everything's blurry."

As I turned loose one of his hands, I asked, "What was she?"

"Strong." He shook his head. "Other than that, no idea."

Witch girl. Come here, said a low voice from somewhere so close to me I heard it in my brain cells instead of my ear.

My shoulders tensed and my heart stuttered. I gripped Darius's hand. "Did you hear that?"

"Hear what?" He turned his sunglasses toward me. "The thunder? It hasn't stopped since we got here."

I let go of Darius and pushed around him toward the room at the end of the hall farthest from the main door. The door was closed, and streaks of gray light slipped out beneath the worn wood. Something about it felt . . . wrong.

My skin prickled from my neck to my toes.

A shadow passed across the light as something moved in the closed room.

I sucked in a breath and grabbed for the door handle, but Darius put his hand over mine before I could try to open it. "Trina, did that bunch of screaming scramble your mind? Come on, baby. We need to beat it before Security gets up here."

"Oh no you don't," said a woman's voice, more sharp and commanding than Darius's mother ever even thought about being. "You just stay put."

Darius and I jumped apart to find Sharon the nurse standing at the table we had just vacated, her frown at full volume. Now that I could see her up close, I realized she was much older than I had thought, with salt-and-pepper hair pulled into a bun and a lined face dappled with age spots on her jaw line. She folded her thick arms over her ample bosom and narrowed her eyes at Darius.

"What are you?" she demanded.

Not who. *What.*

And then her face changed from suspicion to shock as she recognized him. "Oh, wait. You that boy who got charged with murder a while back."

Darius let out a sigh, but Sharon was still talking. "Weird as all that was," she said, "figured you had to have a little Madoc in you."

Keeping himself between me and the nurse so I had to look around his shoulder to see the woman, Darius asked, "How do you know about Madocs?"

"None of your business," Sharon snapped. She turned her attention to me. "And you—you're the pastor's girl. The little witch. What do you want around here?"

"I'm not a witch," I said reflexively.

Thunder turned loose outside, broken only by the *crack-boom* of lightning striking nearby. The lights on Unit C flickered again.

"Then what they calling folks like you these days?" Sharon's tone shifted to teasing, or maybe it was mocking. "You work with potions and powders and charms like the pastor does when he thinks nobody's watching, you a witch, as far as I know."

I tried to think of a good comeback, but she was already back on Darius. "I don't know why you came here hidin', but she don't like most Madocs. She'll never let you stay."

It took me a second to realize that Sharon was talking about the Forest-apparition we had seen, but Darius was quicker than me. "Who is she? That—the—um, is she a ghost?"

"Can't nobody staff Unit C without knowing about Miss Bridgette," Sharon said. "You worked around the hospital for a while. Didn't you hear stories?"

Darius kept his arms at his sides, and I knew he was trying not to look threatening. "No. I didn't come on the units."

Sharon shrugged. "Every part of this hospital has ghosts. She's ours."

"Can you see her?" I asked, wishing I hadn't left my pad and pen on the table beside Sharon.

"No, but some of our folks can." Sharon glanced back toward the unit door, then at us. "She runs off most of the other ghosts, and the people who don't need to be here—like staff who treat the patients mean, and witches who come here for no good reason."

I'm not a witch, I started to say again, but that would have been habit, not truth. What did come out of my mouth was, "I'm on an externship."

Sharon pointed at Darius. "If you came here just to work, you wouldn't have snuck him in."

"It's not that simple—" I began, but she interrupted me.

"It is that simple, and you need to get on out of here. These folks have enough trouble without you scaring them."

Darius didn't move. "Do you have Madoc blood, Miss Sharon?"

I expected another "none of your business," but she said, "My mother did. Not rightly sure how strong it runs in me, but I'm more sensitive to spirits than most folks."

Darius reached back, took my hand, and pulled me up next to him as he asked, "Why are you at Lincoln Psychiatric?"

"I'm here for them." Sharon pointed toward the door of the room where she had taken the unit's only patient. "Been working here over thirty-two years."

Witch girl. Come here. Now.

The voice crawled through my brain. My eyes slammed closed against the cold, dark chills that skittered down my spine, and I had to force my lids up again. When I did, I saw black sparkles in the air around my head.

The sound had come from the bedroom behind me, I was sure of it. I pulled away from Darius and marched toward the bedroom door.

"You stay away from that room," Sharon said. "Nothing good ever happens there."

Darius managed to catch hold of me from behind, then asked, "How come?"

Sharon sighed. "We don't put patients in that room. Miss Bridgette don't like it. And you two better—"

"I heard somebody in there," I said, struggling out of Darius's bear hug.

"Then you as crazy as the people I look after," Sharon said. "It's been empty all year."

She walked straight past me to the room, used her key, and pushed the door open.

I fought back an urge to leap forward into the gray shadows to confront whatever had been messing with me—but when the door swung wide, there was nothing. Just a bed, a wardrobe fastened to the wall, and a barred, screened window taking punishment from the stubborn storm.

Darius stepped into the empty doorway and glanced around. Then he shrugged. "Nothing, baby."

From deep in the center of my mind, something laughed, shooting gooseflesh all over my body.

Menace washed across my senses. I smelled dirt and something coppery, like blood. I plunged my hand into my pocket, grabbed my willow charm, and I held it in front of me like a shield as I muttered the words to a reveal spell I had learned from Addie. It was Greek, or maybe Latin. I had no idea. I knew the sounds and the cadence, not the meaning.

The thing in my head laughed again.

I finished the spell, and my willow charm twitched in my fingers.

Nothing happened.

"Trina?" Darius sounded concerned. "What are you doing with that willow thing?"

He was standing in the room's door with Sharon, and both of them were studying me like I was completely over the edge.

No wonder. I was standing five feet away from them pointing a flimsy willow cross at shadows in an empty hospital room.

The charm twitched again.

Lightning ripped the sky outside the bedroom window, forking down and blasting onto Lincoln's manicured grounds. Sparks flew off cinder blocks and circled my charm. The willow burned into my fingers, but I held tight and kept it aimed into the room, and—

Threads of lightning fired over Darius and Sharon, straight at the corner of the empty room. When they hit the gray shadows nearest the window, they shifted into something man-shaped.

"Witch girl," the thing said in an eerie voice that echoed down the hallway until the patient on Unit C started shouting. "Come here to me."

I felt pulled toward the thing in the corner. I stumbled over to Darius and Sharon as more lightning fired out of my charm. Thin bolts struck the shadow-thing again, and he let out a howl.

Behind me, the patient on the unit started gibbering in his room. Sharon broke away from us and headed toward him.

Darius kept his eyes on me. "What's happening, Trina? What are you seeing?"

The man in the corner took a step toward us.

My heart stopped beating. I jumped forward. Power blasted through me, and a bolt of blue-white fire exploded from the center of the cross.

giggling and giggling and the sound made me want to scream. I watched him swing his iron shanks, seemingly in slow motion. The tips were coated with blood.

The man laughed louder and louder as he swiped at my face and missed, swiped and missed.

"Go faster!" I yelled as I pounded on Darius's back with one hand. With the other, I held out the willow charm. Terror pumped through me, so cold my teeth chattered, so strong it finally fired the oily well of anger way down inside my soul.

"You freak!" I shouted, lips pulled back from my teeth. "Get away from me!"

The man stabbed at me. Screaming without taking a breath, I got the charm high enough to aim it at his face. Fear and rage mingled inside me, and on either side of the man, trees exploded.

I barely noticed, barely processed that I might have done that. Colors danced out of the darkness, brighter than black, then brighter than sunlight, and I shouted one of the few Latin words I knew—the one my father had used before to kill evil things.

"Percello!"

The noise of the bells completely drowned my spell, but lightning blasted again, right above us, around us—

Into us—

Into me.

Electricity snapped and popped through my body, crackling down my neck and blasting heat through my belly. I saw nothing but golden glare as it swept through my arms and into my palms, then into the willow charm. The charm bucked in my grip, but I held it.

Fire flashed out of the tiny willow strands, arcing at the man's chest. The blast struck him square under the throat and knocked him backward.

Chunks of dirt flew as Darius chewed up turf with his shoes, carrying me as if I weighed nothing. The man hit the rain-soaked grass, skidded, got up, and charged at us again.

Darius grunted, and I realized he was climbing steps. Steep ones, narrow, made of stone—the bell tower. He had gotten us to the bell tower!

Hope flared through my entire body, giving me new strength. The world sharpened around me. The bells rang and rang, screaming and screeching, like the metal was pulling itself apart.

The man reached us in two big leaps, shanks extended, boy-eyes wide and insane. He bared his teeth.

I yelled, holding out my willow charm hoping it would keep me from getting sliced to bits.

Darius slammed us into something, crushing my legs against wood once, then twice. The wood gave. We fell through a door-way into a dark, tiled hallway, and a blur of motion swept past us out into the rainy night.

Fire whipped across my vision right before Darius pulled me to my feet. He pushed me farther into the building, his glasses gone, his bad eye glowing ivory white. Colors spilled out of the scars on his face, and his normal pupil expanded until he didn't look human at all.

Then he wheeled, fists clenched, ready to fight.

Imogene was suddenly between Darius and the man. She gave off a maniacal silver light, and her long gray hair floated upward as she raised her hand. Pressure popped my ears and crushed into my cheeks.

Dogs howled, geese honked, wings flapped, and still the bells kept ringing. Shadows spiraled down the bell-tower walls. The biggest dog jumped straight out of the stone, and it wasn't a beagle anymore. It was giant and black, snapping a mouth full of fangs. I kept the limp, smoking willow charm in front of me as if it could do something.

"Darius!" I shouted, and energy lurched into me. The charm twitched. Something yelled above me. I ducked as Levi arrowed past me, straight down from the ceiling. Blackness darker than night hung around him as he rocketed forward, knocking Darius aside and joining Imogene in the doorway. When he saw the man, Levi let out a feral growl almost as scary as the deep snarls of his monster dogs.

The flicker-flicker-flicker of the constant lightning turned the whole scene into a bad old movie as Imogene let Levi go by. His big dog followed, and more dogs and geese burst out of the bell-tower walls and pounded along behind them.

The man shouted, and the sound turned to a screech, then a little kid's scream. He started running. I heard his shoes smack the stone as he fled, the dogs and birds right behind him. Levi stormed after them, the rain closing behind him like gray curtains as he went. Darius had gotten his balance again and charged forward, intending to join Levi, but Imogene held out her arm like a traffic gate and stopped him.

"Let it be," she said in a voice as hard as granite. "You'd just get in the way."

Darius hesitated, but then turned toward me and flicked on the lights in the bell-tower entry hall.

His mouth fell open.

"Trina," Forest said from behind me, just about the time I realized that there was blood all over the tiles around me.

Forest put her hands on my back, and golden light filled my eyes, my senses. I could taste it like dandelion fuzz, and hear it like singing, and smell it like honey. It burned.

Darius pushed gently against my arms, pressing them down so he could get to me, and Forest was drowning me in molten honey, and Imogene was glowing silver.

Something square-shouldered and tall stepped out of the night, knocking Imogene's arm aside and grabbing her around the neck, and I—

I—

I blinked.

My knees started to buckle.

"What did you do to her?" a deep voice demanded, jangling every nerve in my body. "I'll kill you all!"

"Daddy," I whimpered as Darius caught me against him before I hit the floor.

The last thing I saw was my father coming at us, dragging Imogene with him.

CHAPTER TWENTY-EIGHT

Sunlight broke into my dark mind.

Sunlight and pain.

And Addie's face. "Don't you touch her, Xavier. You haven't earned that right yet."

Agony blazed across my shoulders, claiming my back, my spine, and I couldn't breathe. The voices and faces went dim, until . . .

My father's sad expression flashed into view. He was looking at me. Pleading. Maybe praying. His face seemed a little dented on one side.

"It's a strep infection," Darius's mother told someone. "Severe. Yes. She'll return as soon as possible. Your field placement is very important to her." The sound of a phone hanging up.

More sunlight.

"Careful, Forest," Imogene said. "You'll wither like a picked daisy."

Blackness took over again, and from somewhere far away, my father said, "I need to understand."

———————

I dreamed about flashing knives.

Men were chasing me, packs of them, laughing and howling and stabbing, and I couldn't run fast enough, and they wanted my blood, and I was sweating and screaming and I knew I'd never, ever get away.

Pain blasted through me as I fell. They cut me. They never stopped cutting me.

Forest floated across my awareness, only it wasn't her. It was the shadow-Forest from the hospital, washed out and transparent, barely even there.

"They eat you," she whispered, looking sad.

And I died.

———————

"I made him stronger," I said as I sat up on the couch in Darius's living room.

Then I tried to get to my feet.

Addie and Jessie grabbed my arms at the same moment. It took me a few seconds to process that Addie really was there, gazing at me with concern as she and Jessie tried to get me to lie down again. I took in every detail, from her perfectly trimmed hair to her black blouse and the tiny strand of pearls at her neck. She smelled like almond lotion, and she looked alive again, healthy—nothing like the last time I had seen her, after she took down my father—

My father.

I dropped back onto the couch and looked around. "Dad. Is he—"

"He's here," Jessie told me, fluffing the pillow closest to him. "He's out in the back garden with Darius and Ms. Hyatt."

I tried to get up again, but Addie stopped me with firm pressure on both my shoulders. "Whoa, there, Trina. Easy. We have an understanding—for now."

Addie's face was only inches from mine, her dark eyes wide and honest. "Think about it," she added. "Would Jessie be in here if Darius needed protecting?"

"We're good," Jessie assured me.

I eased back to the couch, my head swimming. "Why am I so dizzy?"

"Short version," Jessie said. "You and Darius got pitched through a corner of the other side and chased by some psycho guy with knives. He sliced your back, and the cut got infected really fast. Levi and Imogene couldn't heal it, but Forest has been doing a good job."

I sat up straighter and tested myself by stretching out my arms. A twinge of pain made me wince, but my skin felt solid enough, and my muscles still seemed to be attached. I didn't feel like I had a fever, either.

My attention shifted to Addie, and I lowered my arms as she sat in a chair beside the couch. Her expression was gentle, and she looked calmer and more at peace than I had seen her in a while. Heat and tension filled my chest, and tears welled in my eyes. Just looking at her . . . I hadn't been sure I'd ever get the chance to talk to her again.

I couldn't find words for the hundred questions I needed to ask her, so I went with, "My father. The short version?"

Addie closed her eyes, then opened them, and nodded. "I cracked his head pretty good. It took him three days and all my healing spells to wake up. The second his eyes opened, he panicked about what was happening to you, and we went searching."

"Three days?" That didn't add up. I had only been at Darius's house for one day when we went to Lincoln.

"You lost a little time when you passed through the other side," Jessie said. "Forest and Levi went wonky trying to find you when you vanished out of the hospital, and they almost didn't get you in time."

While I was trying to digest the fact that what had lasted minutes in my perception took days in everyone else's, Jessie continued. "Did you know that your father knows tae kwon do? Should have seen him trying to bust Darius's head when he thought they were hurting you."

I put my hands over my face to fight off a fresh wave of dizziness, and the image of my father going Jackie Chan on my boyfriend in Lincoln Psychiatric's bell tower. For a split second I heard the bells again, so loud they made my bones shake.

"Stay with me, honey." Addie gave my leg a pat.

I nodded and looked up at her.

Addie's frown eased, then came back again. She twisted her hands in her lap like she did whenever she was nervous.

When I twitched and started twisting my own fingers together, Addie met my gaze. She took a breath, then let it out very, very slowly. "He'll want to know you're awake, Trina."

Jessie cleared his throat and made a point of staring out the living-room window, leaving me to make my decision.

"It's not like I can avoid it," I said, my voice sounding so small and young it pissed me off.

Addie and Jessie didn't say anything, and neither of them looked at me.

I twisted my fingers together a few more times.

My father had intended to hurt me when Addie hit him. I knew that. But he had been blinded by rage and maybe other feelings I didn't understand. When he woke up, his first thought had been for my safety instead of his injured face.

Had he really gotten into a fight with Darius and Levi and Imogene to save me? Had I really seen him praying while Forest tried to heal me? My vision blurred, part from emotion and part from dizziness.

I didn't hate him, and I wasn't angry with him. I felt hurt. Confused a little bit. But it wasn't all about me, was it?

"I'll talk to him when I talk to everybody else," I said.

CHAPTER TWENTY-NINE

About an hour later, Imogene stood on the brick patio in Darius's backyard and handed me a brittle yellow newspaper clipping. It was from the *Cincinnati Enquirer*. The headline and date were too worn to read, but I could see that the year was 1929, and I made out the words, "Boy free."

There was a picture of a woman holding tight to a boy in her lap—a boy with a cruel face and dark hair and a mean little smile. Just the sight of him made me shiver in my lounger, even though the sun was hot on my cheeks.

"That him?" Imogene asked.

I handed the clipping back to her, not wanting to touch it a single second longer. "Yes."

"Who is he?" Ms. Hyatt asked. She was sitting in her wheelchair on my left, and Darius sat cross-legged on my right, handsome in his sunglasses and jeans and black T-shirt. When he reached out to take my hand I let him, even though my father was only a few feet away, directly across from me in one of the folding chairs Darius had fetched from his garage.

Addie sat at my father's right hand, with her big bag of potions tucked underneath her chair. Forest was on my father's left, and Levi was standing next to Forest, of course. Jessie stood between both groups, ready to intervene if we came to blows or spells.

"Name is Carl Newton Mahan," Imogene said. "He was from up around Paintsville, in eastern Kentucky."

"That sounds familiar." My father reached for the clipping, and Imogene let him have it before she went and settled herself on the low brick wall holding back a bed of azaleas. It was the strangest thing to see my father in one of his best brown Sunday suits, sitting next to folks with Madoc blood—and not just any Madocs, but Forest and Levi and Imogene, probably the strongest he had ever run across. I couldn't stop looking at his face, his sad, nervous expression, or the way the right side of his head seemed out of line, like Addie hadn't been able to get the bones all back together again.

"I remember hearing about this," he said, shaking his head at the clipping, then passing it back to Imogene. "That boy was six years old when he shot his best friend to death after they fought over some scrap iron they were trying to sell to a junk dealer up in coal country. Youngest murderer ever convicted in this state, or anywhere."

Scrap iron. I shuddered again, remembering the shanks stabbing toward me in the rain, and that maniac-child face on top of a man's body.

"Whole nation got up in arms about how young he was, and the attorney general sent him back to his folks instead of putting him in reform school," Imogene said. "That's when the newspapers forgot him, and his folks brought him west to get away from the trouble."

"But he brought the trouble with him?" Addie said.

Imogene nodded. "Boy was twisted up, even that young. He came to Lincoln when he was twelve, after he tortured a girl to death over to Cadiz. They had to keep him in a room by hisself, or he'd try to kill folks when they slept. He died of consumption afore he turned thirty. I crossed him over."

After a few seconds of uncomfortable silence, Ms. Hyatt shifted in her wheelchair. "So he came back, like my father?"

"Seems so," Forest said.

"Why?" Ms. Hyatt asked.

"It's what the bad ones do," Imogene said. "They linger close, and come back to work whatever wickedness they like best. They're starving for blood and mayhem."

"Did they all have Madoc blood in life?" my father asked. "The spirits that make it back?"

"I used to think so," Imogene said. "Time was, I wondered if only folks with Madoc blood went crazy, or did the terrible things on this earth. But now I know the truth. Ain't a person in this world who can't go bad or lose their wits, no matter what kind of blood runs in their veins. All it takes is the wrong things to happen."

Ms. Hyatt's frown seemed as dark as a thundercloud. "The

ghosts and spirits trying to come back—does that happen in other places, too, or just Lincoln?"

"I don't rightly know," Imogene admitted, "but I suspect we ain't the only ones livin' a few inches too close to hell's own hills."

"But the Madocs came to our area—" Addie started.

Imogene cut her off with a quick gesture. "Those folks, whatever they was, didn't only settle here. This is just one place. Likely there are a lot of others."

My father's face twitched as he considered this.

In the quiet that followed, I tried to imagine a kid awful enough to murder his best friend and torture a girl to death, all before he even turned thirteen. "I think Carl Newton Mahan used the energy in my spells to turn ghost or poltergeist or come back to life or whatever," I muttered. "Perfect."

"True enough, spirits can't usually get solid enough to act." Imogene shifted her gaze to her knobby knuckles, and I saw the slight tremor in her hands. "Like as not, those what want bedlam feel me waning. I used to could send them on their way a second time, before they figured a way to really wreak havoc, but that time's passed, and they know it."

My father's half-broken face stayed blank. His eyes fixed on mine, and for once in my life, I felt like I was reading him, staring at his soul, instead of the other way around.

"That's the real war," I told him. "Good people like us against true evil, not us against people with Madoc blood. Do you get that now?"

He opened his mouth, like he was about to say a whole bunch, but all that came out was a whispered "Trina."

I took a quick breath, and Darius squeezed my hand.

So much emotion in just one word. How did my father do that?

I knew it was the closest he could get to apologizing. A million years ago that would have pissed me off, but right at that moment, it was enough. I nodded to him, and he seemed to relax.

"Before we got attacked," I said to Levi, "Darius and I saw somebody who looked just like Forest in the hospital, on Unit C."

Levi's too-red lips pulled into a frown, and I tried not to look at how his teardrop tattoos glittered red in the sunlight. "Darius told us that."

"Could it be a time thing?" Jessie asked. "Maybe she moved through it and was in two places at once."

Levi shook his head. "Can't happen."

The thought of Forest being in two places at once was way too metaphysical for me, so I left it alone. "Forest—or the thing that looked like her—shrieked when she saw us. The sound had power, and it made Darius visible. I think it also summoned the—that—Carl Mahan, or whatever it was."

"Opened the door for him to come through, maybe." Forest leaned forward in her folding chair. "It sounds like she used sound to shove you out of Lincoln."

"Can you do that?" Ms. Hyatt asked Forest.

A touch of color rose in Forest's cheeks. "I usually just find a thin spot where it's easy to do the crossing. I never tried making my own."

"I tried to fight Mahan with spells," I said, "but they didn't work right. They just made him stronger."

Levi sank into a crouch next to Forest, as if I had just knocked all the strength out of his legs. "So he's strong enough to absorb energy," he murmured. "Guess he's a shade, like Eff Leer was."

Jessie cracked his knuckles. "Can we kill him again, like we did Levi's grandfather?"

"Yes," Imogene said. "Though 'kill' might be the wrong word. We can send his spirit back where it came from."

Levi sat quietly, watching my father, and for the first time ever I saw something in his eyes that looked like fear. He lowered his head, and I swear his shoulders shook before Forest brushed her fingers through his hair.

"Was it him?" I asked Levi, nodding toward my father. "The one who, um, killed you?"

Nobody looked at my father, and Levi didn't answer.

After a minute so long the planet seemed to stop spinning, my father whispered, "It was me."

When Levi raised his head, the tattoo under his right eye seemed brighter than usual, like he was actually crying a tear made out of blood.

I felt like crying myself, or apologizing. I wanted to hit my father or shake him. Then my emotions just shut down, and I wanted to lean over, put my head on Darius's shoulder, and sleep until next week, or next month, and wake up to find out I had only had a nightmare about my father being a killer.

"I was wrong," my father said. "I can see that now. I'll turn myself in to the authorities and confess my crimes."

"That won't make any of this right, preacher," Imogene said. "You never can, not in my books. But Levi speaks for himself."

She got up from the wall without saying anything else and walked out of the yard, heading back in the general direction of Lincoln Psychiatric. I was about to say something about somebody giving her a ride when the world seemed to shimmer, and Imogene wasn't in the backyard anymore.

I stared at the spot where she had been, but I couldn't make a sound.

"Why?" Levi asked, and the sound of his voice made me jump.

"My father started this business after his father got killed." My father cleared his throat. "My grandfather's killer was a man named Purcell Mace. He was a patient at Lincoln, off and on. When he was out, he drank. Seemed like he always knew who had money he could steal. Followed my grandfather out of a bar one night and beat him to death with a lead pipe."

After another pause he glanced up at me, and I didn't look away.

"Mace never did a day's time in jail," my father continued. "They just sent him back to Lincoln, and he died there, but not before he killed one of the folks trying to take care of him. My cousin. Her mother's the one who told us about him, and about other patients they had who could—you know, do things no human being ought to be able to do, and know things they couldn't possibly know."

"Like who had money to steal?" Ms. Hyatt asked.

My father nodded.

"I came to find out there were folks like that all over Never," he said. "Not all of them were patients in the hospital. And I could sense them, or reveal them using spells I learned." This time, he looked at Levi. "A lot of our murders and disappearances—a lot of things that shouldn't have happened—Madocs were at the bottom of them."

Levi still didn't say anything, but I could tell he didn't disagree.

My father shifted his gaze back to me. "With that, and after Mace, I figured they were all bad. Creatures of the devil. So I did what my father taught me to do. I eliminated them whenever and wherever I found them, and I thought it was God's work."

He stopped and looked at his hands. "I thought that's why God gave me the tools he gave me, to rid the earth of the scourge."

His mouth got tight, but the edges trembled.

Oh God. Was my father going to cry? I couldn't hack it if he cried.

But he didn't. He just waited, like he wanted me to say something, but I didn't have any words for him at all. Understanding why he had done what he did . . . it made more sense, but it didn't feel any better.

"What do you want us to do with Pastor Martinez, Levi?" Ms. Hyatt asked. "Call the police? Let it be? You're the one he wronged, so whatever you think ought to happen, we'll help you."

Levi swallowed once and blinked, and I found myself waiting for that bloody tear on his cheek to drip onto the patio. "Seems like right and wrong don't matter much now. What matters is getting rid of Carl Mahan before he hurts somebody else."

My brain tried to latch on to the reality that Levi was looking at the man who murdered him, and that man was my father. If Imogene hadn't been whatever she was—if she hadn't been able to cross spirits back—Levi would be dead right now, and my father would still be killing anybody he thought had Madoc blood.

"I'll stop Mahan," my father said. "Then you can do with me as you will."

"You can't do it alone," Forest said. "He's a shade, and you can't cross him over."

Addie considered this, then murmured, "Maybe we can, if I find the right spell. I'll study my books, and Xavier's, too."

"We don't have time for that." Levi kept his eyes averted. "We'll have to work together."

Right and wrong don't matter much now. The words wouldn't stop running through my mind. I fidgeted with my fingers. "I don't think we can use our spells," I told Addie. "They might work, but they just as easily might give Mahan more power."

"I want to go to the hospital," Forest said, surprising me and everybody else.

Levi turned toward her, his mouth slightly open. "No. That monster's running around loose. We have to think this through."

"That spirit looked like me. She could be related to me—and maybe she could help us with Mahan." Forest touched Levi's hair, keeping her eyes trained on his. "I need to go back to Unit C and find out what's going on."

"Not now," Levi said, sounding stunned and sad all at the same time. "Mahan first, then the shade."

"It's far too dangerous, Forest," my father said, and I heard the protectiveness in his tone.

"If she wants to go, we should take her," I said, feeling a mix of relief that my father was being protective of Forest like she was a real person to him, and frustration that she was getting dismissed so fast. I turned to Darius. "Imogene just went back, right? And Mahan knows he's taking on Levi and Imogene now. He's not going to attack right away, not until he figures out how to beat us. Now's the perfect time."

"Sorry, baby, but I vote with them." Darius gave my hand a squeeze. "We'll go when we've got a plan for taking on that monster."

Addie and Ms. Hyatt didn't say anything, and something in Addie's expression, a resignation mingled with a glint in her eyes, made me keep my mouth closed even though Forest looked crushed.

After a long minute of silence, my father brought up the idea of making dinner before we did any more work. He and Jessie and Darius decided to grill us a meal, and the meeting broke up quickly as they headed off to retrieve hot dogs and ground beef from the Hyatt kitchen. Ms. Hyatt gave directions and instructions, but she didn't go to help, and neither did Addie. Levi stayed next to Forest for a few minutes, then got up to sit on the brick wall where Imogene had been. I figured he needed to be alone with his thoughts.

The four of us sat together quietly until the men were out of earshot, and then I put my hand over Forest's trembling fingers. She was staring at her own feet, and my touch startled her into meeting my gaze. She had tears in her eyes.

"Who do you think she was?" she asked me, her voice shaking.

"It was you," I said. "Unless you have a twin sister."

"Not that I know of," she told me.

"Anything's possible," Ms. Hyatt said, but Forest never stopped staring at me.

"What did your mother look like?" she asked.

The question caught me off guard, and my stomach did a quick little flip. "I don't really know." My eyes darted to Addie. I was never sure how she felt about hearing things related to my biological mother, and I didn't want to say anything that would make her unhappy. I know most kids stayed all torn up about parents who were missing from their lives, but with Addie around, I had never really cared that much. I loved Addie, and she loved me, and my mother, wherever she had decided to go, had made a choice not to be a part of my past or my future.

"My father always tells me my hair is like hers," I said to Forest. "And my eyes, and—oh."

In that moment, we all saw the same thing, and we saw it clearly. The knowledge passed from face to face, lighting our eyes and minds with the truth, and the truth was this:

We had to pay a visit to that spirit on Unit C, for Forest.

We had to find out if it was Forest's mother, and somehow we all knew that nothing was more important than doing this, no matter what the risks might be.

"They think we always need protection." Forest nodded toward the house, where the boys were beginning to bicker about the best way to light Darius's grill to cook hamburgers. Levi was still perched on the wall nearby, off in his own world. "They'll never agree to it."

"We don't need their permission," Addie said.

Maybe they were right, my father and Darius and Jessie and Levi. Maybe it was too dangerous to go near Lincoln Psychiatric, even if Imogene was back in her bell tower. There was always that possibility, but there was also the possibility that we were right, too—that it was important to get to that spirit and gain a better understanding of what she knew about Carl Mahan, and Forest, too.

My father and Jessie and Darius—even Levi—wouldn't help us. They would try to stop us, and possibly destroy any chance we had of finding out what we needed to know.

Addie picked up her bag. Then she cleared her throat and waved a hand at the men.

"Never mind about those hamburgers," she said. "I can make us all a nice, juicy pot roast in under an hour."

CHAPTER THIRTY

A little after sunset, the men of the house—Levi included—succumbed to full bellies and a bit of after-dinner tea laced with some of Addie's best hops and valerian. We figured we had at least a few hours, but with my father and Levi in the mix, who knew. At least we got out the door without a fight.

No one spoke as Addie drove Forest, Ms. Hyatt, and me to Lincoln Psychiatric, which took about fifteen minutes. We used the employee badge I had clipped to my collar to get past the guard at the main gate, and I directed us to the parking lot outside the entrance closest to Unit C.

"I never worked anywhere but the geriatric unit, and that was years ago," Forest said as she and I walked to the heavy metal door that would let us into the basement of the old asylum. "Since then, I've mostly been at the bell tower. Everything looks different now."

I shook out the kinks as I moved, still feeling weird twinges from my fight with Mahan. It was hard to remember that when

Forest crossed spirits to the other side, she stepped out of time. She couldn't really go backward in history, but she could go forward in a huge hurry. Even though she was my age chronologically, she had actually worked at Lincoln Psychiatric years and years ago. It was weird. And it made me wonder about Levi. Forest said he was our age, or close to it, biologically, but when had he actually stepped onto this earth?

We reached the darkened corner of the main building and had to cross out of the comforting halo of a sidewalk lamp to get to the door, where we stopped to wait for Addie and Ms. Hyatt. The sudden rush of darkness made me shiver. My fingers hovered over my pockets, where I had my willow charm and a little bag of graveyard dirt, snakeskin, powdered bones, sulfur, and other things I didn't even recognize. Addie gave it to me because it was one of our best offensive spells. I hoped we didn't have to use it. Aside from just plain not wanting to fight Mahan again, that dust smelled like pepper and cow manure, and it burned like hellfire.

Addie had also given us a bunch of dimes with holes punched in them strung on little leather strips and hung around our necks, wrists, and ankles. She said the shiny silver would go dull or turn black if we got close to anything evil. As Addie walked out of the shadows on the sidewalk, pushing Ms. Hyatt in front of her, dimes glittered all over her body. My father's kill bag rested in Ms. Hyatt's lap, along with Addie's spell bag.

"Won't you get into some kind of trouble with your husband?" Forest asked Addie as she parked Ms. Hyatt in the darkness beside us.

"I already told you, I don't need his permission to do what's right," Addie said. "Despite what he might think, I don't need his permission for anything, and neither does Trina."

"We look like dime trees," I said as I lifted my badge to the sensor outside the door. "If we get caught, Security probably won't call the police. They'll just take us to Admissions."

Ms. Hyatt grunted at that, then laughed.

The lock clicked, and I pushed open the door to let us into Lincoln, into the basement four floors beneath Unit C.

We walked in single file, me in the lead, Forest next, and Addie and Ms. Hyatt bringing up the rear. The door swung shut too fast, and the heavy metallic clank made me flinch.

"What is this place?" Forest whispered as we took in the long hallway stretching out before us. It had brown stone walls and a brown stone floor, just like castle dungeons in fairy stories. A yellowish glow rose from a strip of emergency lights positioned where the floor met the wall on the hall's right-hand side, and on the left—

"That's a cage," Addie said in low, tense tones as we studied the steel mesh making up most of the hall wall on the left. The door to the cage was padlocked, and gurneys and wheelchairs filled the cobwebbed space inside it.

"Storage," Ms. Hyatt said. "Now, anyway. I don't want to think about what it might have been a hundred years ago."

Something thumped above us, and we all jumped. When I looked up, I saw long pipes running the length of the ceiling. Hot water? Gas? Crazy juice? Who knew?

"I'm not finding a light switch," Forest said as she felt among the various boxes at our end of the hallway. "When I worked here, they kept the emergency lights in nonpatient areas on at night. The basement was always deserted, except at break time, when people hit the canteen machines four halls over in that direction."

Forest jerked her thumb toward the hall door closest to us, but it was even darker than this one.

I glanced at the ceiling and remembered something from my social-work supervisor's chattering orientation about the thickness of the stone walls, and how many feet of steel and rock separated each floor. The old hospital doubled as a storm shelter, a fallout shelter, and a disaster center. It was built to be a fortress, back when fortress-building was still an active art. It was nearly impossible to escape, with so many locking doors, and because so many patients used to yell twenty-four hours a day, seven days a week, the engineers had made it pretty soundproof, too. Noises didn't carry very far.

In space, no one can hear you scream, my brain unhelpfully offered, in Darius's voice, no less. I hated him for making me watch *Alien*.

Addie bent forward and rummaged in her bag. She came out with a long black flashlight, which she handed to Ms. Hyatt, who switched it on and let the beam drift up and down the stone walls. Cool air chilled my cheeks as the flashlight chased shadows to the ceiling, then back down to the floor again. The air smelled like wet rock and bleach.

The door rattled, and the bunch of us jumped again.

"Wind," Ms. Hyatt said, focusing her beam on the wheelchairs and stretchers. "We need to stop being silly and find the elevator to get up to the floor where Trina saw the ghost—oh, dear God." Her hand shook, making the light dance.

She had stopped on a silver gurney covered with sheets. There was something under the sheets—long and human-shaped and definitely not moving.

I swallowed hard and tried to breathe, but my throat wouldn't cooperate. All I could manage was a tight, wheezing gasp. Forest caught hold of my hand, and the both of us stared at the sheets.

"It's too small for a body," Addie said with the confidence of someone who worked at a mortuary. "An adult body, at least."

"Is that supposed to make us feel better?" Ms. Hyatt swung the light to Addie's face. "Are you crazy?"

Forest let go of me, took the flashlight away from Ms. Hyatt, and walked slowly toward the cage, shining the beam through the gloom of the cramped space. I wanted to grab her and pull her back, but I glanced at the dime around my neck. Still silver, as best I could tell in the low light. And I'd been to the mortuary, too, a lot of times. Whatever was on that gurney under the sheets, it didn't stink like a dead thing. It didn't have the cold, empty feel of a dead thing. So it was either alive, or it was—

"Plastic," Forest said. Then, kind of amused, "It's Harold."

We all stared at her as she turned, directing the flashlight to her left.

"The first-aid dummy," she clarified. "When I trained here, they used Harold to teach us CPR, how to apply bandages, that kind of thing. The training nurses liked to leave him sitting around in odd spots in the hospital, just to freak people out."

"What a lovely tradition," Addie said, her voice as frosty as the air in the hallway.

"The elevator is that way." I pointed to where Forest had aimed the flashlight. "Past the cage."

Nobody moved.

Something human-sized ran across the hall entrance, flashing in the bright beam.

Forest yelped and dropped the flashlight, and I pounced on it and picked it up, shining it left and right and up and down, but there was nothing. My heart rate accelerated, and the hairs on my body seemed to stand up all at the same time.

It had gotten colder. I could see my breath.

"Patients used to be able to walk around down here," Forest said, puffs of white fog shooting out of her mouth with each word. "Do you think that was one of them?"

"My supervisor said everybody stays on their wards now." The flashlight beam jittered as I tried to keep my hands steady. "Why is it colder? And everybody saw that, right?"

Addie pushed Ms. Hyatt past us and held out her hand for the light. "We saw it," she said as I passed it to her. She did a quick check of our dimes, all of which glittered brightly in the strong beam.

Then she swung the flashlight back toward the hall entrance.

We all sucked in a sharp breath.

Someone was standing there wearing jeans and a red hoodie. The hood was pulled up so we couldn't see the shadowy face inside, but wisps of dark, curly hair spilled out from the open neckline.

The hair looked a lot like Forest's.

"You have to get out," said a soft, frightened-sounding woman's voice—Forest's voice, but not Forest. The jeans and hoodie faded, then got more solid again. "You have to run away from here."

Desperation seemed to lace each word, and I felt it like a current in my own thoughts. It was so cold in the hallway my teeth started to chatter.

Run, my brain urged, or at least I thought it was my brain. The inner voice didn't feel like my own.

I checked my dime again. Still silver. Addie turned her head, just enough to catch my eye, and I saw her hand move to her jeans pocket. Ms. Hyatt was reaching into Addie's bag, slowly so her movement wouldn't be noticed. My hands crept into my pockets, and I gripped the willow charm with my left and the bag of dust with my right.

Run!

"It's time for me to stop running," Forest said, sounding almost as scared as the apparition in the light. "I have to stay and fight."

"There's too much bad around this place," not-Forest whispered, out loud and in my mind at the same time. The sensation made my eyes water. "You can't win."

Addie kept her flashlight fixed on the apparition as Forest said, "Then I'll die trying."

The hooded head came up at that, and the figure pushed back the cloth to reveal a face so much like Forest's that I blinked, even though I knew to expect it.

"Don't say that." The woman's tone was absolutely pitiful now. "Never say that."

Forest approached the figure, hands at her sides, and they circled each other in the hallway entrance.

"You're my mother," Forest said, and the apparition didn't argue with her. "You're not a shade, because you've never been to the other side. You're what Imogene calls a haunt."

Forest reached her hand out, but her fingers passed through the spirit, making a light mist where the woman's elbow should have been. I had seen the ghosts of Darius's grandmothers, but this one was different. It had a slight glow to it, with colors even in the blank spaces, and motion, almost like molecules zinging around at a thousand miles per hour. What I was seeing reminded me more of Darius's white eye than the ghosts of his dead relatives.

"What's your name?" Forest asked.

"Bridgette," the woman answered. "I was born here, just like you." She covered her mouth then, like she shouldn't have spoken.

Forest stopped walking around the haunt and faced Bridgette, still keeping her arms down, obviously trying not to threaten her. "Who was my father?"

Bridgette grimaced and brought a finger to her lips. "Ssshhh. Don't ask. *He* might hear."

My grip on the dust tightened. Somehow, I didn't think "he" was Forest's father. I was pretty sure the haunt was talking about Mahan.

"Is my father alive?" Forest asked. "Could he help us?"

The haunt glanced at the ceiling, then looked sad. She didn't answer.

"Why did you give me up?" Forest tried again. "Why did you leave me to be found and raised by other folks?"

"Because darkness needs light, and light needs darkness. It's the only way." Bridgette reached for Forest's wrist.

Too late, I understood what she was doing as she reached for the carved rowan bracelet that Forest had worn all her life, the one with the smooth iron beads that repelled and burned Madoc essence.

"Watch out!" I yelled, but Bridgette made contact with the bracelet even as I yanked the dust out of my pocket.

"Darkness needs light!" Bridgette cried as Forest froze in place and jerked like she was being electrocuted.

Addie started a spell and I raised my dust, but Forest shrieked, "No! Don't hurt her!"

Bridgette's hoodie and jeans burst into flames.

So did her eyes.

"Light needs darkness," Bridgette moaned, and orange fire licked out of her mouth with each word. "The only way!"

She stared at us with those terrible, burning eyes, and then she screamed.

My hands flew to my ears, and I pressed the bag of dust against the side of my own head. I couldn't help it. Addie and Ms. Hyatt had covered their ears, too. Their mouths were open like mine, and I knew they had to be yelling from the pain like me, but I couldn't hear them.

Forest kept shaking like electricity was filling her whole body, but the flames blasting off the haunt didn't come close to her. This time, the scream at the end of the hall seemed like it would never end.

A dark square opened behind Bridgette, framing her, drawing her backward, sucking in her fire and distorting the edges of her body.

I felt rooted, hypnotized. Forest—

But Forest wasn't struggling, and she wasn't being pulled toward the black square. She seemed to be trying to hold on to what was left of her mother—and then Bridgette burst into bright sparkles. The sparkles flew into the black frame and it snapped shut, cutting off the terrible sound of her cry.

Forest sagged backward, her shoulders hitting the wall, the arm with her bracelet held toward the now-closed crossway. I crammed the dust back into my pocket and ran to her as smoke settled all around us. Heart hammering, I grabbed Forest in a hug and held her. She was ice-cold and shaking and she was crying, too.

"Her mind was overwhelmed by too much power," Forest whispered against my shoulder. "When she touched me, I could share her thoughts. Bits and pieces of the past, and the present— the future, too—but I couldn't heal her." She drew a shaking breath. "She'll be on the other side now, scared to death because it's strange to her."

"Nonsense." Ms. Hyatt and Addie had reached us, and Ms. Hyatt patted my side and Forest's arm at the same time. "There's bound to be women on the other side, just like us here. They won't let her suffer."

She sounded so sure of what she was saying, it was hard not to believe her without questioning. But this wasn't heaven we were talking about. It wasn't hell, either. I had no real idea what the other side looked like or how it felt or how it smelled, or how people acted there, or if there were any people at all. What if it was just clouds—or monsters like Darius's psychotic child-killing grandfather and Carl Mahan?

I kept my arms around Forest until Addie gently pulled us apart. Forest stepped back, and I couldn't see her face in the shadowy light.

Addie gave my shoulder a squeeze, then turned to Forest, took hold of her arm, and lifted it to check the skin around the rowan bracelet. "No burns," she said, letting go of Forest's wrist and lowering the flashlight.

"Thank the good Lord," Ms. Hyatt said, raising her right hand in praise even as she turned her wheelchair and pointed it toward the exit door. "Now, let's—"

"Your God never visits Lincoln Psychiatric Hospital," said a boy's voice from directly behind us. "Only the mad come here."

Addie swore and swung the flashlight beam toward the sound as we all whirled around to see what was talking to us. Forest caught my hand and squeezed my fingers as the flashlight revealed another figure in jeans and a red hoodie. This one was a lot taller and more substantial than Bridgette had been. No flickering movie effects. No super-chilled air. In fact, the air around us felt hotter than it should be, and it was starting to move.

"Trina," Addie said, and the flashlight beam touched the dime around my neck.

The coin had gone black as char.

The figure giggled, and the sound echoed in my guts. My entire body clenched with terror. The figure flicked his fingers, and wind tore the flashlight out of Addie's hand. It burst against the rock walls, batteries and casing and lens cover flying in different directions. The emergency lights in our portion of the hallway winked out at the same moment.

Even through the thick walls of Lincoln Psychiatric, even over the drum of my own pounding heart, I heard thunder and the distant ringing of bells.

A red glow drifted out from the figure, the only light, sick and menacing. I couldn't see much about him except the crimson shadow of his hooded head, but I didn't have to.

I knew that when he pushed back that hood, he would have a little boy's face.

CHAPTER THIRTY-ONE

Deserted.

Soundproof.

Dark.

We were locked in the basement of a fortress asylum with a monster.

Forest and I moved together, on instinct, forming a wall to block Mahan's access to Addie and Ms. Hyatt.

Darius. An image of his face flickered through my mind, stamping itself across my heart. *I'm so sorry. You were right after all.*

If I ever got to see him again, he'd probably kick my ass.

Wind howled into our hallway, rattling the padlock on the cage and sending stretchers and wheelchairs spinning inside the metal mesh. My hair and cheeks felt plastered to my skull, my employee badge flapped against my chin, and the monster in front of us glowed a darker red.

I let go of Forest's hand to reach for my dust, but she said, "Don't."

I had no idea how I heard her through the whistle and screech of that wind, but I stopped my hand. She was right. I didn't need to waste my only real weapon. Had to choose my moment.

My eyes watered as I stared at the top of Mahan's lowered head, then at the iron shanks in his hands.

"Get away from me," Forest hissed underneath the blasts of wind. "Let me handle this." She tried to step in front of me, but I inched forward right beside her.

"Trina, I mean it." Forest sounded scared. "Go back to Addie."

"Not happening." I was two parts terrified and one part pissed, but I wasn't leaving Forest. Addie was behind me doing something to get us out of this mess, I had no doubt.

Colors seemed to sprout from the walls, bleeding silvers and golds and blues and reds down the stone. The wind didn't touch the power coming out of the rocks, or oozing up from the floor.

Was Addie calling the power out?

I wanted to turn around and see where she was, what she was doing, but I didn't dare.

With my left hand, I drew my willow charm out of my pocket and aimed it at Mahan. I willed the power I was seeing to strike me the way lightning had the first time I fought him. I wanted to throw fire out of my charm again, but now nothing happened.

"*Percello!*" I yelled over the wind.

More nothing.

Mahan raised his head, straightened to his full height, and

finally pushed back his hood. His boy's face wept crimson light, like it was covered with blood, and his eyes gleamed red.

I expected him to giggle, or call me a witch.

He didn't make a sound.

He just got bigger.

And bigger.

He filled the doorway now, and space seemed to bend around him, letting him grow. The wind focused itself on him, pulling back into him, feeding him, and I realized Forest had her eyes closed. She was humming.

Something exploded behind me, and I screamed and ducked, holding the willow charm over my head.

Mahan twitched, and as I raised up again, I saw a small, dark hole in his left shoulder. A second or two later, it closed like it had never been there.

"Did I hit him?" Ms. Hyatt called.

"I don't think guns will help," came Addie's tense reply.

"You got a bigger caliber in this bag?" Ms. Hyatt asked, but I didn't hear Addie's response, because Forest started humming too loud.

Mahan lowered his head again until his awful face was almost level with Forest's eyes. He seemed to be listening to what she was humming. The tune didn't make any sense to me. It was giving me the shivers, like nails grating down a chalkboard.

The monster's red eyes flared, focusing fully on Forest. He raised his iron shanks slowly, but he seemed wary of her.

All the wind stopped, and between the notes of Forest's tune, I heard Mahan sniffing like he was trying to get her scent.

Who are you?

The question echoed in my skull until I clamped my eyes shut, but I was sure Mahan wasn't talking to me. Each word carried a power all its own, and I felt myself wanting to answer, wanting to give up my full name and tell Mahan everything about myself.

It was all I could do to keep my mouth shut and force my eyes open again. Forest didn't react to his compulsion; she just kept humming, only it had become more of a chant now, wordless and rhythmic. I managed to hold up my willow charm again, keeping it between me and Mahan.

Addie was chanting, too. I caught a few words, along with the distinct sound of metal rattling against wood and other metal, like somebody was digging through my father's kill bag. The colors on the walls and floor brightened and stirred, sweeping upward like sentient mist.

Somebody pounded on the basement door behind us.

"Let me in!" Imogene demanded, her creaky voice and deep Southern accent unmistakable. It had a resonance that made the walls shake.

I had the only badge to open the door.

In one quick motion, I pulled it off my collar with my free hand and tossed it behind me, hoping I got it near Addie or Ms. Hyatt. They'd let Imogene in, and we'd—

Who are you? Mahan demanded again, and when Forest didn't answer, he lunged toward her.

Silver flashed in the red light as a dagger zinged past me, pulling the misty colors with it as it flew.

Addie's pitch struck Mahan right in his chest, and he grabbed at the hilt and fell backward, growling and snapping his teeth together. Brilliant colors skittered in and out of the wound, but he managed to yank out the dagger and hurl it away from him so hard the blade snapped as it struck stone.

Forest kept right on chanting.

All my anger left me at the same second, leaving nothing but terror in its place. "We should go," I said to Forest. "Back to the door, at least. Imogene's here."

Forest wasn't listening. She raised her arm, and the rowan bracelet seemed to writhe against her skin. I thought about grabbing her, then got even more scared. What if some Madoc superpower of hers burned me alive?

As if to agree with me, new colors bled out of the walls and floors. They pulled toward Forest, joining and joining until they mixed into a black rush of nothingness.

Mahan got his feet. Red flames jetted out from his shoulders, scorching against the old hospital's ceiling tiles. He stormed toward Forest. I heard the door behind us rattle, and I heard Imogene shout, "Get away from them, boy!"

Mahan kept charging forward, staggering and swinging his shanks.

"*WHO . . . ARE . . . YOU?*" he demanded in my head and out loud at the same time, directing his question at Forest but hitting me, too.

"I'm Trina!" I shrieked, because I couldn't help it. My hand shook, but I kept my charm pointed at him, and some of the colors in the hallway swept into the twisted fibers.

Forest's eyes snapped open and spit golden heat, like molten fire shooting off the surface of the sun. She threw out her arms and yelled, "I am my mother's daughter!"

And then she screamed.

I screamed with her, because the sound seemed to tear my skin right off my bones. I screamed and kept screaming as agony claimed me, as every color I had ever seen blasted into me, filled me, ran through me and back out again, erupting into black emptiness as it touched Forest.

Two more daggers whizzed past my head.

And then, suddenly, the world stuttered, then just stopped. No sound. No smells. Hardly any motion.

Addie's spelled throwing knives hung in midair, dripping colors like water.

Mahan ran away in slow motion.

Darkness trickled out of Forest like rain from a cloud, swallowing the hallway.

I turned to find Addie, but I felt like I could barely move, like I was twisting inside drying tar. It took so long. It took forever, but then finally I was looking at her.

To her right, the basement door was open. Imogene was pulling Ms. Hyatt out into the night, away from Mahan, almost frozen in the action, her wild silver hair floating free around her head. Addie's hands were still raised from throwing the daggers.

Second by second by second, her brown eyes ticked toward me. Found me. Widened.

She looked horrified, then agonizingly sad.

Her lips moved, forming my name.

Power flooded out of her in millimeters, then inches. It looked blue. Protective. So strong. So total.

Pressure clamped against my skull, like my whole head was exploding. Something seized me. Not hands. More like a force whipping down across my body. The willow charm flew out of my hand, lifting slowly into the air and tumbling at half speed, a quarter speed, to the stones on the basement floor at Lincoln Psychiatric. It landed on one pointy tip, and began to spin no faster than a warped dream, turning around and around and around—

Colors—

So many colors—

Like stardust falling through a rainbow.

Sound blasted past me—voices, hundreds of them. Thousands.

"She's crossing over," Addie yelled.

Her blue magic energy coated me as the walls melted. The floor turned black. Cold mist slapped across my cheeks, and the world moved again, and people were singing. They were calling to me.

I fell upward into the nothing place Forest had made, only it wasn't nothing, it was everything, and it was everywhere. Strong scents of pine and honey and fresh water filled my awareness. I heard the smells, as though they were laughing. I smelled the moon, too, fresh and pure, and I heard it call my name in Addie's voice.

My skin ripped completely away and came back again, holding a rainbow underneath it. I was outside. We were out in a bright, bright morning, Forest and me, standing in a field. Forest still had her arms out, and her eyes mirrored the sunlight. Soft grass, greener than green, grew up around her shoes, then her jeans, and mine too. Trees sprouted below her fingertips and bloomed and stretched taller. Flowers unfurled and tipped their red and yellow petals toward her.

From somewhere far away, bells rang, and the sound was so soft and beautiful in the midst of the sweet singing that I wanted to cry. The tune was like a lullaby Addie used to sing to me, and I wished she could hear it.

Forest shifted her attention to me. I should have been terrified, she looked so powerful, but I felt giddy instead. She pointed to my pocket.

I reached down and pulled out Addie's pouch, and the laces came open. A tiny bit of dust puffed into the air and formed gnashing fangs, but the yellow powder didn't bite or burn me. It didn't even stink.

Forest pointed again, behind me, and I turned to see Mahan not five feet away from us. He was struggling to rise from his hands and knees as vines twined around him and pulled him back toward the grass. He still had red eyes and his iron shanks—but he also had two rainbow-colored daggers sticking out of his neck. Blood blacker than death spurted down his chest.

When he lifted his baby face to me and roared, I threw the whole bag of dust straight into his hateful mouth.

The yellow powder mushroomed around him, becoming a thousand sets of fangs, chewing and snarling and tearing, and the singing got louder to muffle his bellows of pain. He tried to fight, but the vines and grass pulled him down and trapped him, and the earth itself opened up. He disappeared into a hole and dirt covered him completely, then grass, then flowers, and then he was gone.

My outstretched hand let off reds and blues and yellows and pinks, and dozens of sparkles played about my fingernails, as if cleaning every trace of the dust off my skin. Even though some part of my brain knew I should be horrified, I couldn't do anything but laugh.

I started singing, trying to pick up the words of the lullaby floating all around me. I ran toward the sound, dancing at the same time, reaching for it, and I lost all track of everything except the sweetness of the air and how the colors played and swam through my eyelashes.

Forest's fingers closed over mine. "Trina," she whispered in an achingly musical voice. "I'm so, so sorry."

A single tear sparkled on her cheek. When I stared into it, I thought I could see crystals and worlds and universes.

Before I could sing another word, Forest yanked me back into total darkness, tearing my skin off my bones all over again.

CHAPTER THIRTY-TWO

I didn't think I would ever stop throwing up.

Forest stayed on her knees beside me, holding my shoulders as I hurled and hurled and hurled. It was probably only a few minutes, but it felt like hours. When I finally finished, I sat back and tried to get a fix on where we were.

I didn't see much but sunlight and spinning trees, so of course I puked a little more. It was hot outside, like midsummer sweating hot, and that wasn't helping.

"We're near the hospital," Forest told me as she tugged a piece of gum out of her pocket and gave it to me to get the nasty taste out of my mouth. "We came through in the woods, in that clearing close to the bell tower where Mahan first chased you."

Spearmint flooded my mouth, driving back the nausea, and I chewed the gum for a few seconds before I spit it out. Forest gave me another piece, and I chewed that one, too, until my mouth was all gum taste and no yucky nastiness, then I spit it out and let myself take a nice, slow breath.

It was *so* hot.

Forest was talking about disorientation from crossing over. I could barely put the words together, because I couldn't quit thinking about the field and the flowers and the singing. It had been so *real*—but now . . .

What did it sound like again?

I couldn't believe it was already draining out of my thoughts, like a dream just after waking.

Forest had to be wrong about where we were. We were somewhere south of Never, because it was too hot for September. My money was on a place near the equator, like Mexico, or maybe the Yucatán. My brain was so muddled I didn't really care. We were alive. Mahan was gone. I held on to bits and pieces of what had just happened—the dust attacking Mahan, Addie's knives in his throat, the grass and vines and earth closing over his little boy's face. There was pain and that unbelievable singing, and a lot of sweet smells, but most of the images faded as I tried to remember more about them.

"Just keep breathing slowly," Forest told me. "I'm sorry. I'm so sorry. I had no idea it was even possible for you to cross over like that while still alive."

I thought about Addie's blue energy and the rainbows under my skin, all the power she and I had been pulling into that hallway, and I let out a breath. "Probably had a little help from Addie."

"Yeah," Forest said, and she sounded even more worried and sad.

I glanced up at her, relieved to see that her face—and the

trees—had stopped spinning. We really were in a forest clearing, with hardwoods and evergreens all around us. No sand. No tropical-looking anything. I lifted my face, shielding my eyes against the sunlight, and far across the treetops I could see the unmistakable shape of Lincoln Psychiatric Hospital's bell tower.

A dread I couldn't name and didn't understand bloomed in my sore belly. "We really shouldn't have done what we did," I said. "Even if we did take care of Mahan."

Forest's pretty eyes bored into mine, as if she wanted to tell me something but couldn't quite bring herself to say it outright. I had never seen her look so guilty and down.

"We never should have gone to the hospital," she whispered. "I know you did it for me."

I shrugged. "Addie and Ms. Hyatt went with us. We all thought it needed to be done."

Forest grabbed my hand, and power hummed through her fingers. "I'm sorry," she said again. "You crossed over. I'm so sorry."

"Yeah. Okay. So I crossed over—but you got me back here where I belong." I pulled my hand away and got to my feet because her mood was making me nervous. Besides, I needed to stretch my arms and legs. Nothing seemed to be broken or infected, but my muscles ached with fatigue. "We made a big mistake."

Forest sighed as she stood. "That's the truth. Now here come the consequences."

A sound caught my attention, and I turned toward the edge of the clearing. It sounded like a herd of buffalo was charging through the underbrush. My pulse jumped, and I sucked in a breath to yell at Forest to run, but she took my hand in hers, giving me a jolt of calming, healing energy.

Branches and leaves rustled, and Darius burst into the open. He was wearing jeans and a T-shirt and he looked even more handsome than I remembered. His dark glasses turned toward me and he ran forward, his sweet face breaking into a smile. Before I knew it, he had me wrapped in his arms and he was weeping into my hair, and I saw Levi standing still and quiet at the edge of the trees, his gaze fixed on Forest.

She moved away from us, going to him as quietly and softly as a morning breeze.

"I thought I'd never see you again," Darius said against my ear. "But I waited. I believed."

He kissed my lips, and I wanted to ask him what he meant, but for the next minute or two, there was just him and his strong arms and the way his lips felt soft and firm against mine. When he pulled back, he kissed my cheeks, then my eyes and forehead. "I waited," he said again. "I waited for you, baby."

I leaned away from him and ran my fingertips across the rough stubble on his face. When I moved my hands upward and brushed across some of the scars below his bad eye, my skin tingled. That had never happened before. I glanced at my fingers, then touched his scars again, and the same thing happened.

My instincts were bothering me in ways I couldn't explain. My senses, too. The world around me seemed a little too crisp and well-defined. It was like I could sense the breath of the trees and the quiet whisper of the grass, even feel the heat rising from the loam of leaves and dirt and twigs in the clearing. There was a willow close by. I couldn't see it, but I knew it was there. I could hear the long tendrils of its bent branches singing as it swayed in the soft summer wind. It seemed to be connected to me, even though I had lost my willow charm.

"I bet my father is pissed," I muttered, trying to shut out the oddness.

Darius's face froze. He kept hold of me, but his fingers dug into my waist a bit too deep. "Trina," he said.

He let me go, and I watched the same sadness and worry I had seen in Forest take over his expression. Why was he acting like this? It made no sense. We got in some trouble, and I took a trip to the other side, but we kicked Mahan's butt, didn't we?

Tears formed in the corners of Darius's eyes, and the fuzzy-headedness I'd had since I got back blinked away, leaving me totally focused and aware.

The way Forest kept apologizing, and now Darius, too . . .

I waited for you . . .

Panic flickered against my ribs, and I grabbed Darius's arm.

Truth and consequences. I had been to the other side and come back again. When I had left, it was fall. Now it was summer.

I had gone through time with Forest.

No.

"Where's Jessie?" I glanced around to see if the lanky redhead might come striding out of the forest. "Darius, where is he?"

More panic clawed at me, this time sharper.

"Indiana," Darius said. "With his wife and kids."

My mouth fell open.

No!

Darius didn't look any older. Time couldn't have—

"I'm not aging as fast as most people," he said, as if he could read my thoughts. He pointed to his white eye. "Levi figures it was the damage, that I'll be like him now, getting old so slowly it's hard to notice. You hadn't aged, so you'll probably be the same way."

Wife. Kids. I hugged myself and tried to tune Darius out. *Jessie's old enough to be married. To have children.*

How long? I wanted to ask, but I couldn't. I just couldn't.

Darius tried to get his arms around me, but I stepped away from him and shook my head. Time had passed, time had slipped. I needed to ask.

When I lifted my face and met his gaze, my chin was trembling. "Your mother?"

Slowly, he shook his head. "She's gone, baby. Last year. Diabetes finally got her."

My knees went watery, and Darius had to catch me. He held on, pressing me to him, saying nothing, not even trying to make it okay or make it go away, because he couldn't.

He had waited for me. Time had passed, and Darius had waited. He was still here. He was still mine.

But . . .

I was vaguely aware of Forest coming closer, and Levi. I had so many questions, but I didn't want to know the answers to any of them.

I let Darius go and faced the three of them. Forest looked so miserable, I knew she already knew everything.

Dread was turning me to ice. I felt suddenly tired, like I hadn't slept in years, and I hurt inside and out.

"Take me to my father," I said.

Levi was the only one who seemed to be able to meet my eyes. He put out his hand, and I took it. His fingers seemed thin and too warm, and power crackled between us. Colors shifted across my knuckles, and Levi lifted one black eyebrow but he didn't let me go.

Without saying a word, Levi led me slowly through the trees, with Darius and Forest following quietly behind us. We went past the bell tower. Imogene stood on the steps in a dress that looked like something from *Little House on the Prairie*, her expression a mix of relief and sorrow.

We got into a sleek-looking black truck with vanity plates— *Darius 2*—and left the grounds of Lincoln Psychiatric Hospital.

The drive didn't take long, but then, I had known it wouldn't.

When I first saw the wheelchair by the stone bench, I thought it was Ms. Hyatt. Then my brain and emotions caught up with reality and I ran forward, knelt on the grass beside Addie, ran my fingers across her knobby, arthritic knees, and wrapped my arms around her neck.

She hugged me back so tightly I could hardly breathe, and we didn't move for a long, long time. When she finally pulled away from me and studied my face, I was shocked at the lines around her eyes, the wrinkles on her forehead, and the way her sweet-smelling hair had gone silver. It was still short and curly and perfectly tended, and her smile was still wide and white, even when it was sad like this.

She toyed with my hair for a few moments, and then cupped my face with both hands and said, "Xavier always told me you would come back."

I couldn't find any words, so I kissed her soft cheek.

"It was foolish, what we did." She shook her head, keeping my face firmly in her grip. "Stupid and short-sighted, and you paid for it, Trina. There aren't words for how sorry I am."

"You didn't force me to go."

"I didn't stop you, either."

Her eyes closed, then opened.

Finally, I was able to ask, "How did he pass?"

"Heart attack." Her smile turned wry. "Right in the middle of having a temper fit at some fool who cut him off in traffic. I told your father a thousand times he was headed for an end like that, but did he listen?"

"No," I said, resting my hands on her bad knees, trying not to buckle under the sudden weight of grief and regret. "Of course he didn't."

The colors in my hands were shifting and moving, moving and shifting, and when Addie saw them, her eyes got wider. "Looks like you got power inside you now. Have you tried to use it?"

"No," I told her. "But you gave me some of it. It saved my life when I crossed over to the other side."

She nodded. "Well, then. We have our work cut out for us, figuring out what you can do with power like that."

On impulse, I pressed my palms against her knees. It was like my fingers were drawn to press on certain spots, and as I stared into the colors, I picked out the strand that reminded me of the sunlight that came out of Forest. I willed it into Addie's knees, sensing the unnatural shape of the joints and asking my yellow light to make them smooth and round and right again. My arms vibrated and my fingers tingled, and the yellow light left me in a soft, hot rush.

"Oh," Addie said.

My eyes flew to her face, but she didn't seem to be in pain. Just startled.

After a few seconds, she shifted my hands away. I sagged for a second, surprised by the fatigue that hit me. By the time I got to my feet, Addie had popped her wheelchair leg rests to the side.

She stood, hesitant at first, but as she straightened, her expression moved from worry to amazement to relief. She nodded to me, bending her knees, then straightening again. "Yes, my girl, we have a lot of work to do."

Addie was able to walk me to my father's grave, where Darius and Forest and Levi were waiting.

I knelt in the soft grass in front of the marble etched with his name and the dates proclaiming his sixty-nine years of life and

I stretched out my hand. Dozens of tiny purple flowers sprang open everywhere I touched.

"I'm here now, Daddy," I said, tears blurring the flecks of purple and green. "I came back, just like you told Addie I would."

It was over now, all the struggling and fighting between me and him, but all the trying was over, too. Darius's hand settled on my shoulder, and I covered it with my own.

"He never killed anyone else," Darius told me. "Even the ones who needed killing. He got it, baby. He really did."

I pressed my cheek into his knuckles and let the tears flow.

Behind us, some two miles in the distance, Lincoln Psychiatric Hospital sat soaking up the seconds and minutes and days and years. I had a feeling that the stones and mortar in that old hospital knew all about time—and pain, and power, and other things too terrible to consider while kneeling in the sunlight in a patch of flowers, crying tears for my lost father, with my friends and the boy who had waited for me to come back to him even though the other people in his life had moved on and left him behind.

That old hospital and the horrors skulking in its dark corners weren't through with us yet. I knew that. But for now, at least, the bells were quiet.

Part IV
Fear

Levi

She comes to me in my dreams, in the clearing where Pastor Martinez set me on fire. Birds shriek as she walks, and shadows run away before she touches them. She has a golden light, and it's beautiful.

"There are lots of wonderful places in the world," she says, and her voice is like music. "Why do you stay here?"

In my dreams I always tell Forest the truth, so I say, "I stay here because I'm scared."

She laughs, and the sound makes me happy. Then she looks me over with those brown eyes, and a breeze tickles the curls around her face. "You died and came back to life. You help spirits cross over to the other side, and you kill things that would terrify most people. What scares you, Levi?"

In my mind's eye, I see Imogene and all the power she had when I was younger, and how it's draining away. She started fading the moment she brought me back from the dead, as if it's a price she's having to pay, and I almost can't stand to think about how I've hurt her.

"I'm scared of trying to handle the spirits at Lincoln," I tell her. "I don't know if I can do what Imogene does."

She thinks on this, and the light around her warms me like a campfire. "Reasonable. But that's not why you're hiding. What scares you, Levi?"

I lower my head because I don't want her to see my face.

In my mind's eye, I see Trina and Addie, the witches. They have a lot of power. They might be dangerous. If they take to fighting me, I won't be able to beat them.

"I'm scared of what I don't understand," I tell Forest. "What if I make a mess of everything?"

Forest thinks on this, too. Her eyes are so pretty they make my heart beat funny. "I worry about the same thing," she says. "But that's not why you're hiding."

She stops, but I know she's going to ask me the same question a third time. When she does, I'll have to answer her.

My hounds circle in the clearing, Cain in the lead. I met him the night I died, and he's been with me since then. He must have heard my nerves jumping. When people look at him and the rest of my dogs they just see beagles, but in my dreams, they're made out of shadows, and they're bigger than ponies. They've all got matted black fur like Cain and fire for eyes and bloody fangs. Imogene told me they're barghests, and they usually live on the other side. Our great-greats called them soul-eaters.

Forest doesn't pay a bit of attention to them. She doesn't care about my birds, either, when they come sailing down from the moonless sky. They look like geese, but in my dreams, they're a blur of wings and claws. They've got heads like buzzards, but bodies like women. They're all about revenge and nightmares, but they stay away from Forest. Her light would set them on fire.

I make myself look at Forest, but I have to blink, she's so bright. She's got Imogene's power. I know she does. She's gentle and sweet. She's made out of love. The bracelet on her wrist hangs there like it's mocking me, reminding me that I can't touch her.

The third time she asks me her question, it comes out so soft I barely hear it.

"What scares you, Levi?" she whispers.

In my mind's eye, I see her just like she is, beautiful in more ways than I know how to talk about.

"You," I finally tell her. "I'm scared of how much I care about you."

CHAPTER THIRTY-THREE

Some girls dream about handsome princes who carry them off to live happily ever after.

I'm not one of those princes.

In fairy tales, castles are always bright and pretty and full of unicorns.

Lincoln Psychiatric Hospital isn't one of those castles.

It's a monster made out of stone and brick and metal. It's also a doorway between two worlds—ours, and the place where dead things stay until they face their final judgment. Lincoln doesn't much seem to care what happens outside its thick walls. Time passes, but Lincoln never changes. It's got secrets, and it watches, and it waits.

"You talk about this place like it's alive," Forest said as we walked through an empty ward, checking for anything weird or wrong like we did every evening, when the thin spots between worlds got thinnest. Since we fought Carl Newton Mahan and Trina went to the other side when she shouldn't have, everything had gotten worse. Seemed like every other night something had been trying to claw its way back to the land of the living.

I shrugged. "Lincoln is alive, in its own way. More like . . . aware."

My hand dropped to the belt I was wearing, to the knife Imogene made for me. The handle was steel, but the blade was bone. I never asked her what kind of bone she used. I wasn't sure I wanted to know. It could cut anything, and that was enough for me. Until I met Forest, I didn't carry it much. Usually my dogs and geese did enough to scare ghosts and people into doing what I wanted, but since I met Forest, things had been trying to kill us.

"Lincoln Psychiatric can't be aware." Forest waved her hand around the dark hallway, the light from her skin sending spiders skittering toward dark corners. "It's just a building."

"It's a big pile of rocks built on poisoned ground." I glanced at her, trying not to get goofy because she was so pretty. "Blood rituals back through time and all the patients that lived and died here—you can't imagine. These walls have been soaking up pain and crazy for as long as they've been standing."

Forest's brown eyes laughed at me. "You're saying it's a building with issues."

"Yep."

She moved slow, but she kept smiling. "So, is the old asylum on our side, or not?"

That made my chest go cold. In the back of my mind, I heard the tower bells ringing, and I thought about the times I'd had to fight some bad ghost or strong Madoc spirit. Lincoln was built to help sick people, but it seemed like the hospital had gotten sick itself. I didn't know if it was trying hard enough to keep the door closed on what was dead and gone.

I let myself look at Forest. "I don't know."

We were on the top floor, and the only light came from the bulbs along the baseboards. They glowed blue, barely enough for me to see the hardwood and tile. We had to be careful of all the furniture set around to make the place "homelike," as if anything could. Each step we took echoed. I kept my hand on my knife.

"Did you see that?" Forest's voice made me jump, and I looked where she was pointing.

Silvery smoke flowed across the painted cinder-block wall, marking the spot where a ghost had just been. I squinted in the darkness. Whatever the ghost was, it was so weak it didn't leave much in its wake.

"A leftover," I said.

"They aren't leftovers, Levi. They're people." Her sharp tone stung, even though I knew it was coming. "Or they were."

If I sighed, she'd give me a sermon about manners, just like Imogene. If I kept my mouth shut, she'd go right on frowning. If I said the wrong thing, she'd think I was mean. I wanted to knock my head against the nearest table.

"You're . . . right." That was the best I could do. "Sorry. But whatever it was, it didn't have much power."

Forest let out a breath, then nodded. "Should we go after it? Try to cross it over?"

I studied the dark corner where the smoke was fading away.

Only a little bit left. It was probably a kid. There had been lots of kids here across the years, and I still found them sometimes. Kids liked to hide, even when they were ghosts. Once upon a time, I would have called my hounds and birds, but now Forest would get pissed if I did that. She'd think it was awful to scare a kid, no matter that the kid wasn't alive anymore.

The muscles in my gut got tight. Thanks to knowing Forest, I kinda thought that was awful now, too. She was making me soft.

"It can wait," I muttered.

I think she smiled.

We started walking again, and I made sure to keep the shadows pulled around us. I hadn't always been careful about being seen, but Forest thought that was mean, too—letting sick people get a look at me when other folks might not believe them when they told what they saw. She was probably right.

Darius and Trina were working the ward below us, and Imogene and Addie had the basement. We each had little willow charms in our pockets. The witches had made them, and said they'd get warm if something bad happened.

My gaze slid over to Forest again.

When I first found her, I thought she was just another pretty girl with a touch of Madoc, but she'd proved me wrong right quick. She could see thin spots to the other side better than me, could cross over and come back easier than me, and even make her own thin spots. She was getting good enough that she didn't lose much time when she did it, either. I kept saying she might get as strong as Imogene, but Imogene said no. She said Forest would be stronger.

"Levi? You're doing it again."

"Doing what?"

"Getting lost in your head and looking pissed off. We're patrolling, not skulking."

"I don't skulk."

She laughed at me. I wasn't sure why.

We walked around a corner to face a unit door, and my skin went prickly. The lights in the old asylum went dim, and right about that time, Forest pointed to a spot way down the hall.

"Look," she said. "There's that ghost again."

CHAPTER THIRTY-FOUR

About fifteen feet ahead of us, pale silver light danced in the hall. In the middle of the glow, I saw what looked like a little boy. He was skinny, maybe three feet tall, and wore a buckskin suit like Davy Crocket. The curls on his head made him cute as a bug, but behind him, the door to the next ward blinked like an old movie.

I didn't like it. I backed up a step and grabbed Forest, taking her with me.

The kid watched us, his eyes a little too glowy and white for my comfort.

"What?" Forest pulled away from me as my fingers burned from touching her. Smoke came out of my fingernails, and my gut clenched against the pain of the blisters rising on my palm. That bracelet of hers, it only got stronger with time.

"Why did you hurt yourself? It's a kid," she said. "Not a dragon. Just a cute little boy."

"That's what it looks like, yeah." I still didn't like it. The kid was brighter than he should have been, given the smoke we saw on the wall a while ago. I suspected he was trying to fool us. Now he was standing between us and the door.

Forest hunkered down beside me to get a better look at the kid. "What's your name, sweetheart?"

"Don't talk to him." I clutched my knife even tighter and reached out for my hounds and birds.

"Are you seeing something I'm not?" Forest asked. "Has he got some kind of glamour?"

"No, but—"

"Then don't be paranoid."

I barely heard her. My thoughts whipped through every type of ghost I had run across or read about in Imogene's records. Something that liked to look like a kid. Something strong enough to trick us. Nothing came to me.

"This might be a shade, back from the other side," I said to her, as quiet as I could. "Don't get close to him."

The boy's blank eyes glittered at Forest. My hounds started baying, and I caught the distant thunder of wings and honking.

"What are you doing?" Forest sounded mad. "Are you trying to scare him to death?"

"He's already dead." I didn't take my eyes off the boy, not even for a heartbeat, as I pulled my knife and squared my feet in case it came to a fight.

The boy smiled at Forest.

I bared my teeth.

Shadows flickered on the walls around the kid—and they weren't my shadows. Something . . . I felt—

My thoughts clouded, and my elbows got heavy.

Why did I pull my knife on a little boy? He didn't have empty eyes. He had blue eyes, and pink cheeks, and curly dark hair.

"He looks cold," Forest murmured. "I wonder if we could find a blanket no one's using."

A blanket. Yeah. I should go and get one. The kid was probably freezing. He might need shoes, too. Probably a small size, but I wasn't sure. Those feet looked pretty big. And they were growing . . .

I blinked.

Those feet belonged to a grown man. A man wearing moccasins. And the Davy Crockett buckskin, it wasn't cute anymore. The pants and shirt had fringe like old Kentucky mountain men wore—the really badass guys who lived off the land and would kill you just as soon as look at you. The boy, now he had long hair and a beard that went all the way to his waist. When he grinned, I saw rotten nubs where his teeth should have been.

He turned solid, not like a ghost at all.

Oh hell.

He was a shade, and a strong one.

Cain and the rest of my hounds exploded through a thin spot and charged across the ceiling, howling and pulling the geese along behind them. The birds arrowed down, forming a ring around the scrawny man.

"Levi?" Forest sounded scared. "Who is that? *What* is that?"

"Get behind me," I told her through clenched teeth, gripping the knife as Cain dropped his beagle glamour and put his huge black body between me and the shade.

Forest got up and scrambled back where I told her to go.

"Hey," I called, and the shade jumped toward me, knocking Cain into the wall. The dog cried out in pain.

The shade swung a tomahawk at my head, laughing like a fool.

"Stay back," I yelled at him, filling my voice with all the power I had. He didn't want me, I could tell. He was aiming for Forest—but he wasn't going to get her.

Cain snarled as he hefted himself off the ground. At his second growl, my hounds and geese jumped all over the shade. The dogs snapped and barked, and the geese flogged his head with their wings so hard he had to raise his bony arms to save his face. Then he started laughing again and grabbing my birds and wringing their necks. Cain darted in and out, snapping at the shade's legs and ankles, but he landed a kick square in the dog's face.

"Go!" I shouted to Forest as Cain yelped. My other hounds fell back, keeping a wary distance. "Get through a thin spot and find Imogene!"

I had no idea if she heard me over the noise. The shade threw down bird carcasses and jumped at me again. The tomahawk whistled past my face, missing my nose by a hair. I stabbed out with my knife, but didn't hit him. Cain growled and grabbed the shade's elbow in his teeth, turning him long enough for me to catch a breath.

Behind me, Forest started to sing. Then she shrieked. The sound was enough to shatter my skull, and the world started to shake. My skin ripped at my bones, a thousand pains sliced through my soul. I almost dropped my knife on the floor.

The crazy mountain-man shade threw Cain aside, sending him spinning down the long hall on his belly. He swung that tomahawk again, again, getting closer each time as I jumped away. I could smell the stink of his breath. His eyes had gone wide and wild, and I knew. This one killed just to watch people die. He liked hurting people.

He lunged, and this time I swung my knife true. The bone blade caught him in the chest and ripped him throat to waist, spilling his guts all over the tile.

He never stopped laughing as he kept coming at me.

I swung my knife again and got him across the face, blocking his tomahawk swing at the elbow. Blood spurted down his face and mouth, coating his rotten teeth. His eyes went cloudy. Cain launched himself through the air, a flying black ball of fury. The barghest sunk his teeth into the shade's ruined side, pulling and ripping and shaking his massive head.

From somewhere behind me, Forest shrieked again, and I felt a thin spot rip open and drag against me. The willow charm in my pocket started shaking, then burst into flames, scorching through my jeans and burning my leg. My heart hammered, and I backed away from the staggering, bleeding shade.

He tried to swing his tomahawk again, but fell forward instead. Right when he would have knocked me down, I dodged. He hit the tile, sliding in the ruin of his own insides, and the rest of him started to fall to pieces. Cain stood over him, snarling and chewing the pieces to even smaller bits.

Forest let out a fresh scream, and this time the whole hospital seemed to shake.

Energy crashed into my back, shoving me forward. I pinwheeled over the smudges of the shade and tipped face-first into my own hounds. My nose and shoulders hit fur, then bashed into the tile. The dogs whimpered as my knife clattered against the wall, then shot out of my grip.

I shoved myself up without stopping to breathe or think, but my head was spinning. I couldn't get my bearings.

"Forest!" I yelled as I turned and staggered toward the curtain of whirling darkness that had opened in the middle of the hallway.

My heart almost stopped beating when I saw her.

She was on the other side of that curtain, lying in the arms of a mountain man much bigger than the shade I had just brought down. Massive. He loomed over the hallway, his furred and feathered cap throwing shadows in every direction. The guy's white face was painted with red slashes that looked like bloody handprints. He had Forest clenched against his buckskin-covered chest, but didn't seem to notice the blisters rising on his hands.

Behind him, in dusky moonlight, I could see a crossroads. There was a pole there, and something on the pole.

It might have been a head.

"Cain!" I yelled, and the barghest scrabbled across the bloody floor, trying to reach the thin spot.

Forest turned her head to me as I lurched toward her, and her eyes met mine. She looked scared. And mad. And—something else. She was trying to tell me something, but I couldn't read her lips. What did she want me to do? Charge the shade? Grab her? Find my knife and cut the bastard's face off?

The rest of my hounds followed Cain toward Forest, and the few geese who hadn't been torn in half flew at the shade's head. The mountain man let out a growl and dropped Forest. He held out his hands and stared at his smoking fingers, finally realizing he was burned everywhere he'd touched her.

I tried to move faster, but my legs buckled and threw me off-balance. Cain slipped and slid, careening into the rest of the dogs.

The mountain man's lips curled as he batted geese out of the air. Then he kicked Forest so hard I felt the hurt in my own ribs.

"I'll kill you!" I shouted as I crawled at him.

Forest didn't make a sound as she collapsed to the ground.

My fists clenched, and I managed to pick up speed. A hundred feet to go. A littler farther, and I'd be there. Cain was right beside me.

Forest gave me a sad look—and this time I knew what she said.

Good-bye.

All of a sudden, I knew what she meant to do.

"No!" I powered toward her, holding on to Cain's fur for balance as I closed the gap. "Don't!"

Not fast enough.

Forest let out a shriek so loud and long I thought my brain

would burst. The mountain man's wild eyes got even wilder. He bellowed back at her. The hospital shook and bucked, and I fell against Cain as dust blew off the walls and ceiling.

I had to get to Forest. I got up and crawled again, even though my insides clenched at that world-ripping sound.

"Forest!" I got my head up to see her one more time, curled into a ball at the mountain man's feet, eyes closed, mouth open, her scream going on and on and on.

My dogs got their footing and barreled at the thin spot just as the man kicked her so hard her back probably snapped.

Cain moved in front me, dragging me forward as the thin spot shivered once, like a ripple across a pond.

Then it closed with no sound at all, leaving Cain and me alone in the hall.

CHAPTER THIRTY-FIVE

The world went so still and quiet my eardrums threatened to burst.

Then Cain howled, and I howled and I hurled myself at the space where Forest had been, digging at the empty air. She couldn't be gone. Not like that. No.

"Forest!" I kept calling, but she didn't answer.

Voices hollered over Cain's wild barks. Probably guards or nurses. I had no glamour now. I didn't care.

I had lost her. I didn't get to her in time. My eyes slammed shut as I tried to sense a thin spot, here or anywhere close by.

Nothing came to me. I couldn't even catch a hint of the big spot at the top of the tower.

No. She couldn't have. I felt sick and reached out my mind again.

More nothing.

Forest had shut down all the thin spots in the whole hospital.

She had made sure that big bad shade couldn't come through, but now she was trapped on the other side. I had no way to reach her.

Cold numbness settled in my bones. It took me some time to understand that the voices calling my name were real, that Imogene and Trina were in the hall with me. It took me more time to see that they were waving their hands—and bleeding.

Cain licked my hand, then nipped it, and the flare of pain brought me back to right here and right now. I realized that Imogene had scratches and holes all over her body. Something had been at her—maybe a bunch of somethings. I stumbled over to my bone knife and grabbed it off the floor.

When I turned back to Imogene and Trina, I saw that Trina was burned like she had stuck both arms in a campfire. The skin on her hands was puckered an angry pink, and a gash marked her right cheek. I glanced left and right, looking for Addie and Darius.

"Where—" I reached out with my senses, sweeping through Lincoln Psychiatric Hospital, searching for the familiar flares of energy.

"They're gone, boy," Imogene said as she tended Trina's wounds with touches and bursts of golden healing light. "Forest and Addie and Darius. All three got taken."

"The whole hospital's going ballistic." Trina's voice sounded jittery. She looked jittery, too, until she sat on the tile floor. "They're counting patients and locking doors—and the arrows! I don't know who or what shot them. They looked like people, but they weren't. And they weren't really here! My powder blew up and burned me when I threw it at them. They took Darius. They took him, Levi!"

"Shades," Imogene said, her voice sounding flat and calm compared to Trina's. "Weak ones, and from a long time ago, by the way they were dressed and painted up like a tribe. They couldn't come through from the other side, but they shot me full of holes and swiped Addie before the thin spot shut itself." Her gray eyes blazed, making her look younger. "They're closed, boy. All the doors in Lincoln. Sealed off tight."

My senses swam in circles. Trina's dark eyes glistened with hurt for Addie and Forest going missing—and Darius. Darius was her heart, just like Forest was mine. She turned that terrible gaze on me, blazing with witch power and a little bit of crazy born out of grief. "We have to go get them back. We have to get them *now*."

"There's no way to get to the other side," I told her, feeling that same grief-crazy creeping up on me. "Forest killed the thin spots."

"Then you'll just have to open one," Trina told me loud enough to make Cain growl.

My eyes darted to the hall door as people started hollering about earthquakes and cracked walls and broken windows. "Imogene and I always use the thin spots Lincoln makes on its own."

I smashed my hand against the nearest wall, feeling bones snap in two of my fingers. I didn't care. It didn't even hurt, but Cain whined anyway and came to lean against my legs. My bones would heal, and too fast. Since Imogene had brought me back from the other side, it was like I kept her healing inside me, working all the time.

"Who took them?" Trina demanded. "What do they want?"

Imogene said nothing. For a few seconds I saw the shades again, the skinny one and the big one, dressed up and painted like pretend Indians, their faces full of all kinds of hate and meanness.

"They're killers." I squeezed my broken fingers so the pain would punish me for failing Forest, but the bones were already starting to heal. That made me twice as mad. How could I be so indestructible when Forest was gone and maybe dead? I wished I could break myself into pieces.

"If they were bad enough to make the newspapers, or if they came through this hospital, they'll be in my books," Imogene said as she limped toward the far hallway door. "Let's get to looking. We'll have to walk the whole way, since the thin spots are gone."

Trina let out an angry yell, then turned to me again, her dark eyes blazing with purpose. "Forest's mother could make thin spots. Her *ghost* could do it—and you're telling me you can't?"

"I can't," I said, wishing like anything I could.

"But if Bridgette could do it, then somebody else has to be able to!" Trina grabbed hold of my arm like she meant to force me to agree with her—and I wanted to.

Forest . . .

Everything inside me hurt, but Trina didn't care. She shook me and glared at me, and her stubbornness only made things worse inside. In all the history Imogene had written since she could move a pen on paper, Forest and her mother's shade were the only folks who had ever been able to make thin spots.

Trina saw the hope draining out of my face, and she let go of my arm. "What about thin spots in other places in the world? There have to be some, right?"

"Mayhap," Imogene said as she opened the door. "Mayhap not. Levi and I, we're from this place. I don't rightly know if we could pass through some other place's thin spots."

Trina swore and put her face in her hands. Her shoulders shook, but I didn't dare touch her. I didn't know what to say to her, anyway. She hated me now. I could feel it, and I didn't blame her. I was worse than useless.

After a time, Trina lifted her face, and her hands curled into fists as she lowered them. "Well, we haven't searched the whole hospital yet, have we?" Her gaze shifted from me to Imogene and back to me again. "This place is different. It's not totally normal. Parts of it may be hidden from your senses—like the tunnels, when Darius's grandfather and his witch tree broke through, right?"

Imogene held the door open for us and frowned. "They came through a thin spot as was already there. They didn't make one."

The hospital seemed to give up a bit of light, showing me Trina's tear-stained cheeks and the desperate sparkle in her eyes. She was refusing to give up hope. Maybe I needed to borrow some of hers, and at least try to hold on to some possibility that I could reach Forest.

I nodded to Trina as I laced my fingers into the black fur at

Cain's neck and gave it a tug, pulling him toward Imogene and the door. "Let's go figure out who we're dealing with. Then we'll decide what to do next."

It took a while to get to the bell tower, Imogene was moving so slow. It was like the last attack on Lincoln had drained her near to nothing. When I tried to give her a little healing, it didn't do much good. The rooms where she stayed and tended her books, they were darker than they should have been, even when we turned on the lights.

Imogene directed me to some shelves and had me pull down two books marked *Before* on the spines.

"These can tell us about stuff I never seen," she explained. "Things that happened afore my time that I heard about from live folks or spirits. Given how those shades were dressed, we'd best start looking as far back as we can."

I sat down at a table with Cain beside me and opened a volume, just like Trina did. I started squinting at Imogene's scrawl, trying to push away every thought about what might be happening to Forest. My mind kept sweeping back to her being hurt, or maybe dead. I was barely able to read.

Cain whined at my strong feelings and rested his head against my knee.

Each page in Imogene's books had two dates, one for when she heard a story and wrote it down, and one for when the events of the story actually happened. There were lots of paragraphs about Madocs, like the too-tall skeletons found in nearby graves. Each sentence I read made me that much madder. None of this was what we needed.

"This is about a flood in 1773," Trina grumbled. "Not much help."

Imogene nodded and kept reading her own book. I went back to mine. Mixed in with stories about witches and bad spirits that plagued Never and the whole South, I found Imogene's first scribbled tries at sorting out all the spirits she was seeing at Lincoln Psychiatric.

~~Spirit~~ Ghost—Sad bit of soul what got lost on its way to the other side. Naught more than fog, trapped around where it got made. May take on a bit of shape if it stays too long.

Ghast—Full of mischief afore it died. Probably a kid. It's got more shape and stays around where it got made, but can move a bit.

Useless to me right now.

Forest . . .

Not long after the mention of ghosts and ghasts, I finally hit on something that got my attention:

Bloody Harpes

1775—Micajah "Big" Harpe and Wiley "Little" Harpe. Cousins born up to North Carolina. Strong Madoc line. Bad as they come. Burned up farms, defiled women, stole from soldiers.

*1780—joined the redcoats just to kill folks.
Took up with a group of Cherokee raiders.
Kidnapped women and married them by force.
Next ten years, had two kids each, killed by
their daddies.*

*December, 1798—come into Kentucky to keep
killing.*

My eyes focused sharply as I squinted at Imogene's scrawl. These two freaks, Micajah and Wiley Harpe, had gutted men and stuffed their insides with rocks to sink them in the river—and what they had done to women, it didn't bear thinking about.

"These guys murdered their own children," I muttered, and Imogene and Trina raised their heads. "The Bloody Harpes. And they ran with some twisted Cherokees for a while, which might explain the arrows and face paint, and the weak shades who got Darius and Addie."

Imogene closed her book, and my heart started beating faster. "I remember those stories. Over to Russellville, Big Harpe bashed his own baby girl's head against a tree to stop her squalling." She shook her head. "They slipped capture a long time, 'cause their Madoc blood gave 'em a sense of when they was followed."

"Who were they?" Trina asked. "And what happened to them?"

Imogene's answer came quick. "This country's first known serial killers. Little Harpe got killed by his own band of thieves for the bounty, but Big Harpe went down harder."

"'Legend has,'" I read from Imogene's notes, "'Big Harpe ran afoul of some folks with power down to Natchez, Mississippi, at a place called Witch Dance. They cursed him as he went back to Kentucky, and he finally got caught. One of the posse what took him down got vengeance for his murdered wife and baby daughter by chopping off Big Harpe's head whilst he was still awake. The posse stuck the head on a pole at a crossroads near Henderson, Kentucky. The place is called Harpe's Head to this day.'

"That's him, then." I pushed the book away from me, thinking about what I had seen behind the mountain man when he took Forest. A pole at a crossroads—maybe with a head on it.

"So, Big Harpe's got her. And he's got a grudge against witches," Trina said.

"A big 'un," Imogene agreed as she pulled the book out of my hands and started running her finger down the list of Harpe wives and children who hadn't got murdered, following the bloodline. "If you believe the tales, it was a witch who finally pulled his skull off that pole and ground it to powder for a potion."

Trina and I were quiet for a long minute, until Trina said what we were both thinking. "Did the Bloody Harpes come back now because of me? Did they pick me out as a witch when I went to the other side?"

Imogene got up and walked to a shelf and pulled down a volume, opening it before she even got back to her chair. "Mayhap," she muttered, but I didn't hear much conviction in her voice. "We don't always know what makes a shade strong enough to cross when it does, but those that's bad are always trying."

"It's a good bet the shade I killed was Little Harpe," I said. "And the one who took Forest was Big Harpe." The thought of Forest in that killer's filthy hands gave me pain in my guts. Had he already murdered her, or made her wish she was dead?

"Mmm," Imogene said, and changed books again. She was after something, but whatever it was, she wasn't letting on yet.

"Let's go." Trina stood. "We've got a name. Maybe we can call him out."

"You got a ritual for that?" I asked her. "Because without a thin spot, we won't be calling anything out from the other side."

Trina just stared at me, and I knew she was getting mad. Imogene didn't seem to notice her at all as she got up again and this time pulled down three books, from three different shelves. She opened them all at once.

I got to my feet and went to watch what she was doing, Cain following behind me. Imogene's knotty fingers flew across the pages so fast I could barely follow. She flipped sections, closed first one book and then the next, until—

"Here." She tapped an entry.

Trina came to stand beside me, and she was the one who read it out loud. "'Bridgette Harper.'" The entry had admission dates for Lincoln Psychiatric, and a star by one of the dates with the note "baby girl born" scratched out to the side.

Trina's eyebrows shot up. "Bridgette—as in, Forest's mother?"

Imogene nodded.

"Harper." I stared at the name, and then at "baby girl born." "You don't think—"

"I do." Imogene closed the book. "Most of the Harpe folks changed their names to outrun what happened. Some changed it a lot and moved west, like old Wyatt Earp's folks. But some stayed local and just went with 'Harp' or 'Harper.'"

"But Forest can't be one of them," Trina said. "She's not evil."

"Evil gets chosen by the person, not the blood," Imogene said. "She'd be the balance to her great-greats, as good as they were bad, by her own choice. Big Harpe likely feels he's got some claim on her, and having her might make him strong enough to do things we ain't seen from a shade afore."

"Is he right?" I asked.

"Can't say. But he was big into blood magic." Imogene's frown deepened every line on her face. "I'd bet he thinks he can use Forest somehow, make her open thin spots for him to come and go as he wants."

Trina shook her head. "She'll never do that."

"Then he'll kill her and try to take her power for his own," Imogene said matter-of-factly.

That should have scared me stupid, but all I could think was, *Forest might still be alive.* If that bastard needed her for something, maybe he hadn't killed her. My hand dropped to the back of Cain's neck, and I slid my fingers deep into his matted fur.

Trina grabbed my other arm and dug her fingers into my wrist. "Let's search the hospital."

"Couldn't hurt to try." Imogene's voice came out as cool as a winter midnight. "Find what spirits you can, and ask what they know."

"You're not going?" I asked her, fighting back a wave of worry.

"I'm tired, boy," Imogene admitted. "I think I might do more good here, readin' over the books."

That felt like a lie, and Imogene didn't meet my eyes when she said it. Instead, she turned her attention to Trina. "What you got left in your witch bag, girl?"

"A few powders to slow down an attack," Trina said. "And my willow charm."

I winced at the thought of her charm. It was a lot bigger than the willow circles we had carried, and strong with Addie's magic. Problem was, when Trina used it, it was about as predictable as lightning strikes in a thunderstorm. That thing might help us, or it might blow us to bits.

Trina seemed to read my thoughts and shrugged. "It's better than nothing."

Before I could offend Trina any more, I gave a whistle to Cain, and he looked up at me with his red-fire eyes.

"Hunt," I told him.

The hound stared at me for a second. It had been a while since I let him take the lead, since Forest didn't like scaring things, even ghosts.

Cain's jaws pulled back and his tongue lolled out in a nasty imitation of a human grin. He thrust his nose against the floor and whuffed a breath, scenting the tile. From there he moved to the record-room door, then on out into the bell tower. Trina followed him, but I stayed long enough to give Imogene a hug and a kiss on her wrinkled cheek. Her eyes looked as dull as rain clouds, and her skin had a chill, but she smiled at me.

"Go on with you," she said. "Find that girl and bring her back."

"I will," I said.

As I left the room, I heard her whisper, "You better."

CHAPTER THIRTY-SIX

Hope rushed through me even though I knew we were likely on a fool's errand. Cain led us across the grounds and into the hospital, then up some steps.

I knew he was leading us to a spirit who likely couldn't help us a bit, but what if . . .

Over the years, Lincoln had kept its doors locked in lots of different ways. They were using fingerprints now. Staff stuck their thumbs against a pad by the handle, something beeped, and the locks turned loose. I didn't need any of that. I poured my power into the metal door, willing the black fog to pull out bolts and loosen connections. When I thought I'd done enough, I gripped Trina's hand and pulled her through with me. Cain barreled in behind us, then ran ahead as the door's mechanism went solid again.

We followed him onto a ward filled with patients. There were men and women, old folks and young folks, all circling around like they were getting ready to leave for a meal or a group session or something.

Cain went straight to a younger girl with blond hair, oily skin, and vacant eyes. A faint silver glow around her told me she had some Madoc blood. She didn't care that a barghest was drooling on her feet, but when she saw Trina and me through the glamour I'd put on us, she pointed and hollered and backed against the blue wall. My heart gave a twinge as I imagined how mad Forest would be about me scaring the girl, so I whistled for Cain and held up both my hands to show the girl I meant her no harm.

She only hollered louder.

She'd probably need a shot. Forest was always telling me how the shots hurt and how the medicine made people slow and confused.

There's no excuse for scaring people when you don't have to.

Yeah. I got that, but I wasn't very good at not scaring people, especially without Forest there to bug me about it all the time.

A few seconds later, the hospital staff had the girl surrounded. They talked to her quiet-like, but her eyes stayed glued to Trina and Cain and me. My feet seemed to grow roots where I stood, but Trina thought faster than me. She walked straight up to the girl, slipping between hospital staff so easily they probably didn't even notice the breeze.

"It's okay," she told the girl. "We're not here to hurt you. We're just looking for some people."

The girl's crying eased to puppy whimpers, and she focused on Trina. Her eyes seemed too wide and her face too flat for how scared she was. I got the idea she was hearing things even as Trina tried to talk to her.

Trina gave me a quick, sharp look over her shoulder. "Can't you help her be less afraid? Use some healing or something?"

I shook my head. "Won't work on folks who are sick in the head. Trust me. I've tried."

"Oh." I couldn't see Trina's frown, but I heard it.

The girl whimpered louder, and a nurse went to get the medicine. We were running out of time with this one. She likely couldn't tell us anything that would help us get to Forest, but I kept right on hoping.

"Have you seen anything unusual today?" Trina asked the girl. "You know, like us?"

The girl just stared at Trina, her mouth open and chin trembling.

As the nurse came out of the medication room toting a syringe, Trina tried again with, "Has anything else scared you today?"

The girl's eyes darted from Trina to the ceiling to the wall. Her jaw clenched, then turned loose, and her teeth chattered for a moment. Then she leaned away from the staff who were trying to make her happy and told Trina in a whisper, "*He* did."

"Who?" Trina got closer to the girl. "Who is he?"

The girl pointed down the hall away from us, toward the corner that led to the far section of the unit. "Him," she said, nodding like we knew who she meant. "He came when the walls rattled, but I think he's been here before, lots of times, only we just couldn't see him."

"She's talking crazy," Trina said. "I don't think she knows anything."

"What does he look like?" I asked the girl, careful to stay in front of Cain just in case she decided to notice the monster dog and start shrieking again.

The girl's eyebrows lifted, and she laughed and waved at Trina's face. "Her," she said, and laughed again. "He looks like her."

I held back a sigh as the nurse arrived with the girl's shot. The girl raised her arms like she was going to fight, but Trina shook her head. "Let them help you. It'll make you feel better."

The girl kept her fists up for second, but then she put them down. The nurse and some helpers got to her and put the shot in her hip, and I didn't know whether to feel glad or pissed. I knew the girl was scared to death by us and the shot and whatever else she was hearing or seeing—but would the medicine make things any better for her?

What would Forest think?

It hurt to wonder, so I walked away, taking Cain with me. Trina hesitated, then followed. When we rounded the corner in the direction the girl had been pointing, we didn't find anything. The hallway was empty, the rooms deserted. I felt like I had swallowed hot iron, my throat burned so bad. I knew the girl wasn't right in the head, but I guess I'd wanted her to be telling the truth.

I stared at the locked double doors leading to the next unit as Cain sniffed the floor.

"Let's go up first," Trina said. "I hate the basement."

"And you say you're searching for something." The deep voice behind us made us both twitch and turn so quickly that we bumped into each other.

The blond girl with Madoc blood stood behind us, swaying because the shot had already made her sleepy. Her eyes were partway closed, and a guy in hospital scrubs hovered close. Now and again he had to touch her elbow or catch her at the shoulder to keep her from collapsing.

"You need to go to bed," he told her. "I'll help you."

The girl pulled away from him and called him a name. He didn't fight her or say anything back, just kept her on her feet as best he could.

Cain slid between me and the girl, growling low in his throat.

"Did some nasty demon voice come out of that woman a second ago?" Trina asked, eyeing the sleepy patient. "When she said something to us?"

"Yeah." I studied the girl, feeling wary and glad Cain was there, and that I still had my bone knife tucked in my belt. "Didn't even sound female."

The girl watched us through half-shut eyes, then glanced at Cain. "The Lord is my light and salvation. Whom shall I fear?" Each word sounded raspy and deeper than the one before. "Certainly not you."

Her features shifted like sand until she looked stern and old. The tight lines of her face made me feel sick. Something had gotten ahold of her now, for sure.

I drew my knife as Cain snarled.

"Move back," I told Trina.

She ignored me. She had her head cocked, like she was

listening to her own voices. "Light and salvation—that's Psalm Twenty-seven," she muttered. "From the Bible."

The girl's face worked like she was fighting whatever had taken hold of her words, but she lost in a hurry.

"Get out of the way," she said, and the words echoed with hisses and scorn. She was talking to Trina, who pulled her willow charm from her pocket and held it in front of her.

"Don't!" the thing in the girl growled.

Cain snapped his jaws, flinging drool as my heart thumped. I didn't know what scared me more: the possessed girl, or that charm.

"Show yourself," Trina demanded.

The charm didn't do a thing, and the girl laughed, too low and too long. Then she swore and sagged toward the floor. The guy in scrubs caught her before she hit the tile, scooped her up, and began carrying her toward her room as he hollered for help.

Trina kept holding up her charm, but her arm shook. We both watched as some of the ward staff vanished into the girl's room, followed by a nurse who stepped in and closed the door. Cain padded away from us, stopping just in front of the doorknob. He stood very, very still, tail out, nose extended, until he reminded me of some kind of Satanic pointer dog.

Even after a few seconds of quiet, I still had my knife raised, and Trina had that charm pointed at the closed door.

"Why was she talking like that?" Trina asked.

"Possessed by a spirit," I said.

"Possessed?" Trina held her shaking arm even straighter. "Like in *The Exorcist*? You and Imogene never said anything about ghosts being able to possess people."

"Yeah, we did. Remember Captain James? We thought maybe he was possessed."

Trina snorted her opinion of that.

I lowered my knife, then tucked it into my belt. Best to set a good example. There was nothing to see here, and nothing more to learn.

The moment Trina lowered her willow charm, the door to the girl's room burst open.

Trina yelled, and so did I. Cain scrambled backward, and Trina and I leaped sideways as a black cloud boiled out of the girl's room. It rolled toward us, covering the floor and walls and blotting out light as it came.

I lunged toward the cloud before it could get to Trina.

The storming darkness splashed across me. It felt like buzzing ice water, stinging and freezing as it clawed its way under my skin, into my body, into my being. I shouted and swung my fists through the vapor, but it didn't do any good. The cloud poured into me.

My heart thundered and my body rattled until my teeth knocked together. Images and feelings and ideas blasted against my thoughts. I pushed back, but inky waves crashed over my awareness. I saw Trina—truly *saw* her. Somehow I knew her as a baby, and I could tell how much stronger and older she was now. I was pissed. In a rage. Happy. Surprised. I couldn't hear, and yet I could hear everything.

"Reproach hath broken my heart; and I am full of heaviness," my mouth said in a low, awful voice. "And I looked for some to take pity, but there was none."

"Psalm Sixty-nine." Trina had her charm back up, only it was pointed at me now. "What are you playing at?"

Cain turned on me, his fire eyes wild with uncertainty. He bared his teeth and growled at me. I tried to will him to back down, but I couldn't direct my thoughts or say a word on my own. Disgust and disapproval stacked up in my chest until I thought my ribs would crack from the weight. These were not my feelings. I wanted to yell and rip myself away from whatever had taken hold of me, but it was way too strong.

Move to the door.

A command I couldn't resist. I stumbled toward the end of the hall, then reeled like the ground was cracking underneath my feet. The metal double doors stood in front of me, then parted like cold mist. I staggered forward—

And fell straight into hell.

CHAPTER THIRTY-SEVEN

My knees cracked against tile even as my hands grabbed for the back of a chair to break my fall. Bright colors blinded me, and my ears popped like somebody had thrown me down the side of a mountain. I tried to find Trina in my mind, or reach out to Imogene, but they were closed away from me.

The spirit yanked me to my feet, and I found myself face-to-face with an older lady dressed in a pink housecoat and slippers. Hundreds of tiny black bugs crawled all over her. Thousands. Maybe millions. She screamed and scratched at them, and blood dribbled around the scurrying legs and wings.

My insides churned. I tried to reach for the woman to scrape the bugs off her, but my fingers stayed locked around the wooden slats of the chair back. My head forced itself to the left, toward a guy sitting in a chair in the doorway of his room. He looked to be maybe twenty, with thick brown hair and a beard.

You can't hide! boomed a voice from the ceiling, and the guy winced. The ceiling hissed at him, then muttered in different voices I couldn't make out. He stared at his feet, and his face turned to a mask of terror.

I let go of the chair and turned away from the guy toward an older man with a crew cut and big, wide eyes. He was walking quickly toward a black wall in the center of the hall. The wall looked wavy and wrong, and when he reached it, he spun around and walked back toward another wall just like the first one. Faces popped out of the walls, groaning and twisting and moaning. Holes opened where their eyes should have been. The man tried not to look at them, but when he did, he choked out little screams and walked faster.

You can't hide! shouted the ceiling. *They're coming. Do you understand? You can't get away. You're dead!*

The *scratch-scratch* of scurrying bugs muffled the ceiling's yelling, and I could have sworn they were chewing on something. My eyes flicked back to the woman they were attacking and saw blood dripping off her fingertips and pooling on the floor in front of her bug-covered feet.

If I could have covered my ears and slammed my eyes shut, I would have done it, but instead my body fell forward, barely missing one of the walls full of faces. Arms reached out of the tarry depths for me, fingers closing inches from my nose.

I staggered one step past the walls, then two, then three and four, until I stood in front of a much older lady. Her loose gray hair looked wet, like she'd been sweating, and she waltzed in a small circle as tinkling music played. It seemed faraway and old-fashioned, and she looked so sad I wanted to cry for her.

On I went down the hallway, in control of nothing. On my

right, a middle-aged man wearing paint-flecked jeans swung his fists at bats that dived at his shoulders and face. On my left, a young guy listened to whispering voices telling him he was rich and famous. He laughed and nodded, and a girl in a chair a few feet away yelled at him to be quiet. Then she went back to chattering at a black shadow beside her. The shadow said something about killing her family, then shook a fist at her as she started to cry.

How dare you ignore their agony? asked the voice in my head. *Look upon their suffering and deliver them!*

I had walked straight into the land of the insane and had no road map, no clue where to turn next. I couldn't focus on anything but the sad, scared people around me. I didn't know what the voice wanted, so I just kept moving, following commands I felt more than heard.

My head turned left, and I saw images of people in rooms and in hallways, blurry shapes, so many of them. They were packed together like cordwood, and when I looked into their hollow eyes, I could see that they were sick, all of them. They surged at me, grabbing at my shirt, dark mouths open in silent screams.

Another door seemed to spring out of nowhere, and I fell through it into a deserted ward. The baseboard lights flickered and shut off, leaving the hall in darkness. My ears throbbed. My eyes bled tears that dripped onto the tile floor. I felt like my soul was shredding. For a few dread-filled seconds, I thought the bugs were coming for me, and the ghosts, and the bats and faces and shouting ceiling tiles.

How dare you ignore their agony? the voice asked again, louder, and full of so much righteous anger I wanted to cover my head.

"Please," I managed to say. "Let me go."

They beg for release, too, those poor people. The voice in my head was definitely a man, and he was furious. *They plead for mercy, and you don't act. You, with all your power. Do they mean nothing to you because they're still alive?*

"If I could help them, I would." My words sounded slurred and hollow. "I've tried."

Disgust and loathing ricocheted through my bones. *Lies!*

This time my mouth wouldn't move. Helpless to explain, I conjured an image of the first sick person Imogene and I had tried to heal at Lincoln Psychiatric Hospital. It was a kid, a boy about nine years old. Imogene had told me it wouldn't work, but I had to try, and she knew I had to do it in order to learn.

I relived the way we had sent our healing power into him and tried to fix his broken thoughts and stop the voices he heard. I showed the thing in my head how the healing had backfired, tearing away the boy's skin as he screamed, leaving nothing but his spirit to cross to the other side.

Tears crowded the corners of my eyes. "See? There's no way to fix it. When I tried, my power healed him the only way it could—by moving him on."

The spirit got quiet, but I felt its anger.

"We tried one more time with a grown-up, thinking we might have better luck, especially if we worked together." The effort of forcing out sentences left me doubled over in the darkness, gripping my own guts like they might fall out, but I could tell the thing in my head knew what had happened next.

The man died.

"Yes."

You're telling me your healing power can't repair mental illness.

"We can fix problems in the body, but not the mind." The cramps in my belly eased a fraction, enough for me to try to stand. "We didn't think killing mentally ill people was okay, so we stopped trying to help them."

A new emotion built in my chest, something like grudging understanding, maybe even agreement. The grip on my mind eased another fraction, and standing became easier.

What about all the lost souls trapped in these walls?

"I didn't know there were so many," I said. "Imogene's said as much, but I can't see them for myself. Not that clearly. I have to get help from my dogs or Imogene, if the spirit doesn't have any Madoc to it." Something like hope filled me up. It wasn't mine, but I thought I knew what the thing in my head wanted from me now. "If I ever figure out how to see as good as Imogene does, I'll do what I can to help them."

The next sensation I had was close to surrender. I didn't know whether to be grateful or angry, but I never got the chance to choose.

CHAPTER THIRTY-EIGHT

I was about to ask who was in my head and what it really wanted and needed when Imogene burst onto the ward, pulling Trina by the hand. Cain thundered through right after them. As the metal door turned solid behind them, Trina jumped at me with her willow charm, plastering it against my chest.

My eyes went wide as Cain whined and pawed at my feet.

The fact that I didn't explode from Trina's charm surprised me. The wood felt cool and peaceful—until Trina said something in Latin. She looked directly into my eyes as the braided wood jolted me like electric paddles. "I mean it, Daddy," she said. "You get out of Levi right now!"

I braced myself against the witch power slicing out of that charm and directly into my chest.

Daddy? I thought. *Oh, wait a minute. No way. No. Freaking. Way.*

My brain wouldn't go there at all, so I stopped trying.

"No need for threats," my mouth said, and my bones wrenched, my consciousness blinking along with the lights. "I'm going."

Cain brushed his fur against my fingers, and I held on to him. Sweat broke across my neck and forehead. I wanted to knock Trina's charm away. I didn't think I could stand it, but it was working. Like some spirit-knife, it cut the black cloud right out of me until it hovered between us.

Trina lowered her charm.

Imogene caught my elbow and steadied me before I fell. I waited for Trina to blow up the cloud, but she just stood there with her arms at her sides, staring at the glittering ball of darkness. Cain snarled softly. I knew that, like me, he was debating whether to jump on the spirit and rip it to shreds, but something about Trina's expression held us back.

"You might as well take your real shape." A tear leaked from the corner of Trina's eye, though her voice stayed strong. "We all know exactly who you are."

The cloud shifted, then slowly drew itself into the form of a tall man dressed in a black suit and tie. I stared at the big hands, remembering them with and without the knives he'd used to stab me to death. His bald head and smooth, dark skin seemed almost solid, yet still translucent.

Specter, I thought, since he was strong but didn't have any Madoc in him. Even as a spirit, Xavier Martinez had dangerous eyes, black like coal.

My murderer had taken over my body. That gave me the cold

shakes, and it pissed me off something fierce. I pulled out of Imogene's grip and drew my bone knife, wondering if it would cut him.

He didn't seem to notice me at all. Pastor Martinez gazed at his daughter, and something like a smile played at his lips. "You grew up beautiful, little girl."

Trina's mouth worked as she exerted a mighty effort not to burst into sobs. I could tell she wanted to say a hundred things to him and ask him a hundred more, but she knew we didn't have that kind of time if we meant to save Darius and Forest and Addie.

"How long have you been here?" she managed to whisper to the remnant of her father.

"I don't know." The pastor glanced about the hallway. "Time isn't trustworthy in this place. There was a disturbance today, though, and I gained enough energy to take action."

"When the thin spots closed," Imogene murmured, "the other side must have lost its pull on him."

Trina took several quick breaths, still fighting with her feelings. "Addie's in trouble," she said, getting straight to the problem. "She's trapped on the other side, and so are Darius and Forest. A serial killer's shade took them."

The pastor's blazing stare shifted to me. "Can't you go after them?"

I shook my head. "Forest closed the thin spots."

Pastor Martinez considered this for a few moments, and I saw some of Forest's logic reflected in his eyes. It was a horrible thing, yes, but in the end, the world was safer without those thin spots.

Why not leave it that way? It was like he was saying I should leave things just like they were.

"I won't," I said, my fingers tightening on the hilt of my blade. "I *will* find a way to get them back."

"You think he'll murder them?" the pastor asked like he didn't feel a thing. "This killer? Is that why he took them?"

Misery flared in my heart and on Trina's face and in Imogene's eyes. I had to close my own eyes before I said, "I don't know."

"Don't lie to me, boy!"

My eyes flew open. "Yes. He'll kill them. He may have already."

The pain of saying that out loud nearly broke me. Every piece of my mind and heart yelled for Forest, and I wanted her beside me right now. I needed to see her. She couldn't be dead. I wouldn't believe it.

The pastor studied me, and I saw the moment when he decided I couldn't do anything to save the people I loved. He didn't think I could do much of anything at all.

Heat shot through my muscles. It was time this fool understood what I could do—what his killing me had wrought, once Imogene brought me back from the other side. I sheathed my knife and stood straighter, growing taller as I let go of the little bit of glamour I usually kept, even when I didn't need to be invisible to most folks. "You killed me. You owe me for that. And you owe me for every Madoc you've killed who didn't need to die."

Trina's small gasp hurt me, but my anger made me strong.

"I don't owe *you* anything—" the pastor began, but I interrupted him without flinching from his glare.

"Help me get to the other side." My voice echoed when I spoke, getting louder and lower with each bit of glamour I released. "And maybe I'll see fit to forgive you."

"You don't have the power to forgive me anything, boy."

My rage escaped in a long, low growl that brought Cain to full alert beside me. I banished all glamour from anywhere around me and heard Trina gasp again as she saw Cain's true form. I towered over the specter of Xavier Martinez, more than a foot taller than he was. My skin glowed with the light Imogene had given me when she brought me back from death.

The pastor's eyes fixed on my face, and I knew he was horrified by my tattoos, the bloody teardrops under my eye that had marked me from the moment I took a breath after his attack. Times like this, when my feelings got so strong, the tattoos bled, slow and steady. The air around me crackled, and I had a sense that Lincoln had come awake.

The hospital was watching me.

I felt the heat of the fire blazing in my own eyes, just like Cain's. "I was born at Lincoln, just like Imogene," I said as black mist rolled off my arms and shoulders. It could heal or hurt, that mist, and I let it hang in the air all around me. "This is *my* place to tend, from its walls to the bell tower to the trees outside, all the way to the fences. You've done wrong in my place, pastor, and I do judge that, and Imogene and Lincoln itself will back me up if you want to fight about it."

The pastor's mouth fell open, but he didn't say a word.

"One more thing," I told him. "Don't ever call me 'boy' again."

Why had I let this guy kill me? Why had I let him possess me? It was stupid, and it wouldn't happen again. I knew it, and so did he.

After a few more seconds of quiet, the pastor said, "I'll do what I can to help you—but only if you don't take Trina out of . . . out of the world I know. I don't want her on the other side again."

"Agreed."

From somewhere behind me came Trina's angry shout, followed by, "I should get a say in that!"

"No," Pastor Martinez and I said at the same time, but it was what we didn't say that probably hurt her most. Once before we had asked the women we cared about not to take a risk, and they had ignored us. Trina ended up going to the other side and losing a lot of years, and she never saw her father alive again.

I pulled in my power and turned to her. "Please, Trina. You can help me search, but when it comes time to go after the Harpes, that needs to be my job. I can fight better if I don't have to worry about you."

It wasn't completely the truth and she knew it, and so did the pastor. I was worried about her safety, no question. But I was also worried what her witch power might do on the other side if it misfired. If Forest, Darius, and Addie were still alive, Trina could as easily kill them as save them.

"I'll do everything I can to bring Darius and Addie back to you," I told her. "I'll find a way. I promise."

Trina swallowed hard, but she gave in and stopped arguing.

All the manners Forest had been drilling into me gave me the presence of mind to say, "Thank you." Then I turned my attention back to the pastor. "Have you been to the other side—even touched it a little?"

His brows pulled together. "I've seen a glimmer of it, but it was like watching a movie. I think I watched it for a long time but never stepped inside. Does that make sense? I was always trying to get back here, to help Trina."

It did make sense. The pastor had been existing in a thin spot, and he might have come through it just as Forest closed them—or maybe right after.

Please let it be after.

"Can you show me where you saw the movie?"

Again, he had to think hard, like he was rifling through his whole brain. "It's below here," he said. "You have to go down."

"Great," Trina muttered. "I should have known, because I really, really hate that basement."

I reached out to take Imogene's hand, but she shook her head. "Can't, boy. I'm sorry. I'll be heading back to the bell tower."

She took a breath, and I knew she had left something unsaid. That made me nervous. I glanced at Trina, who looked as nervous as I was. For the first time since she and Trina made the pastor's spirit let me go, I really looked at Imogene. She had gone sheet-pale, and seemed a lot thinner than she ought to be.

My knees went a little weak, but Imogene patted by arm. "You've known it was coming, and a long time at that. I'm just like an old battery, running out of juice. I don't get to choose when my lights go out, and neither do you."

"No." It was all I could say. The sadness behind it was too much to stand. She had schooled me to do what I could in her stead, and I'd known she was losing power, but I never thought it would happen so soon.

I couldn't—she couldn't—

"Boy, you can either stand here and moon over nature finally taking its course, or you can go fetch your girl and your friends." Imogene's smile was the only thing about her that kept its full strength. "I'll get myself back to my rooms and my books."

"Will you be there when we get back?" The question came out of me in a little boy's voice, but I couldn't help it.

"Mayhap," she said. "If'n you hurry."

CHAPTER THIRTY-NINE

Trina and Cain and I wound down three sets of twisting stairs, following a specter into the absolute darkness of the basement.

I had pulled some of my glamour back into place so I wouldn't make Trina so nervous. Even though she was glad to see her father's spirit, she still seemed pretty close to a meltdown over Darius. As for me, about Forest, about Imogene—

Couldn't do it.

I had locked myself down, feeling-wise.

When we reached the first basement hallway, Trina walked into the blackness beside me, quiet as a cemetery headstone. Her eyes tracked her father's spirit, which was the only tiny bit of hope we had. Her hand stayed in her pocket, and I figured she had hold of her willow charm.

It took me a minute or two to realize we weren't walking through the basement I usually saw, with its offices and canteen and storage rooms. This basement had a life to it I had never seen before, yet I didn't feel any power other than mine. I didn't smell the mold and cleanser and formaldehyde and mixture of potpourri, carpet freshener, and spritzing mint scent machines that always made me cough.

The walls had become shadows, pressing toward us as we moved. No patients called out or moaned from above. No plumbing whooshed or clanked. The air system failed to rattle. I wasn't sure I had ever heard the asylum so quiet.

It seemed as if the hospital were watching us again.

Our breathing echoed with the soft slap of our steps, and now and again the sound of dripping water fractured the unnatural silence. We came to a corner and turned. A bit later, we turned again. Minutes passed, then more minutes. The darkness got even darker.

At the next hallway crossroads, the shimmering form of Pastor Martinez hesitated. "I'm not certain," he said in a whisper as Cain eased to his haunches beside him. "Nothing seems familiar to me."

Trina hugged herself and sighed.

On instinct, I rested my hand on the stone wall—and jumped.

The rock should have been cold, but it was warm, as hot as any human body. A faint, steady rhythm tickled my palm and fingertips, and I yanked my hand away. My muscles tensed even as my mind tried to pitch out what I couldn't believe.

"What is it?" Trina asked, her voice just a mumble in the quiet.

"Lincoln," I said, though I didn't really know what I meant. "It's . . . the asylum. The walls—"

She put her own palm against the wall, and seconds later pulled it back, her eyes going round with fear. "Levi, that's a heartbeat."

"Impossible," said the ghost of the pastor, but he hushed himself before I could say anything. Here we were, a preacher's spirit leading a witch, a barghest, and a guy who had come back from the dead through halls too dark to be real. "Impossible" had no place here.

I knew the building had weird awareness sometimes. I was the one who had told Forest the hospital was alive, that it had been soaking up crazy for years. But I hadn't meant it like this.

So, is the old asylum on our side—or not?

My breath came too shallow, and the last thing I wanted to do was put my hand on the warm stones again. I cursed myself for being a chicken, then reminded myself that Forest was worth anything I had to face, even a haunted hospital threatening to come to life.

I set my jaw, lifted my hand, and placed it against the rocks.

They pushed and pulled against my fingers.

Breathing.

Easy now. My chin lifted, and I stared into the darkness of the stones, directing all my attention at the pulse inside.

"I need your help," I said to the wall—to Lincoln itself. "We need to go to the other side, and we can't find a thin spot. Will you lead us?"

The stones rose and fell under my palm once, then twice. The third time felt more like a sigh than a breath, and somewhere far to our left, a light flickered and came on.

"Is this assistance, or is it a trick?" Pastor Martinez asked as he stared at the light.

"It is what it is," I said. "Which is more than we had a minute ago."

"This isn't okay." Trina's voice shook as she spoke, causing her father's spirit to turn to her and reach for her arm.

His fingers passed through her elbow and she shuddered—but then she smiled. She sounded so much younger when she said, "Daddy."

"Come on," I told them. "Let's get a move on."

I whistled for Cain and walked toward the lit-up hallway without waiting to see whether they'd try to argue. After a minute, I heard them following along.

When I got to the cages full of gurneys and wheelchairs, I felt a surge of heat in my chest. It was right here that I had lost Forest once before, when she slipped into the other side for years, trying to kill the shade of a murderous little boy. Was the asylum helping me, or trying to keep me off-balance?

Maybe it wasn't good to trust something I didn't understand. I turned and walked back toward Trina and the pastor, intending to go back the way we had come, but a rattling in the drain behind me brought me up short.

Cain growled as I turned to stare at the circular metal drain cover, which was about as wide across as a softball. The light over the drain got brighter, and it rattled again. The screws on either side loosened, and Trina and the pastor backed away.

I pulled my knife as the cover bucked, then clattered off to the side. A tongue flicked out, then disappeared. I gripped my knife tighter as Cain crouched beside me. A large, blunt snout thrust itself out of the drain, red as flame, and attached to a wide, triangle-shaped head.

The snake oozed upward, heaving itself inch by inch, foot by foot, into the hall. It was orange and red, with a diamond pattern so bright it glowed.

"Kill it," the pastor said, his tone full of disgust.

I was just about to stab at it when Trina said, "It's just a corn snake. Not poisonous. It eats rats and mice. All that slithers isn't always evil."

No doubt Forest would argue for the snake's life just like that.

The corn snake made a wet slithering squelch as it stretched itself between the drain and the edge of the hall door. Another snake followed, and another, and another, and another, each redder than the last, until they formed a scaly, writhing blockade between where I stood and the direction I had been attempting to take.

Cain backed out of his crouch and whined.

"For, behold, I will send serpents, cockatrices, among you," Pastor Martinez offered.

"Your Bible's so cheerful," I shot back.

The pastor actually chuckled. "A little fear is good for the soul."

"Says you," Trina muttered. "Levi, I'm thinking we're not supposed to go that way, unless you want to hack up a bunch of reptiles that don't have any quarrel with you."

The light in the hallway switched off, hiding the snakes. I swept my knife toward my feet but didn't feel any scaly bodies.

The tip of the blade tapped the stone floor, and as though I had summoned it, a light in the hallway behind me switched back on, showing me that the snakes hadn't moved.

My breathing was a bit too loud for my pride. I slowly raised my knife as if to salute the ceiling. The walls expanded slightly, then contracted, and in the far distance, the *thump-thump-thump* of its eerie pulse made me swallow hard.

I sheathed my bone knife and turned away from the snakes, leading our group in the direction Lincoln Psychiatric seemed to want us to go. We passed into the lighted hallway, and as we reached the end, the light flickered once and went dark. The long fluorescent ceiling bulb in the next hallway flared to life instead.

We were definitely being led.

The only question was, where?

And what would be waiting for us when we got there?

CHAPTER FORTY

This is the place," Pastor Martinez said as the ever-changing lighting led us into a long hallway that I recognized. He pointed down the long stretch of tile that ran past the canteen where I first saw Forest to a room used to store clothes for Lincoln's patients.

My chest ached from the memory of Forest's voice.

Stop! You with the dogs. Knock it off! Hey! Guy in the duster. I'm talking to you!

She had caught me completely off guard and made me tell her my name. She had thought I was a patient. Not the most epic or romantic beginning, but it was something.

"Levi?" Trina's voice came to me from far away, and I realized I was standing in the dark with my hand on the clothing room sign.

A sliver of light shone from beneath the door, the only break in the absolute black of the hallway, and the meaning was clear enough.

Go inside.

It only took a few seconds to disrupt the essence of the wooden door, let Cain in, and pull Trina in behind me. The ghost of Pastor Martinez followed easily.

I don't know what I expected—a blinking neon sign screaming THIN SPOT, or some kind of spirit that could make one—but what we found was clothes. Lots and lots of clothes. Stacks of T-shirts, socks, sweatshirts, bras, underwear, dresses, and suits. Cain nosed at a rack in the center of the room that held a few nicer dresses and suits. The room smelled like perfume and laundry detergent.

My heart sank.

I looked around, and so did Trina and the pastor. I even ran my fingers along the thick cream-colored paint covering the cinder-block wall at the back of the room.

Nothing.

Not even the breathing and heartbeat of the stone walls at the front.

Forest grabbed Decker right here in this doorway. She caught him by the ankles and dragged him back into the hallway. Then she burned me with that bracelet. The confusion of that moment—and the high of seeing her full-on for the first time . . .

Forest . . .

My fingers curled. I wanted to smash my fists through the cinder blocks and beat my way to the other side. On impulse, I drew my knife, walked to the back of the clothing room, and stabbed at the wall. Nothing happened save for the noise of the blow and mumbling from Trina and the pastor. The impact sent shocks up my wrists, all the way through my shoulders.

"Levi," Trina called, still from far away, but I just stabbed the back wall again. This time, I poured a little power into the blade, and the knife dug straight into the cinder blocks. Chunks of solid mortar struck the floor, sending up clouds of dust.

A chill passed through me, and Pastor Martinez inserted his ghostly form between me and the wall. He had his hands raised, but I was already swinging the knife down a third time. The tip of it swiped him from shoulder to hip, and he stared, wide-eyed, as he came apart like a punctured balloon.

"Daddy!" Trina screamed. "Oh God!"

She rushed forward and shoved me aside, grabbing for the mist that was her father. I staggered and caught myself against the wall. Cain didn't rush to help me. The barghest was backing away, his round eyes staring at the preacher's fading form.

Trina came away empty-handed, but she didn't stop trying. She just kept grabbing and started to weep. "Don't leave me again. Don't you leave me like this! Daddy!"

Xavier Martinez gazed at his daughter and tried to patch himself up by tugging the mist this way and that. He knew he was losing the fight, though, and soon enough he held out his arms for Trina.

She rushed into them and passed straight through, staggering into the wall I'd been tearing up with my knife. When she turned around, she looked so sad and angry I felt like the biggest ass in the universe.

"I'm sorry, honey," the pastor said. "I had intended—I wanted so much to—but it wasn't meant to be. Don't cry, baby. I'm so sorry."

His voice grew more faint with each sentence.

"Do something!" Trina yelled at me. "Stop this!"

I gaped at her for a second, then tried to help as she had asked. I sent my black mist toward the specter, willing it to heal. The pastor kept right on breaking into bits and fading away. He was nothing but shoulders, arms, neck, and head now. The rest of him was vapor, blowing to nothing each time we let out breaths.

I shed my glamour and reached out with my hands, but I couldn't touch him. "Wait a minute," I said. "I didn't mean any harm. I'm sorry, sir. Please stay with us."

Trina tore the knife out of my grip and stared at it. The second she touched the blade, the mist of my power fell away from it. She threw it down and turned back to her father.

His face was still there, his eyes fixed on her. "I love you," he said to Trina. "You are an amazing young woman."

"I love you," she whispered.

And he was gone.

Sparkles lingered in the air for a few moments, then winked out of existence. Trina lowered her head, shaking all over.

Guilt sank into every bone in my body. What could I do? I couldn't think of a single word to say. When I did, the best I could come up with was a lame, "I had no idea, Trina. I didn't—"

"Shut up!" she roared, clamping her hands over her ears until I stopped talking.

She had her back to me when she dropped her hands to her

sides and started moving, so I didn't realize she was pulling out her last few potions and her willow charm. I didn't even process that she was picking up my knife again until she already had it, until she held everything in her hands at once.

"My father was right all along," she said hoarsely as she whirled on me. "You *are* evil."

"Wait." I held up both hands as Cain ran to me, growling.

"I can't believe I didn't see it before now." Trina glared at me. "Darius, Addie—both gone. And now my father. Again!"

Her hands trembled, and the glass jars holding her potions rattled. I held her gaze and didn't argue with her. I didn't apologize, either, because it wouldn't have been enough.

She started talking again, but this time, she spoke in Latin, then in French. Two of the three potions started to smoke. The third sparked when she muttered something in German.

"You could hurt yourself," I warned, backing away from her until my shoulders hit cinder block. Cain came with me, hackles raised, but his fire-eyes stayed on the jars in her hands. Even the barghest knew she might as well have been holding bombs.

Trina acted as if she didn't hear me. Her willow charm throbbed as it turned a deep, dark green. The handle of my bone blade started to glow.

Trina's appearance shifted. She became a woman in a purple robe, her head wrapped in silks. Then her form flowed into an old woman dressed in red, her ancient face so wrinkled I could barely see her angry eyes—her dangerous eyes—lit with the same gleam the pastor had when he stabbed me to death. Faster now, she changed shape again and again, into short women, tall women, round women, thin women, all colors, all ages. Were these her great-greats? Other witches? I had no idea.

Cain tried to lunge for her but his body seized, turning him into an angry statue, his fanged mouth open and dripping.

Trina's eyes closed, and her voice got louder. She was all the women at once now. I couldn't even make out her true face or voice anymore.

I stood my ground, partly from determination, and partly out of certainty that I would die if I so much as twitched.

I'm sorry, Forest.

She was counting on me to rescue her, and I was going to let her down again. I'd never see her another time in this life, and that felt worse than anything. And Imogene—she was depending on me, too, to do her work when she finally faded out of this world. What would happen to her? What would happen to Lincoln, to Never, and everywhere?

I'm sorry, Imogene.

Trina's eyes opened, only I saw no eyes. White light poured out of the spots where they should have been, and out of her mouth. She raised her potions and her charm and my knife, and hurled them all at me.

The spelled dust and twisted willow and bone struck me full in the chest, and colored powder exploded around my shoulders and face.

There was a sound like a truckload of dynamite hitting a bridge, then nothing, then a giant sucking-rushing-pulling that whipped me backward and smashed me straight through the cinder-block wall.

Agony blasted through every inch of my being as my skin tore away, my bones broke, and my body blasted into pieces.

I screamed, but all I could hear was Trina's laughing.

Then I was . . .

Gone.

CHAPTER FORTY-ONE

Somewhere, bells were ringing.

Heat burned against my cheeks. I tried to turn away from it, but it followed me.

Light pierced my closed lids, stabbing into my eyes until I woke up hollering, swinging my arms and bucking against the ground. Pain gripped my arms and legs, and I had to cover my face before the blazing glare set my skin on fire.

My chest crushed inward with each breath—but I *was* breathing.

That thought grabbed my attention at the same moment the light blinked off like it never existed. The bells went quiet, too. When I had the guts to pull my hands away from my face, I found myself staring at my bone knife. It was driven into the dirt beside me. I struggled to sit, then I touched my nose and eyes, my stomach, and my knees—all still there. I wasn't in pieces.

I was whole, and I was sitting in the middle of a dirt cross-roads beside a pole with a rotting head on top. The moon showed across the rounded tops of the Kentucky hills, and as clouds drifted across its face, I knew I'd come to Harpe's Head, right about where Forest had been pulled to the other side.

How was that possible? We hadn't found a thin spot, and I'd hurt the pastor, and Trina—Trina had snapped. She had spelled me with all her power.

She had killed me again.

I died.

That's how I got to the other side: I came the natural way, no thin spot required.

I didn't remember what happened after the first time I died, the time between dying and when Imogene brought me back. Did I feel this alive then, too?

"Forest," I yelled, looking around. "Forest!"

I yanked my knife out of the ground, wiped it on my jeans, and shoved it into my belt. Pine trees whispered in the night breeze, but I didn't hear anything else.

Where was Big Harpe? Would I be able to sense the shade if I tried?

I reached out with my mind, but caught no hint of Forest or Darius or Addie or Big Harpe. Maybe I couldn't sense spirits anymore, since I was dead, too.

"But Forest isn't dead," I told the spooky, clouded moon. "And Darius is okay, and Addie, too. Harpe's around here somewhere, and he's got them."

I wanted to charge into the pine trees and start searching, but I could hunt for hours or days or weeks and not find a thing. I needed to think. I needed to—

Heat touched my back, and light spilled around me.

I froze, hand on my knife.

The light pulsed and got hotter. It seemed to be daring me to turn, to look into it. I drew my knife and eased around—and dropped to one knee, the knife falling from my limp fingers.

There in the distance I could see the bell tower of Lincoln Psychiatric Hospital. Not possible. But there it was, etched against the sky and hiding the stars. From way at the top came the light—and sure enough, the bells started to ring.

The light moved away from my face to touch a pine tree near the edge of the crossroads. Next to that tree, in the white glow, I saw a path.

Great.

Following the asylum's directions had already gotten me killed once today, but it had also brought me where I needed to be.

The light touching the path pulsed, and I picked up my knife, jammed it into my belt, and started walking. As I headed toward wherever I was being led, Forest's voice echoed in my memory.

So, is the old asylum on our side, or not?

Good question.

And one I was about to answer.

CHAPTER FORTY-TWO

The light from Lincoln Psychiatric's bell tower led me along the path, deeper into trees and grass of Kentucky's rolling hills. I turned corners and more corners, until I finally came to the edge of a clearing that looked a lot like the one where Pastor Martinez had set my body on fire.

This one was bigger, though. And darker. The second I got to the edge of it, the bell tower's light faded and then winked out, but that was okay. I was more at home in the darkness anyway. The only thing I could make out was a black, cabin-like shape, and next to that, a fire.

Big Harpe was standing by the flames.

As I walked toward him, I realized it wasn't really a fire, at least not the campsite kind. Harpe had built himself an altar out of pine branches and rocks, and he'd lit the outer branches. Forest was tied up on the altar, surrounded by the fire. The golden light she always had in my dreams—dreams that came from the other side—was barely visible in the gloom and shadows.

That light meant she was alive. She wasn't awake, but he hadn't killed her yet.

"Thought you'd come," Harpe said. He seemed even bigger than I remembered, and he radiated a black, awful power I'd never felt in any shade before. "Thought you'd be dead, though."

He laughed.

I wondered what the hell he was talking about. I *was* dead, wasn't I? I looked down at myself like an idiot. I didn't look dead, but who knew?

"If'n I kill you here, you'll be gone forever, and you won't be troublin' me when I take my kinfolk's power and cross back to where I belong."

Take Forest's power. So Imogene had been right—Big Harpe thought he could somehow steal Forest's ability to open thin spots. But how?

As I studied him, I could guess. I could see it in his insane eyes. He thought he could consume Forest somehow and absorb all that she was, all that she could do. Was there some ritual for that, something he learned in Witch Dance before he got cursed?

Or is he just going to keep it simple and cook and eat her?

I wanted to throw up.

The mountain man's skin seemed to glow in the moonlight just before clouds rushed across the sky, and his painted face split into a grin as he raised a tomahawk and aimed it at my head.

I barely dodged in time. Before I could move, he threw another. This one hit my chest blunt side first, stealing my breath and knocking me backward.

That *hurt*! Could dead people feel pain like this?

Out of habit, I drew on my power and eased the pain enough to gasp some air, and cold energy surged through my veins. So I did still have some abilities. On instinct, I rolled left, and a tomahawk buried itself in the dirt beside my head. I rolled again, this time getting to my feet and pulling my knife.

Lincoln's bells rang, the sound vibrating in my teeth.

Big Harpe roared. He yanked two more tomahawks from his leather belt and charged at me.

I ran at him, drawing my knife back for a plunge.

Shadows lurched around me, and I used my power to push them back. It didn't work. I stumbled and fell sideways out of Big Harpe's range as he charged past and kept on running. I only fell for a second, but when I got up, I realized the shadows were those weak shades, doing Harpe's bidding. Two larger shades rushed out of the trees to jump me, and wind started to blow. Seconds later, lightning cleaved the sky and thunder rumbled.

Rain exploded over the clearing as though the two bigger shades had brought it with them as they sprinted toward me, and Big Harpe was already turning to charge at me again. Dread spread through my muscles like extra weight. Lincoln's bells tolled above the storm, booming between peals of thunder, echoing around cracks of lightning.

Go, I told myself, focusing on Big Harpe and ignoring the new shades. If I could take him down, Forest would be okay. *Go. Go!*

I pulled my knife back and ran at him again. Shadows leaped at me, shades dressed in buckskin with painted faces and wild eyes, biting and clawing. Big Harpe was coming. He would split my skull with a tomahawk before I even got close.

Teeth sank into my ankle, then tore away as the first of the tall shadows pounced. Not on me. On the weak shades. A dark, muscled arm slashed at the shade that had bitten me.

Lightning flashed and daggers glinted. I thought I saw a reflection off dark sunglasses.

"Darius?" I called out. "Addie?"

No one answered.

The shades fell away in the driving rain, lost in the chaos of the storm.

Big Harpe roared a blood-freezing battle cry.

Knife in ready position, I limped toward him, closing the distance faster and faster.

Forest, I'm coming. I wished she would wake up and run. If she got herself off that burning altar, I'd throw down my knife and let Big Harpe chase me through the woods while she got away.

He let out a bull's bellow and swung a tomahawk at my head. I pulled up short and ducked under it. His arm swung wide. He almost lost his grip on the second tomahawk.

Almost.

He got his balance and swung at me again. His arms were longer than they had been, and he was moving a lot faster. I had to leap back to avoid taking the blow in my face. As soon as my feet hit the ground, my bitten ankle gave. I rolled away as Big Harpe thumped past me.

Before he could turn around, I was up again, circling him. He stopped and glared at me. Then he shook his head like he was trying not to hear something. Uncertainty flickered across his features.

Lincoln's bells kept ringing in the storm. Could he hear them?

A jagged fork of lightning lit the clearing, and I felt the bell tower watching. Could Big Harpe sense that, too? The old asylum wanted death. It was waiting for blood. I wasn't even sure it cared whose.

Could I die again here? Could he?

I was going to find out.

Big Harpe took a swipe at me with his last tomahawk, and the blade opened a gash from my shoulder to my neck. I barely felt the pain, but blood poured down my chest. Drawing power instantly got harder. Sweat broke across my forehead and ran into my eyes with the rain. I kept my knife high and focused on Harpe's midsection. He would move again, and this time, I wouldn't be distracted.

His right hip twitched, hinting at his next move, and I lunged under his swinging tomahawk. My knife struck him below the left side of his rib cage and sank deep, drawing a roar as I leaped backward out of his reach.

"Stop talking," he snarled as he swung at me a second time and then a third, each attack going wild.

Who was talking? I hadn't said a word. Did he mean the bells? Or—

Harpe's eyes flashed, full of the madness I had seen every night I walked through Lincoln looking for spirits.

"Shut your mouth!" He jumped at me, his tomahawk cutting my leg before I could react.

Whose voice was he hearing?

I tried to lead his swings, to move myself between him and Forest, but at the second I would have cut off his access, Harpe dodged around me and jumped toward the altar.

I charged after him, but he caught me with a backswing of the tomahawk's handle. The wooden hilt drove into my gut, snapping ribs and crushing out my air. My knife went flying. I tumbled sideways, smashing into a pine tree, and my vision went dark. The world went too quiet, and I couldn't hear the bells anymore.

For a few seconds, I could do nothing but gasp for air, but then I dug my fingers into the dirt and shoved myself to my feet. Darkness still swam across my vision, and I had to double over. Letting out a choked yell, I made myself stand, reaching for power, drawing all I could from the darkness of the other side. Cold anger filled me, my vision improved, and the agony in my ribs eased enough for me to stand straight again.

Not fifteen feet away from me, Big Harpe stood over Forest, his tomahawk raised.

Forest lay completely still, oblivious to the doom above her.

CHAPTER FORTY-THREE

Ice formed on my heart, and I didn't try to get my knife.

"Don't," I told Harpe. "I'll do whatever you want. Just name it."

"Get on your knees," he growled.

Simple enough. I dropped to the ground. My eyes wouldn't leave Forest, or the few inches between the tomahawk and the faint but steady pulse in her throat. "Whatever you want," I repeated. "Just turn her loose."

Harpe's whisker-covered lips curled into a sneer. "That won't be happening. I need her blood. If I take it into me, I can do what she does."

My insides lurched. "It doesn't work like that."

"So you say." Harpe's pupils dilated, and he shook his head. "What?"

I didn't know what to say, because I couldn't hear what he was hearing.

His expression darkened, and his next growl came out so low

and guttural that the hair on the back of my neck prickled at the sound. "Leave me be!"

I didn't think he was talking to me.

The tomahawk over Forest's throat twitched. Harpe stared past me, then at me. "Make them leave," he demanded.

I swallowed. This wouldn't go well, but I had no choice but to ask, "Who?"

"Them!" Harpe shouted, gesturing to a spot over my shoulder. "My children never give me peace!"

He's hearing the voices of the babies he killed. I didn't think he was hearing actual ghosts. The voices were in his head. My eyes stayed on the sharp edge of the tomahawk as he slowly lowered it to rest against Forest's neck.

He stared at that spot over my shoulder.

"Leave me be!" Harpe shouted again. "I'll kill the lot of you!"

I thought about telling him he already had but realized there was no reasoning with insanity.

Harpe mumbled to himself under his breath, then shouted something unintelligible at his imaginary kids. I kept myself motionless and reached out with my mind like I did at Lincoln to sense spirits. There was so much coldness here. So much darkness. I had to find a way to send it where I wanted it to go.

The storm around us suddenly cleared, and moonlight poured through the pine trees again. Behind Big Harpe, an all too familiar shape came into view. Lincoln Psychiatric's bell tower showed itself again, windows blazing with white light.

The light danced through the clearing, and Harpe flinched

away from it. His gaze fixed on me, and he screamed, "I've eaten witches for dinner. Your tricks don't work on me!"

He drew his tomahawk across Forest's shoulder.

"No!" I lunged forward, reaching for her.

Forest moaned as blood streamed onto her arm. Big Harpe grabbed the collar of her blouse and yanked her off the altar, away from me. Then he held her like a rag doll as she bled. Droplets struck her jeans and then the ground as I forced myself to stop trying to get to her. Harpe had figured out how to control her, how to hurt her and kill her without ever touching her skin and being burned by the power of her bracelet.

Rage coursed through me at the sight of her dangling helplessly in his huge fist. I couldn't see straight. I couldn't speak. I barely heard his muttering because I couldn't tear my eyes away from that horrible sight.

Then, below Forest's feet, grass sprouted and unfurled. My mouth fell open. Did I really see that? Yes! And there again—grass, and flowers poking up, too, blooming in the night. Yellow ones and red ones and even a few white petals, too.

Every place her blood struck the ground, life appeared.

The light from Lincoln's bell tower focused on her, appearing to pour into her, feeding the golden glow rising off her skin.

Imogene!

A fierce ache throbbed in my heart. My grandmother didn't have energy like that to give. She was using herself up to save Forest.

Big Harpe stared at the new plants coating the ground. Then

he lifted Forest and opened his mouth wide, like he meant to bite off her face.

Forest seemed to draw strength from the life breaking out beneath her. Her lids fluttered, then lifted. Tears welled at the corners of her eyes, and when they fell onto Harpe's face, he screamed from the pain of the holes they burned.

Forest looked from Harpe to me, then whispered, "My mother said darkness needs light."

Darkness needs light? What did that mean? As if in answer, the bell tower's beam shifted from Forest to me.

"And light needs darkness," Forest said, her words sputtering out even as Harpe got himself together and made to bite her again.

She reached up and touched Harpe's face with both hands, and his skin started to sizzle. He shrieked and tried to throw her down, but she gripped the sides of his head and didn't let go. I ran forward, not caring how badly I got burned if I could only tear her free. I had to jump to reach Harpe's arms, and when I grabbed hold, my fingers closed around Forest's bracelet.

Energy tore through my body, all the dark and cold I had touched on the other side. We fell free, rolling together across the clearing until we hit a pine tree. I jumped to my feet and pulled Forest with me, not caring about the fire she ignited across my hands.

"Watch out for Harpe," I said to her as she yanked loose from my grip to keep from hurting me. "He's behind you."

We turned and saw him sagging against his collapsing altar, holding his head and screaming.

"His face," Forest said, and I realized what she meant.

Most of Harpe's chin and cheeks were missing.

Forest looked at her bracelet, then at me. The beam from Lincoln Psychiatric's bell tower fell squarely on Harpe, and he screamed that much louder.

The bells rang.

We started toward him. He didn't even try to run. He never saw us coming.

When we reached him, Forest raised the arm with her bracelet and made a fist. After one last glance at me, she closed her eyes. Then she reached as high as she could and punched Harpe in the gut.

Her golden light expanded, and her hand blazed right through his flesh.

Harpe roared, but before he could move, I reached up and clasped my fingers around the rowan and iron. At the same time, I reached out and touched the darkness and the coldness again, feeling the energy of death itself flowing through the other side. Grinding my teeth, I willed it through my burning fingertips.

It rushed outward, stronger than any blast of lightning. Black fire seemed to come from everywhere at once, but Forest stood beside me, unhurt. Her light joined with my darkness, and my darkness joined with her light.

I screamed with Harpe as we burned, my hand and his gut, then his legs, chest, and shoulders. Flames burst from his eyes and poured out of his ears and mouth. His hair caught like kindling and flared.

He fell away from us, his screams turning to the roar of flames as his corpse went up in smoke and his essence broke into bits of dark energy. His gray ashes littered the grass and flowers grown so recently by Forest's blood, and then the ash disappeared as the grass seemed to turn greener.

Big Harpe was gone. I could feel it. No remnant of his spirit remained at all. We wouldn't have to deal with him trying to come back, not ever again. I had had no idea the dead could die, that spirits could be completely destroyed. I wondered if Imogene knew that.

Probably not.

She'd have a lot to write down in her books.

My fingers smoked, and when I let go of Forest's bracelet and looked at the skin of my hand and arm, it was crisp and black and ruined. I was beyond pain, beyond screaming, beyond caring. Forest was with me, alive and safe.

I swayed, light-headed, but I smiled at her.

She smiled back.

CHAPTER FORTY-FOUR

Forest kept looking at me and smiling as she raised her fingers, dipped them into the blood on her wounded shoulder, and brushed some of the red liquid across my devastated hand. Cool relief rushed up my fingers and washed across my wrist, then traveled all the way to my elbow. Like the grass, new flesh grew straight out of the ash, forming into the skin I had always known.

Maybe I wasn't as dead as I had thought.

"Thank you," I whispered, flexing my healed fingers.

"You're welcome." Forest's golden light filled the wrecked clearing as her shoulder wound closed before my eyes. My ankle mended itself in the next few seconds, and my ribs, too. Just being close to Forest healed me completely.

"You're good at using the energy of death to work with spirits and travel back and forth to the other side," Forest said. "Imogene and I, we use the energy of life. Darkness and light. I guess my poor mother had a vision of the future, but she was too disturbed to understand what it meant."

We stood together, inches apart, so close I could feel the heat rising off her skin.

Would it kill me to kiss her?

Probably.

Would it be worth it?

Definitely.

She raised a finger to my mouth and almost—*almost*—touched my lips. "Think of it this way. If we work together, we'll be really hard to beat, now that we know what we can do."

"Forest!" a woman called from somewhere in the pine trees.

Forest laughed as she lowered her hand. "That's Addie."

Another voice shouted, and I knew it was Darius.

I had to struggle not to grab Forest's hand and hold it as we turned toward the trees to see them coming. Both of them looked okay, though they had torn their shirts to bandage various cuts on their limbs. When they reached us, Darius bent over and put his hands on his thighs to catch his breath. After a few seconds he looked up and said, "Levi, this place sucks. Can we go home now?"

"You can, I think, if Forest makes a thin spot. But I can't. I died again when Trina blew me up."

Darius's eyebrows lifted above the rims of his glasses. "You must have pissed her off really, really bad."

"I accidentally killed her father," I said.

"Dude." Darius looked confused. "The pastor was already dead."

I shrugged. "Long story."

"Can you take us home, child?" Addie asked Forest.

"Yes," she said. "And pretty close to the moment we left. I've gotten better at the when of things, but the where . . . that could get a little dicey." Then she pointed at the distant bell tower. "What should I do with that?"

"Leave it," I told her. "Lincoln makes its own choices."

They went through the thin spot Forest had created one at a time, Addie first, then Darius. When Forest stepped aside for me to go next, I shook my head. "I can't."

"You can."

I thought about Imogene, and how her bringing me back from the other side had started her long decline to nothing. "I died in the human world. That's how I crossed to the other side to help you. It's not right for me to go back. If you take me, it could hurt you."

"Silly." She smiled at me and moved into the thin spot, pulling me by the belt loops on my jeans. "You're Imogene's grandson. Death's afraid of you."

I didn't have time to argue with her, because in the next second, we stepped into the records room of Tower Cottage on the campus of Lincoln Psychiatric Hospital. I sucked in a breath at the shock of coming back from the dead—*again*—and blinked at the walls around me.

The dull plaster and old paint looked normal enough. Darius and Forest seemed to be themselves, and Addie, too. The room hadn't changed since I saw it last, with its ledgers and files and books, but Imogene wasn't there.

No . . .

Trina was sitting at her desk, motionless. She had bandages wrapped around both hands and wrists, and she was gaping at Darius, Addie, Forest, and me as we lined up in front of her.

"Good to see you, baby," Darius said.

Trina stood.

I moved back, and Darius laughed.

I expected Trina to run to Darius or her stepmother, but she charged at me. I threw up my hands to ward her off, but she wrapped her arms around me, buried her face in my neck, and sobbed.

"I'm so sorry," she said. "I didn't mean—I wasn't—I never thought I'd see any of you again."

Forest gave me a get-with-the-program look, and I hugged Trina. Maybe a little stiffly, but I did it. "It's no big deal." I waited for Forest's nod, and when she gave it to me, I managed to get myself out of the tangle of Trina's arms and point at her bandages. "What happened to your wrists?"

"Your giant ugly dog got mad when I blew you up," she said.

"Ouch." Forest winced.

"Cain!" I looked around. "Where is he?"

"Locked in the clothing room," Trina said. She pointed at the tattered legs of her jeans. "I hope."

Then she forgot about me and launched herself at Darius.

Addie and Forest glanced around the room, and Addie frowned. She looked at me, her eyes narrowing. "Where's Imogene?"

All the sadness I'd been fighting rolled over me at once, and I coughed when it choked me. I barely got out my stupid answer of, "I don't know."

Then the door to the records room opened with a creak, and Imogene slowly limped into the room.

"I'm still here, boy," she said. She gave Forest a wink. "We got a little work to do, you and me. Can't leave until my business gets finished."

When she saw me looking from her to Forest, searching for some sign that healing me and bringing me back had cost Forest the way I thought it had cost Imogene, my grandmother said, "Leave it alone, boy. She just helped your nature along a bit. Given time, you'd have figured out how to bring yourself back. That's the curse of being my grandson—you have to stay alive until the good Lord's through with you."

"I . . . ," I started, but couldn't find any words.

"I been tellin' you for years, Levi," Imogene said. "You're just too stubborn to hear me. My time's passing, that's all. You didn't hurry it, and you can't slow it down." She patted my arm. "Even with all the attitude you put out, I'd rather have you as not."

Before I could say anything else, Addie and Forest embraced my grandmother. I just stood there staring at her, but I could breathe again. Imogene was still here. My world hadn't split itself in two just yet, and I was so grateful.

When Forest finished making over my grandmother, she stayed close to me, and whenever she moved away, I followed. I couldn't help it. I didn't want to let her out of my sight.

Later, when the sun had moved toward afternoon, my stomach proved how alive I was by growling and grumbling until I had to admit I was starving. Forest and I went out for lunch. We stuffed ourselves with burgers, then tacos, then pizza and ice cream on top of that, and then we went back to the rooms we kept at Darius's house and slept the day around until the sun was ready to rise again.

When I got up, I checked on Darius and Trina and Addie, then gave Imogene a call at the bell tower. Everyone was still fine and safe and happy.

I showered, then met Forest on the front porch in the gray light of dawn. A warm breeze stirred her damp curls as she stood in front of me, close enough to touch, but far enough away to keep me from going completely nuts.

Her voice was musical when she asked, "Want to go have coffee?"

"My place or yours?"

"Funny." She flicked a wet strand of hair out of my face, then held one finger just above my teardrop tattoo. "It's a good thing you make me laugh."

"Meet me at the top of the bell tower," I told her, and she laughed again.

"Ooh, scary as always." She tapped my tattoo and sent a jolt of warmth through my entire being. "You like to live on the edge."

Less than an hour later, we stood together at the top of the spire, looking out across the greens and yellows and whites of spring in Never, Kentucky. The old asylum seemed to hum beneath us, ancient and watchful as always. For today, at least, it noticed us, and it seemed happy that we were there.

Forest warmed me with her nearness, and when she turned to me, I smiled at her as if I had no worries.

This one morning, I really didn't.

She brushed her fingertips against the back of my hand, and I drank in the burst of heat. I gazed into her eyes, helpless and not even caring, and I realized I had no reason to hide from Forest any longer.

When I brushed my lips across hers, I laughed away the sting. "Darkness needs light, and light needs darkness."

She leaned forward, and her breath tickled my ear. "I'm taking off my bracelet tonight, Levi."

For a long, long time, I couldn't stop looking at my light, and my light couldn't stop smiling at her darkness.

Then I reached up and gave the nearest bell a gentle push.

It rang softly, just for us.

ACKNOWLEDGMENTS

In my Acknowledgments section, I usually thank my readers, so let me start there. THANK YOU, dear readers, for exploring my story. I hope it brought you excitement and joy, and a few moments of total creepy-crawly sensations. I have always loved spooky horror, short on gore but high on scream value—the kind of story that leaves you hunched over a book on a rainy day, twitching each time you hear a strange noise. Thanks also to Victoria Wells-Arms, the best editor ever, who is moving on to greener pastures as an agent. Let this be a prediction: you will do very, very well. Last but not least, thanks to Erin Murphy, my longtime agent, for believing in weird directional changes, and to Laura Whitaker, for taking on a project midstream and putting up with all my quirks.

I would also like to take the unusual step of thanking a place. No, not my current place of employment, which I affectionately call the Old Asylum. Certainly, it is historical and beautiful and magnificent, and . . . late at night . . . with the lights low . . .

profoundly creepy in its own right. However, the Old Asylum wasn't the primary inspiration for the setting in this tale. I based Lincoln Psychiatric on my memories of the original Middle Tennessee Mental Health Institute, born in 1852 as the Tennessee Hospital for the Insane and torn to the ground, while many sobbed in 1999, to make way for a Dell assembly plant. For most of its life, it was known as "Central State," and it didn't become MTMHI until around the late '70s or early '80s. MTMHI was a monolith of my childhood, and anyone raised in or around Nashville could immediately drive without a single wrong turn to the former grounds. MTMHI also had a role in my early professional life. Almost all mental-health practitioners in the mid-South area spent time training at MTMHI, with the ancient buildings and the ivy and the gigantic rosebushes and the terrifyingly rattletrap cage elevators—and the tables used by Civil War generals to read maps and plan strategies. It was a place of pain and healing, of darkness and light, of change and hope and mystery. Progress must happen, and, no doubt, the new facility constructed in 1995 serves its patients in much more comfortable surroundings.

Still, the world lost something when "Central State" was erased from Nashville's map. RIP to the original Old Asylum and all of its wonderful and terrible haunting tales. I hope I did it some justice with these stories.